A Dream
in the Dark

Also Available by Robert Justice

They Can't Take Your Name

A Dream
in the Dark

A Novel

ROBERT JUSTICE

NEW YORK

Copyright © 2024 by Robert Justice

All rights reserved.

Published in the United States by Crooked Lane Books, an imprint of The Quick Brown Fox & Company LLC.

Crooked Lane Books and its logo are trademarks of The Quick Brown Fox & Company LLC.

Library of Congress Catalog-in-Publication data available upon request.

ISBN (hardcover): 978-1-63910-817-6
ISBN (ebook): 978-1-63910-818-3

Cover design by Elizabeth Yaffe

Printed in the United States.

www.crookedlanebooks.com

Crooked Lane Books
34 West 27th St., 10th Floor
New York, NY 10001

First Edition: July 2024

10 9 8 7 6 5 4 3 2 1

To
Clarence Moses-El
and
Lorenzo Montoya,
survivors of the greatest injustice in our
justice system.

PART I

I tried to talk to the nation about a dream that I had, and I must confess to you today that not long after talking about that dream I started seeing it turn into a nightmare.

—Martin Luther King Jr.

SHE HAD A DREAM

Liza loved letters.

Or at least she used to.

When her father, Langston Brown, was wrongfully convicted and sentenced to death row, letters were their lifeline.

In between her short, once-a-month visits to Stratling Correctional Facility, longhand letters were the way she kept him updated on his granddaughter's latest achievements and what she was doing to secure his freedom.

Liza kept the missives secured in a firebox underneath her bed, the only real connection she had to her father after his wrongful execution for the Mother's Day Massacre.

Now, as the assistant director of Project Joseph, she still received letters from death row. Those claiming to be innocent inundated the young innocence project with dozens of requests every week. It was Liza's job to cull the herd. She hated this part of the job. In front of her sat two brown boxes, one marked NOW, the other LATER. This first step in the process was like being asked to remove her own teeth without anesthesia.

Later, she and her team would sort the scam artists from those who were truly innocent, but it was this first step that left

3

her insides feeling like an overbaked pretzel knot. Liza knew all too well that innocent people were convicted, but with so many letters and such a small staff, she had to distinguish the urgent innocent from the innocent who were in for life or soon to be dead; the innocent who were "just" doing time for crimes they didn't commit from those facing life in prison or an imminent date with the needle.

Sitting at her desk, she looked at the pile of letters that her volunteer assistant had opened, unfolded, and paper-clipped the way a child looks at a medicine spoon full of cherry red liquid: inviting but, in the end, bitter going down.

Liza had taken the job last year, shortly after her father's execution. When Langston Brown was convicted, she had surrendered her singing dreams, gone to law school, and devoted the next decade of her life to clearing his name. Though it was a dirty cop and a corrupt system that had failed him, Liza still held herself responsible for not trying hard enough.

As Liza reviewed each incarcerated person's letter, she envisioned her dad sitting on the other end of the pen. Each opened envelope represented somebody's someone—somebody's son or daughter or daddy.

It was Liza who labeled the two boxes. When she placed a letter in the box marked LATER, she told herself they were not rejecting that person but simply saying no for now. When Project Joseph grew and had more resources, *then* they would get back to these poor souls who were "only" serving decades for crimes they didn't commit. The focus for now needed to be on those who were facing death in prison or an impending death date. As for the ones she placed in the box marked LATER, she prayed God would give them strength and that upon their release they would have enough hope in their souls to enjoy life with what liberty they had left in the pursuit of a meaningful measure of happiness.

This morning, the first letter she picked up whiplashed her heart as she read.

Dear Ms. Liza,

Your father said you might help me too.

What kind of sick joke is this? Liza thought. But instead of tossing the letter into the trash, she kept reading.

> *I met Langston when he was on Stratling's death row. We would chat through the fence when they let him out of his cell for his daily hour. He was so proud of you; said that you went to law school just so you could get him out. While it bothered him when you gave up singing, he never stopped talking about how good a lawyer you were going to be and how great a daughter and mother you already were. I am truly sorry for what they did to him. Your father was a good man, the best of the best of us.*
> *One time I said to him, "After Liza gets you out, then maybe she could help me." He said, "I bet she will." And that's why I'm writing.*

That was exactly why Liza had taken this job. She hadn't gone to law school because she wanted to be a lawyer. The idea of preparing and arguing a case held no attraction for her. All she'd wanted was to save her father's life. Now that she'd passed the bar exam, her failure had become her fire. Her goal now was to help people like her father, people like this man.

> *Ms. Liza, I'm going to cut to the chase. I'm innocent, and I can prove it. My old neighbor was assaulted and hurt real bad. Her attacker, before he violated her, literally beat*

her blind in both eyes so she couldn't identify him. I feel horrible for her, but I'm not the one who did it, and with your help, I can convince the court.

I'm twenty-eight years into a forty-eight-year sentence. It's 1992—by the time I get out, I'll be an old man living in a new millennium. That is, if I make it that long.

Liza knew she should stop reading. However sad the story, whatever proof he might have, he was not facing death. But she couldn't summon the energy to toss his letter into the box marked LATER. Liza knew the reason: this man had known her father. She kept reading to feel connected to him again.

Because of overcrowding in Colorado prisons, they moved me out of state. I'm now down here in Huntsville, Texas. Coming to see me would be a long day's drive for you, so all I'm asking is that you write me back and say that you'll look at my case.

Like I said, I have proof that I'm innocent, the best kind. But for now, all you need to know is this: when my neighbor first talked to the police, she said she couldn't identify her attacker because it was too dark, and then, after he beat her, she couldn't see anything. THEN the next day she told the police that she knew who it was, that I was the attacker. In court, the only evidence they presented was her testimony, in which she said I was the one who committed the horrible crime.

When my attorney asked how she could be so sure, she said that when she went to sleep that night, she had a dream and her dream revealed to her that I was the one.

That's it! I WAS CONVICTED ON A DREAM. Ever since that day, her dream has been my nightmare.

Liza, your father believed you could help me. I hope he was right. Perhaps you can do for me what you tried to do for your daddy.

Sincerely,
Moses King

Liza's shoulders sagged as her lower back sank into the chair, a tear leaving a trail of eyeliner down her cheek.

She knew the box she should put his letter in. She'd been told by Garrett that their work needed to be practical, not sentimental, because Project Joseph needed to focus on only the most pressing cases, cases like her father's with an innocent person facing a syringe full of poison if the project didn't fight for them.

Liza looked at the two boxes in front of her—the NOW and the LATER; the urgent innocent and the innocent that could wait.

She thought of Dexter Diaz, a man whose case she'd presented to the selection committee just a week ago. Convicted and sentenced to life without parole at the age of fourteen, he had exhausted his appeals and was serving life with no hope of parole. He too needed her attention.

But Moses King had known her father; her father had known Moses King.

Liza's eyes ticktocked between the boxes.

I have proof of my innocence.

They all said that.

I was convicted on a dream.

How did that happen?

Her dream has been my nightmare.

She folded the letter and slid it into her purse.

She knew what she needed.

Liza needed Eli.

THREE'S A CROWD

These days, fury was Eli's food.

Eli scowled out the window as he cursed the cars that sped through Five Points. Even when they sat at one of the corner's many red lights, he knew they failed to see the neighborhood and the people who lived and worked there.

After Antoinette's death, he'd set out to restore The Roz, hoping it would become a beacon for Black people in Denver and they could return to their historic home in Five Points and remember who they were, even if it was just for an evening. Even more so, Eli had thought reopening the iconic jazz club would restore *him*, or at least keep him distracted from thinking about Antoinette.

But all he saw was her absence. That and the stack of bills, the uncleaned grease traps, and the never-ending maintenance money pit The Roz has become. Owning a century-old building was like trying to keep a terminally ill patient off life support.

Just the other night, the power had gone out while Tyrone and the band were in the middle of their second set, leaving the standing-room-only crowd in the dark. By the time Eli ran to the basement and reset the tripped breaker, the mood was ruined and people started leaving as they remembered the real world they needed to return to.

This morning, as Eli stood behind the bar watching the midmorning traffic navigate the five-street intersection, she stood behind him, pressing. Her weight and warmth felt good to him, the massaging of her hands even better. She wrapped her arms around his waist and slid her fingers under his shirt and behind the top button of his pants.

Fredricka was a manicured woman. It was clear she had people tending to every detail of her body, like the neatly cut and trimmed putting greens at Cherry Hills Country Club.

She was making it a habit of stopping by to see how he was doing. But Eli knew that with Fredricka, nothing was accidental.

This morning she leapfrogged past idle chitchat and joined him behind the bar.

"Freddie, please. Stop."

She left one hand tucked in his waistband while the other roamed north toward his chest. The light touch of her nails on his skin stirred his hibernating desires.

He was weak, and she knew it.

The warmth of her body coupled with the smell of her designer perfume created an almost irresistible concoction, and Eli dared not turn around and face her. There was no fight in him, so he reached for his wedding ring.

He'd started wearing it again about a week ago. As Fredricka's nails caressed his chest, Eli fingered the gold band, turning it clockwise around his ring finger. On their first anniversary, when Antoinette asked Eli what he wanted for a gift, he'd requested that she engrave their wedding date on the inside of his wedding band. When she asked if he was afraid of forgetting, Eli told her that he expected to be with her until he was too old to remember anything and, when that day came, he wanted to make sure he had something to help him remember the day they said *I do*.

"Fredricka, enough." Eli managed a loud whisper.

She pressed in harder with her chest, and Eli could feel her full weight as she wrapped both arms around his waist for one last squeeze. Then she released him, stepping back and leaning against the back counter of the bar.

Eli turned and faced her as she ran her fingers through her blond hair and tucked it behind her ears.

"Freddie, what do you want?"

"I want to know when you are going to take me down to your underground hideout again."

"I need you to stop."

"I will. For now." She pouted her red lips.

"Thank you."

"But I still want you to take me on a trip down below. I want you to show me those journals."

Eli should have known it would come to this. Fredricka was Denver's most relentless—and ruthless—news editor, and she needed to keep her stable of investigative journalists well fed.

Eli had done things, and Fredricka knew his secrets. He knew that if it weren't for the fact that Fredricka wanted him more for herself than she wanted to put him on the front page of the *Weekly Word*, he'd already be in jail.

"Eli, I need to see them. You know I can't let you keep the mother lode to yourself."

The front door creaked open, rescuing Eli.

It was Liza.

Eli walked around and greeted her with a smile and a hug. In her arms, he took a breath, grateful for the reprieve of her unexpected visit.

"I don't believe the two of you have met. Liza, this is Fredricka. Fredricka, meet—"

"Liza Brown, daughter of Langston Brown. Yes, I'm so sorry for your loss."

"Thank you. That means a lot," Liza responded. "And thank you for the exposé you ran, clarifying for the entire city that Daddy was innocent."

Eli tried to figure out the expressions on their faces. It was almost as if Liza and Fredricka were familiar with each other or at least had met before, but if that was the case, neither was letting on.

"Please, let's all have a seat. Coffee, anyone?" Eli asked.

"Thank you, but no," Fredricka said as she grabbed her purse, which cost more than some people's cars, and made her way toward the door. "Liza, nice to have finally met you."

"Yes, and you as well," Liza replied as the door closed, leaving them alone. Turning to Eli, she said, "I'll take you up on that coffee."

"Black with two sugars on its way."

Liza removed her coat and took her normal seat at the bar.

Eli removed his wedding band and tucked it into his pocket.

WHISKEY SOURS

Eli poured a cup of coffee for Liza and a shot of whiskey for himself.

Liza pointed at the clock. "It's barely past nine. Getting started a bit early, aren't we?"

"Did you know it was a Black man who invented this stuff? Yup, was a slave."

"What's that got to do with the price of sliced bread?"

What she really wanted to ask about was Fredricka. Not that she was the jealous type, but Liza was convinced that Fredricka was a threat, a lioness in the grass waiting for an opportune time.

Six months ago, she'd followed Eli to the cemetery and watched from a distance as he sat slumped next to Antoinette's headstone. She could no longer deny it: something in her heart had reawakened when she met him. Not only was he easy on the eyes, but he was more than easy to be around. Eli made her feel like she didn't have to hide anything. With Journey's father, she'd always felt like she was onstage, and even though she'd performed to the standards he set, she still hadn't been enough for him to stick around for them. But already Eli had made her feel like she was enough.

When Liza had followed him to Antoinette's grave and watched as he continued to grieve, she knew she was willing to wait. That he was worth the wait. It was then that she realized that she too was being watched. Fredricka was there also, and even from a distance, Liza could see the dismissiveness in her glare.

"I've got a lot going on since you left me—too much."

His words felt like a boxer's opening jab, not enough to daze her but strong enough to let her know there was more where that came from.

Eli took a gulp of whiskey.

"Leave you? I didn't—"

"Since you left, everything is falling apart. I can't keep up."

It was as if the burn of the whiskey in the back of his throat formed words that flamed even hotter.

Liza watched as Eli poured another shot, this time a double.

"You used to keep everyone organized. Now they just come in when they want."

This time, he took a sip.

"I can't spend my time grippin' and grinnin' with the customers because I have a list of problems as long as Colfax."

The reference immediately transported Liza back to her childhood. Whenever they'd leave Colorado for family reunions in Kansas City or St. Louis, the drive began and ended with Colfax Avenue.

"This is the longest road in America. Starts all the way at the mountains and goes all the way to the cornfields," Langston would say when leaving. Upon their arrival back in Denver, Liza would try to beat her dad to the punch and shout from the back seat, "Colfax, from the cornfields to the Rocky Mountains." Her mother would laugh, and Langston would wink at her in the rearview mirror.

Liza watched as Eli returned the almost empty bottle back to its spot on the shelf. Every bottle still sat perfectly aligned, now not so much because of Eli's obsessive tendencies but because there was a layer of dust that carpeted the back bar, leaving bare circles where the bottles belonged.

"They keep saying they're late because of the cops, something about stop-and-frisk." Eli jumped subjects. "Then there's that new place across the street. That dude doesn't care about this neighborhood or our history, just cares about the money, but our people are still going there. I get it, he's bringing in the latest and greatest, nothing wrong with that. But what's wrong is *him*. And I don't know why people can't see that."

Eli was angry, and as he took another drink, the only thing Liza could think to do was reach out to him, her hand on his forearm. She knew it was never a good idea to come between a drunk and his liquor, but she also knew that she was witnessing something more than debauchery—this was grief.

She gently guided his arm back to the bar top and the glass away from his lips.

"Everything fell apart when you left."

"Eli, I'm right here."

"But not every day like I need—"

"You know why I needed to go. Remember what you told me after they killed Daddy? You said there are more, and you don't know how right you were. There are more than you could have ever imagined. Langston Brown was not the first, but I have to do what I can do to make sure he was the last."

Eli loosened his grip on the glass, and Liza guided it down the bar, out of his reach.

"Liza, I know. I remember why you had to go."

"Good, because that's why I came to see you."

YOUR PLACE OR MINE

"I need your help," Liza said as she picked up her coffee and strode from the bar to a nearby table.

It took Eli a moment to register Liza's words, because, as she made her way, he noticed she was wearing a new pair of jeans. As she sat down, they invited him to join her from behind the bar. It was only when Eli sat across from her and away from his whiskey that he noticed she was also wearing a headscarf.

When Eli first met Liza, headscarves had been a part of her daily attire. Between taking care of her daughter, Journey, and fighting for her father's life, she'd had little time for herself, so a collection of scarfs were her hairstyle of choice. However, after Langston's death, she started doing her hair again. Each time Eli saw her, something had changed. Within a month, she'd go from a short bob above her shoulders to long braids nearly reaching the top of her jeans. She'd even experimented with color matching her extensions with the tattoo on her chest and left arm. Liza's hair seemed to be the way she was making up for years of lost dreams. Today, however, her scarf-wrapped hair crowned her chestnut face and shoulders while silver hoop earrings swung freely.

Eli chastised himself for unloading on Liza like he had. Her covered hair should have been a signal that her life was such that she wasn't taking time for herself again.

"About my tone earlier, I'm sorry. I don't mean to blame you, but I'm just—"

"In pain, I know you're still hurting." Liza put her hand on Eli's arm.

"More than you know, but I'm here for you. What do you need?" Eli asked.

"There's this guy." Liza took a short sip of coffee.

The pause was long enough for Eli's heart to descend below his naval like an out-of-control elevator. Now he was angry at himself for removing his ring.

Eli watched as Liza reached into her purse, fetched an envelope, and handed him the letter.

"What's this?"

"This is Moses King. He says that he and Daddy were friends in prison."

As Eli read, his heart began its ascent when he realized the man Liza was referring to was someone in prison asking for her help.

"Wow. How many of these do you get?"

"Dozens every week, and I read every one of them, but this is the first one like this," Liza replied.

"This is heartbreaking, but I'm grateful that he has you and the project to help him."

"That's the problem. We can't help him. He's supposed to go in the LATER box."

Liza had told him that the hardest part of her new job was deciding who they could and could not help and how she had created the two-box system to ease the process.

"He's not on death row or even a lifer. We can't help him, at least not yet."

Eli looked back at the letter and saw that Moses King was doing forty-eight years and had finished a little over half of that.

"Eli, I know what I'm supposed to do, but he knew my dad, and Daddy told him I could help."

"What did Garrett say?" Eli asked.

"I haven't asked him, because I already know what he'll say. First, he'll remind me we can't help everyone and that we need to do for the few what we wished we could do for the many. Then he'll give me his speech about not getting emotionally involved."

"I'm guessing too late for that."

"Eli, my heart was hooked as soon as I read the first sentence, plus he says he has proof of his innocence."

"Don't they all say that?" asked Eli.

"Yes, but as crazy as it sounds, I believe him."

"He says they convicted him on a dream. How does that happen?"

As Liza speculated, a young white man wearing a blue hat and baggy pants snagged Eli's attention. He was the owner of the newest nightclub on the block and the latest target for Eli's anger.

"Who's that?" Liza asked as she looked out the window.

"Nobody. I'm sorry for getting distracted," Eli steered his attention back to Liza and the letter. "I can see how this is tough for you, but you said you needed my help. I'm not sure what I can do."

"Eli, *this* is what I needed. When we used to talk at the end of each night while I was working here and trying to get Daddy home . . . you don't know how helpful that was to have someone—to have *you*—to process with. I've missed that."

Eli also missed Liza. The two nights each week when she sang were the only times she was at The Roz. While this was bad for The Roz, it was dreadful for Eli.

"So I just needed to talk this through like old times. Now I know what I need to do."

"What's that?"

"I need to at least look at Moses King's case, read some transcripts, and see what's going on. Problem is that it's most likely a dozen boxes of files and I have nowhere to put them. Can't have them delivered to the office where Garrett will see and can't take them home either. That would cause my mom too much pain."

After Langston's death, Eli had helped Liza and Journey move in with her mother. Elizabeth helped with Journey, and Liza could look after her mother.

"Mom is supportive of my work, but if I brought this home, someone who knew Daddy, I think it would be too much for her."

"Well then, it's settled. You're moving in with me."

"Well, Eli, I appreciate the offer, but don't you think that's a bit of a leap for our relationship?" Liza quipped. "Plus, I've seen your place. You hardly have room for yourself, let alone me and Journey."

Eli raised his hands in surrender. "What I meant to say . . ." He was stuttering. "I mean, I'm not asking you to move in with me."

Eli could tell from Liza's wry smile that she had no plans of helping him out of the hole he'd dug.

"Eli, I didn't know you were such a tease. How could you get a woman's hopes up like that, only to dash them to pieces?"

Eli was grateful for how Liza always seemed to help him find a reason to smile.

"Let me start over," Eli said. "The boxes. All the files from King's case—you can move them into my place."

"I know that's what you meant." Liza touched his arm again. "But seriously, Eli, you don't have the space. You live like a monk. Can't be over three hundred square feet, barely enough room for your sink, refrigerator, table, two chairs, and your radio. I still can't figure out where you sleep and where the bathroom is . . . or are you somehow sleeping and bathing here at The Roz?" Eli watched as Liza gestured around. "You snuggling up on the shelf in the storage room?"

"I'll have you know, my dear, at my place, there's more than meets the eye." He paused as she looked at him questioningly. "I know I don't have much room, but there's enough for a few boxes. That way you can keep them out of sight of Garrett at the office and your mom at home."

"Eli, you are kind, but I wouldn't want to intrude."

"No worries. They won't be in my way, and you can stop by anytime and grab the files you need. I can even give you a key. You know The Roz is my life. I'm here all the time anyway."

Eli watched as Liza closed her eyes in contemplation. She was a good woman, and he knew it. Problem was, his heart belonged to another good woman, Antoinette, and she was dead. Though she'd been gone for almost five years, the hands on the clock of his grief refused to budge. His heart was a time capsule, holding him hostage to an everlasting now, an unending moment of despair that displayed ever-present reminders of what he no longer had.

Liza opened her eyes and caught Eli staring at her.

"Eli, I came here because I needed help. I just didn't know what kind of help I needed. Keeping the files at your place is perfect. Thank you."

Liza's hand was now on Eli's wrist in gratitude. Eli's other hand was in his pocket, holding his wedding ring.

A WRETCH LIKE ME

After Liza left, Eli found and finished the whiskey she had tried to keep from his lips. He then poured himself another shot, dark rum this time, and began flipping through a ragged-edged copy of *The Wretched of the Earth* by Frantz Fanon.

Eli prided himself on being able to pick up any book from his late mentor's library and remember the underlined quotes word for word, but last night his favorite quote from the book had eluded him. Today, he resolved to find the passage and recommit it to memory.

He was procrastinating.

What really needed Eli's attention was the to-do list that sat on the bar top underneath the glass of liquor. The Roz had been Eli's way of running away from his grief after Antoinette's death. It was their dream before she died. Afterward, he'd hoped it would be a lifeline to their love. Bare minimum, he'd figured that a life behind the bar, tending to the joys and woes of others, would distract him from his own loss.

Reality had been quite the opposite, as Eli quickly discovered that the only thing harder than renovating The Roz was running it. He was totally unprepared for a life of navigating employee schedules, payroll checks, and taxes. He knew how to pour a beer and pop a cork, but lately his customers were requesting more-exotic concoctions that only a trained professional could provide.

As the sweet bite of the aged rum calmed his worries, he knew better than anyone that some days he drank more than he sold.

As Eli looked up from searching Fanon, once again the young white man with the blue hat and baggy pants caught his attention.

Five Points was changing. The historic heart of Denver's Black community was seeing an influx of the children of Europe. A few years ago, Eli had been at an intersection just outside Five Points, waiting for the light to change, as two leather-vested children of Europe on motorcycles sat at the red light. One shouted to the other while pointing down Welton Street, the main thoroughfare through Five Points, "Why don't we cut through there?"

The other replied, "Are you kidding me? I like my life!"

But now some of Europe's offspring were seeing opportunity among the children of Africa. Five Points offered hundred-year-old houses with character, original wood floors, and a mortgage at half the price of a house in Highlands Ranch.

Then there were people like the blue-hat, baggy-pants guy. It was no secret that young people in the suburbs were the ones who listened to and purchased most rap music, but this guy was taking his appreciation to a whole new level.

Eli glanced at the sign above the man's club. In the shape of a large blue hat, it announced the name of the owner and the club at the same time—CHANCE'S PLACE. The marquee below read *Hip-hop extravaganza! NWA and Public Enemy—VIP after party with Chuck D and Flava Flav.*

While Eli didn't know who the groups or performers were, he knew that something didn't feel right about the blue-hat man.

Plus, at Chance's Place they had fancy cocktails with names like Kool Moe Dee and Jam Master Jay. While Eli was game for a little competition and knew the history of The Roz's friendly and even ruthless rivalries, his unease was with Chance's disposition. To Eli, it felt like he'd arrived in the neighborhood in a spirit not of appreciation but of exploitation. A spirit that Eli felt the growing need to exorcise.

Eli waited until the baggy-pants child of Europe disappeared through the front door of his club before he stepped out of The Roz and onto the sidewalk.

If Five Points was the heart of Denver's Black community, then these streets were the arteries: Welton Street, Washington Street, Twenty-Sixth Avenue, and Twenty-Seventh Street. All flowed from the five-point intersection and led to the surrounding neighborhoods—Curtis Park, Whittier, Cole, Clayton, Skyland, and Park Hill, the various chambers of Denver's Black heart. The lifeblood of these neighborhoods was the people, but lately there had been more white blood cells than normal. Eli was pretty sure what was happening to their heart wasn't healthy.

He leaned against the doorframe and returned to flipping pages and scanning the familiar scribblings of his mentor.

"Hey, brotha, what are you doing with that book? Don't you know what they say about us?"

Eli looked up to see Brother X, a thin, charcoal-skinned man wearing a pressed suit topped off with a bow tie, standing on the corner opposite The Roz.

"What's that, my man?" Eli shouted back.

"Haven't you heard?" Brother X replied. "We don't read! That's why they say. If you want to hide something from a Black man, just put it in a book!"

They both laughed, and then the man raised his hand, offering a brown box. "Bean pie?"

"Not today, my man. I'm still working on the one from last week," Eli said.

"All right, my brotha. As-salamu alaikum."

"Wa alaikum salaam," Eli replied as he sat down on the curb and continued scanning the book.

Bass boomed, rattling Eli's chest. Chance's white BMW with its oversized rims and state-of-the-art sound system, complete with subwoofers filling the trunk, was his signal to all that he was a successful club owner. Eli, on the other hand, didn't own a car. He'd sold it as part of the purging process after Antoinette's death.

Chance rolled down his tinted window and shot a glance in Eli's direction. Eli determined to not react to his dismissive smirk. The BMW lurched west, and by the trailing sound of the bass, Eli could tell that Chance turned north out of Five Points headed toward LoDo.

Eli was searching Frantz Fanon's classic work from back to front, flipping the pages one by one with his left thumb. He found the passage he was looking for on the first page, underlined in the familiar hand of his mentor.

Eli closed the book and his eyes. He thought about the changing dynamics of his neighborhood and the influx of the children of Europe and the condescending look in Chance's eyes as he sped away. He thought about how the police had moved from harassment to more heavy-handed tactics and wondered if the rumors were true that they were still searching for the priest they felt was responsible for the death of their brother in blue. He thought about how to ask Fredricka to leave him alone, but with what she knew about him, Eli needed her on his side more than he needed her out of his life. And then there was The Roz. Both it and his life had become unmanageable.

Eli's jaw clenched. The rum was no longer helping.

He opened the book again and recommitted the quote to memory: *Decolonization is always a violent phenomenon.*

After a quiet evening at The Roz, Eli went home, lit the single candle on the small table in his kitchenette, and poured a glass of wine. Though Antoinette had been dead now for almost five years, he still found comfort in his ritual of sharing a glass of wine and the events of his day with her. Tonight, however, Eli was not in the sharing mood. After finishing most of the bottle and staring, for the better part of an hour, at the empty chair bearing her burnt-orange scarf, he extinguished the candle and descended the ladder to his underground abode.

With the hatch door closed to the above world, he began his nightly ritual.

Mind.

He placed Fanon back in its place on the bookshelf and then turned his attention to the bottom shelf, which contained items he should not have: the journals of a dead police officer named Slager. He read as Miles played, hoping he might find something that could help Liza with the King case she'd told him about. It still baffled him that someone could end up in prison because of a dream.

Body.

The chain that held the heavy bag to the steel rafter resonated like the bass from Chance's BMW as his fists hammered it, angering Eli even more. With the alcohol wearing off and sweat running down his brow, Eli figured it was only a matter of time before he and Chance collided.

Spirit.

Eli turned off the record player before *A Love Supreme* dropped and turned on a police scanner he'd purchased from RadioShack. Sleep was far from his mind as he lay down on his cot and fingered his prayer bracelet.

Eli was prepared to leave, dressed in dark-gray sweatpants, a black T-shirt and hoodie, and tennis shoes to match.

He lay there and listened to the various exchanges between dispatch and officers throughout Denver until he found his target for the night. Grabbing a palm-sized pair of binoculars, he headed up the ladder out the door into the night.

WHY WE CAN'T WAIT

The next morning, Liza was back at her desk with a new stack of letters from prisoners vying for the attention of Project Joseph.

The two boxes taunted her like dual Goliaths, and she wasn't sure that she had one smooth stone, let alone a sling.

Liza had believed she was going to bring her father home. She'd gone all in, quit Julliard, made it through law school and fought for him with everything she had, only to watch his dream of a cleared name—and hers of having him back home with her mother, all of them giving Journey a stable and loving launching pad for her dreams—be doused like fire in the rain.

She had failed.

Believing in her father's innocence and devoting everything to prove it to the world hadn't been enough—she hadn't been enough. And now she was trying to help the loved ones of others when she couldn't help her own.

Liza eyed the new stack of requests in front of her and then noticed the name on the top letter—Moses King.

Dear Ms. Liza,

I couldn't wait until I heard from you. In here, all I have is time. What did the soap opera used to say? "Like sands through the hourglass, so are the days of our lives."

That's life in prison. Everyone in here is a falling granule, forced and jostled so close that we bruise each other as we funnel through the narrowing glass of time. If we were sand on the beach, we'd still be anonymous nobodies, stepped over and stepped on, but at least we would have blue sky above and dreams of far-off lands. But here we fall in slow motion, and out of desperation, we claw at each other for fear of descending into the unknown.

Liza had thought a lot about time.

Adorning her chest was an elaborate tattoo of an ornate thirteen-hour pocket watch floating like a life raft upon an indigo ocean. It had taken three sittings and even more payments, but it was a masterpiece. When her father was in prison, it represented the thing she wanted more of—time. More minutes to fight and strategize; another moment to hear his voice and feel his presence. If only there had been a couple more hours in every day, then maybe she could have set Langston free so that one day he might walk her down the aisle. More time was what she'd prayed for, but what would have been a blessing to her was a curse for Moses. The last thing he wanted was a few extra hours of monotony in every day.

Ms. Liza, I know I sent my first letter yesterday, but I can't take the chance of you saying no without having all the information.

First, while days are long for me, they are short for my mother. Over the course of my sentence, I've seen her go from walking to a wheelchair. When I saw her last, she was sick. Even with her oxygen tank and the low altitude of Texas, she could barely breathe. You'll see what I mean when you meet her. She's close to meeting our maker, and I don't want her to die without seeing me free again.

Also, I told you I have proof of my innocence. Well, here it is: the real perpetrator sent me a letter a few weeks ago saying that he felt bad for me and that he wanted to help. Ms. Liza, he confessed to everything. I need you to take my case before he changes his mind.

Your dad was one of the finest men I've had the privilege of knowing. I believe God brought him into my life so that eventually you could help me.

Isn't that why you picked the name Project Joseph?

I didn't use to be much of a religious man, but Langston told me the story about how in the Bible, Joseph was an innocent man in prison for a crime he did not commit, but he was eventually set free. Liza, I am Joseph, but so are you.

I know you remember what Joseph said when he got out of prison: "What others meant for bad, God meant for good, the saving of many lives." Is that why you chose the name, because in him you see yourself too? You wake up every day knowing that when your dad went to prison, so did you. And now you hope that what others meant for bad can result in you saving many lives. I believe I am one of those lives you are supposed to save.

Please, I have his confession in writing, which means I can get a retrial and get home to my mom. And when I do, I will forever be yours for the cause of freedom.

Sincerely,
Moses King

Liza embraced the letter like a graveside widow holding a folded flag. But the tears that filled her eyes weren't born of sadness or loss. No, what she felt was nothing short of rage for the hopeless war she had been recruited into—a war in which the tally of innocent people would never be known. If there was one, there were most likely many, too many to count.

She thought about Dexter Diaz. He was now the focus of the project. He'd been just a kid when they convicted him, but he'd received an adult sentence of life without the possibility of parole. Dexter was one of the many lives that she was now supposed to save.

But how could she not look into King's case too? For a friend of her father, she could at least examine the evidence and read the letter of confession. She'd already decided on this the day before, but today was the day to turn her resolve into action.

Liza put down the letter and picked up the phone on her desk.

"Hello, I need you to send me the case files for Moses King with all due haste."

She wrapped the cord around her finger as she waited for the person on the other end to find their bearings and respond.

"Who am I? My name is Liza Brown. I'm Moses King's new lawyer."

REID WHO?

"Sixty-five times!"

Dr. Garrett was standing at the whiteboard with a marker in his hand and fire in his voice. He was a tall man with a face that looked like it deserved wire-rimmed glasses and a personality that demanded a sports car. His personality won that battle.

Liza admired him as a professor and even more now as a colleague. She'd arrived at law school with the single-minded focus of exonerating her father. Little did she know that not only would Garrett join her in that fight, but he would also eventually recruit her to fight for others by hiring her as the assistant director of Project Joseph.

Today was their Monday morning strategy session, where they reviewed pending cases, brainstormed tactics, and introduced the small but mighty team to any new cases they were going to tackle.

Their conference room was a classroom they'd confiscated from the law school. Besides Liza and Garrett, there were four other people in the room. Lee Goldstein, a seasoned defense attorney, had retired from his practice but served the project on a pro bono basis as lead counsel between rounds of golf at the Wellshire Country Club. Liza was forever grateful for how he'd served her father and fought for him to the very end. To Goldstein's left sat Janet, a highly competent paralegal who was also a stay-at-home mom of toddler twins boys; she often said that she volunteered at the project in order to have grown-up, non-child-centered conversations to look forward to on a semi-regular basis.

The final two team members, Megan and Jennifer, were third-year law students who did the grunt work for three credits a semester. They sat across from Liza.

"Sixty-five times," Garrett repeated. This time he wrote the number on the whiteboard for emphasis.

He was talking about their newest client, Dexter Diaz. The prior week Liza had championed him as their next case.

A decade ago, Diaz had been convicted of the savage beating of a twenty-nine-year-old special education teacher. Out of love for her students, she'd moved to the largely Hispanic neighborhood in Northwest Denver to be closer to those she served. On the morning of New Year's day, a neighbor had found her dead in her front yard with her dog standing guard, her blond hair stained red with her own blood.

The police arrived and followed a blood trail to the open door of the small house she shared with her boyfriend. They surmised that the beating had begun in her house, first with a shoe, and ended in the front yard, where she'd received blows to her head from a softball-sized rock.

The police closed the case in a matter of days when they found Dexter in the passenger seat of the victim's car on a joy ride with a friend. The prosecution said the motive was simple: Dexter and his friend wanted the victim's car and were willing to do anything to get it.

Garrett underlined and circled the number on the whiteboard. "That's how many times he denied having anything to do with the murder over the course of the interview. Sixty-five

times, he told the detectives that he didn't do it, but they refused
to take no for an answer. They bullied him like a pack of bad-
gers until he confessed, and now he's doing life without parole
in Canyon City."

"Did they use the Reid technique on him?" asked one of the
law students.

"Yes, they lied to him," Liza responded. "Told him they had
proof that he did it and asked him loaded questions meant to
trip him up. Even told him he was going to be sexually assaulted
in prison if he didn't tell the truth. It works great on guilty suspects but even better on innocent people, especially juveniles."

The law students scribbled on their yellow legal pads.

Liza remembered her shock when she'd first read about John
Reid, the psychologist who coerced a confession from the husband of a murdered woman. The man recanted the next day but
was still convicted. Later, another man confessed, and it was discovered that the husband was in fact innocent. Reid, however,
became an international interrogation expert, wrote a textbook,
and started a company training thousands of law enforcement
officials in his nine-step interrogation technique, in which the
detective confronted the suspect, saying they had clear evidence
of their guilt, and slowly led the suspect to tell the truth. It
was accomplished through direct confrontation and questions
designed to make the person feel like confessing would be the
right and moral thing to do.

"It's psychological warfare," Garrett said.

A vein blistered on his forehead, and Liza knew what was
coming next. She didn't flinch as he threw the uncapped marker
across the room, leaving another red ink mark on the gray wall.

"Dexter had no chance. He was just a boy. Who sentences a
kid to life without the possibility of parole?"

Liza understood his anger. It was righteous. Dexter had
been only fourteen years old when the detectives coerced a

confession out of him, and he'd spent his teens and twenties in adult prison.

"There's a videotape of the confession," Liza noted. "We'll need to dissect it by the second in order to make our case."

"Dexter fits our mission. He's the reason I started this project. And"—Garrett turned toward Liza—"Ms. Brown will run point on this one."

Liza nodded in gratitude. She was all in.

However, Garrett didn't know she was she was all in on Moses King as well.

JAYWALKING

Liza was a rule follower. Even as an adult, she still waited for the light to change and the silhouette outline of a person to glow before stepping off the curb and into the crosswalk. The thought of representing Moses King without Garrett's approval made her feel like she would break out in hives. Today she was hoping for a green light.

With the strategy meeting adjourned, Liza and Garrett were alone in the conference room. After he retrieved the flung dry erase marker from the floor, Liza began her case for helping Moses King.

"Hey, Doc, got a moment?"

"I was going to ask you the same thing," he said. "I know this is your first time taking the lead, but we'll all pitch in. Don't hesitate to ask for help."

"Appreciate the support," said Liza. "It means a lot that you would trust me with this case. I won't let you down."

"We have to get this kid out. Last week, after you submitted his case for consideration, I went and visited with him. He's a little rough around the edges but doing fairly well, considering all he's had is criminals to keep him company. Can you imagine losing over a decade of your life for something you didn't do?"

Liza winced.

"I'm sorry. I didn't mean for it to come out that way. You can relate better than any of us here. You've lived it."

Liza signaled her understanding with her eyes. Garrett was a bit like sandpaper, but his heart was good. When she's read Dexter's letter, she'd known she wanted to help him. He'd lost the formative years of his life. When he should have been learning to drive and going to prom, they'd left him to fend for himself in adult prison.

"This kid's been through it," Garrett said. "But hopefully we'll see the day when we get to walk him out of prison and back to freedom."

Liza nodded in affirmation.

"Anyway, you had something for me too. What's on your mind?"

"Well, I was wondering if you would allow me to take the lead on not one, but *two* cases."

"One case is a handful and a half. How do you think you could juggle two?"

"Yeah, hear me out, Doc."

Liza told him about Moses King. She explained that the real perpetrator had reached out to him, confessed, and offered to help. She left out the fact that King had shared a connection with her father.

"All I'm asking is that you let me look into the case a bit more and, if it's promising, we take a shot at both. That might mean Goldstein misses a few rounds of golf, but I think it's worth it."

"Liza, you of all people know how much work this is. Just one case is going to stretch us."

She knew what she was asking. Fighting for her father had consumed her, but she was ready for the early mornings and sleepless nights. She'd even convinced her heart to buckle tight and hang on for the emotional roller coaster that went along with taking responsibility for someone's life.

"Maybe we could share the load." Garrett softened. "What's he facing? Life or the needle?"

"Neither, but—"

"You know why we have our policies." Garrett's eyes narrowed. "You helped write them. Someday we'll be able to do more, but if it's not life or—"

"He's as old as Daddy was, and they gave him forty-eight years," Liza blurted. "There's a good chance he's going to die in there."

Garrett's silence spoke for him, and Liza heard him loud and clear.

She had already decided she was going to help Moses King, but she'd thought it was worth trying to get Garrett's stamp of approval. That would have saved her having to sneak around, and if he'd given the thumbs-up, she could have recruited a few more law students to help her read through the mass of materials and formulate a plan of attack.

"I understand," Liza said, as she gathered her purse and oversized tote bag.

She had hoped for an easier way to go about this, but she knew how to juggle. She'd been doing it all her adult life. As a single mother, she'd kept all the balls in the air: multiple jobs, Journey's homework, and attending hearings for her father. She'd made sure her daughter didn't miss a meal or any of her dance classes and recitals down at Cleo's. She wasn't just juggling balls; she'd also been spinning plates as she finished law school, visited Stratling Correctional Facility to see her father, and, in the last year of his life, managed The Roz while also organizing a protest against the governor.

Liza knew how to multitask, but she'd hoped the most intense days were behind her. Thankfully, she knew she wasn't alone. Her mom would be there to help with Journey, and she knew she could count on Eli as well. While she would have liked a green light from Garrett, she was going to keep moving forward and face whatever traffic came her way. If she could pull this off, then she'd have the privilege of walking not one but two men through the doors of freedom.

CALLING TYRONE

The Roz was packed, but Tyrone, the bandleader and star saxophonist, was nowhere to be found. The band was onstage, stalling for time by trading leads between the keys, bass, and drums.

Eli called Tyrone's apartment, but his roommate said he'd left around seven, plenty of time to arrive and prepare for the nine o'clock opening set. But now it was almost ten, and the crowd was as impatient as sprinters waiting for the starter's pistol to sound.

Eli hit Tyrone's pager one last time with an emergency 911 code and The Roz's number and, after waiting a few more minutes, went with plan B—Liza.

Thankfully, it was Friday night, and she was in the building. Liza usually sat out on the first set of the night and then joined Tyrone during the second and third. That way Eli could keep people eating and drinking as long as possible.

Tyrone's unique arrangements and genius on the saxophone coupled with the Liza's beauty—both physical and vocal—made them a must-see combination every week. Friday and Saturday night reservations at The Roz were now booking weeks in advance.

Eli's eyes found Liza's, and while he was worried about Tyrone, he knew she would more than salvage the night. Her formfitting black dress, silver hoop earrings, and eyeshadow that matched the indigo blue of the tattoo on her chest and left arm captured the room's attention as she ascended to the stage. The room hushed before she arrived at the mic.

"How are you all doing tonight?"

The crowd greeted her with whistles and applause.

"We are so sorry for the delay, but I am here, and I promise to make it up to you. First of all, any hors d'oeuvres you order during this first song are on the house. Just make sure you tip your hardworking waitstaff. They're doing their best to take care of you. And second, the band and I are going straight till one with no breaks. We are going to make sure you have a good time."

Liza winked at Eli, and Eli nodded his indebtedness.

Liza cued the band and moved her hips the way every woman wished she could and every man prayed would never stop.

Eli still felt guilty about how much he enjoyed looking at Liza, and even more how much he enjoyed himself when she was around. In addition to her beauty, this talented singer, intelligent lawyer, and charismatic leader was also an understanding friend. Liza was good for him and he knew it. His heart still belonged to Antoinette—she was still the woman of his dreams and his first thought every morning—but Liza was becoming a close second.

While the band was holding its own and Liza was making good on her promise to the audience, Eli tried calling Tyrone again.

He was beyond worried. Daily he was hearing stories of the police targeting people, stopping and searching them for jaywalking and ticketing them for flicking cigarette butts. This was why he was on the hunt. Eli was convinced that the heavy-handed tactics of the police were more than the result of a few. It felt widespread, but there had to be a ringleader.

While Eli was also open to the possibility that he was just paranoid, the harassment in the community seemed to focus on the young male offspring of the children of Africa. Nineteen-year-olds and twenty-somethings like Tyrone were enduring excessive police attention. Whatever the motives of the police might be, the madness needed to stop, so Eli continued to reread Slager's journals, hoping he might discover whether the late dirty detective had a partner in crime, hoping that his late-night prowls would eventually turn something up.

Liza and the band were nearing the end of their first song and people were putting down their glasses so their hands were free to applaud when the front door to The Roz flew open. Two young Black men carried a third through the room and laid him on the front of the stage.

Tyrone had arrived. Unconscious.

WAKING THE DEAD

Eli ran around the bar and shot onto the stage.

Tyrone was alive, but he looked dead.

There was a gash on the side of his head about the length of a stick of gum, and his blood-soaked hair made it difficult to see the depth of the wound. Thankfully, he was breathing.

He was wearing his blue suit.

After hiring Tyrone, Eli had taken him to Harold Penner's Fashion Emporium.

"Tyrone, every man needs three things—a good suit, a nice watch, and a wise woman." Eli spoke the same words he'd received decades prior from his late mentor, Father Myriel, who'd lost his life before he could see Eli with any of the three. "Today we get you the suit. Pick out whatever you want. I want you looking as smooth as Coltrane on that stage. With your first paycheck, get yourself a watch. A man who has time instead of time having him is a man who commands his destiny."

"What about the wise woman?"

"Son, she's on you," Eli had quipped.

Eli appreciated that Savoy and her husband allowed him to do these sorts of things for his nephew. He and Antoinette had never had children after their miscarriage. But as they reached their midthirties, their desire to try again had begun to overtake their desire to avoid pain, and if Antoinette were alive, Eli was sure he'd be a father by now. Antoinette's sister, Savoy, and her husband were great parents and able to provide for their three children, including Tyrone, but Eli was grateful that they seemed to understand his fatherly needs and allowed him to help occasionally.

That day, Harold Penner's had been running a two-for-one special, and Tyrone picked out two suits—one black and the other blue, in honor of Louis Armstrong.

"Unc, how did that song go—'What Did I Do to Be So Black and Blue'?" Tyrone had sung his best impression of Armstrong's growl.

The song captured the question on everyone's mind as Tyrone lay motionless on the stage. Eli eyed the red blood that soaked his white shirt and blue tie. The knees of his pants were torn, revealing scraped craters where black skin had once been.

The shocked crowd pressed toward the stage behind Eli. Those on the balcony looked down from the rail. Liza appeared with two cloth dinner napkins and a glass of ice water that she'd grabbed from a stage side table. She laid the squares on top of each other and poured the glass of ice water on top of both napkins. The water soaked through to the bottom napkin. She tied the top napkin so it held the ice and handed it to Eli.

"Here, put this on his head."

She took the wet bottom napkin and wiped his face. Tyrone's eyes shot open when the cold water touched his skin.

"Stop. Leave me alone." Tyrone's hands were blocking imaginary blows as he scrambled to his feet.

"Tyrone," said Eli.

"Get off me, man, I didn't do nothing."

"Ty, look at me. You're at The Roz. You're safe."

Tyrone's eyes darted from Eli to the people to the ceiling, then to the drums and the upright bass. He startled when Liza touched his hand.

"It's me, Ty. Can I put some water on your face?"

"Where is it?" He continued to scan the room. "What did they do with it?"

"Tyrone, what are you looking for?"

"My axe. Where's my axe?"

"Here it is, Tyrone," said one of the young men who'd laid him on the stage.

It looked like someone had used the tenor saxophone for batting practice. The keys and levers were bent or missing altogether. The circular bell looked more like a crescent moon, as if someone had stomped on it.

Tyrone collapsed.

"I'm calling the cops," a man in the crowd announced.

"No!" Tyrone said, back on his feet. "Do not call the police."

"But Tyrone, look at what they did to you. We need to call 911."

"No," he insisted, looking around the roomful of brown faces. Everyone was wearing their Sunday best. "We can't."

He stood with his left leg forward and his knees bent, eyes still darting, still ready to fight. "You all don't get it, do you? You come here in your fancy cars and tailored suits, but then you leave. We're all Black, but not all of us in the room have to feel Black."

Eli winced. Something didn't feel right about his nephew calling out his customers like that, but he had to admit, he didn't disagree, and even if he had, now wasn't the time to say anything about it.

Eli stood on the stage and put his hand on Tyrone's shoulder. "Tyrone, please sit. Let us get you some help."

"I need to go." Tyrone grabbed his saxophone. "Just forget it. You all don't care anyway; just go back to your fancy houses in Aurora and Green Valley Ranch—and you, Mr. 911, just go back to that nice place you got in Castle Rock and act like nothing happened. When you're gone, some of us still gotta live here—in Five Points, the heart of the Black community. Isn't that what they say?"

"Tyrone, listen. Let the cops sort this out."

"Unc, who do you think did this?"

Tyrone stormed out, and his friends followed.

As everyone made their way home, Eli headed out to find who had harmed his nephew.

MOVING IN TOGETHER

Eli opened the door to the morning the sun in his eyes and Liza on his stoop. On the sidewalk behind her sat a dozen or so file boxes.

Eli had been home only a couple of hours. Since the incident with Tyrone, he'd stepped up the frequency of his nightly patrols. He didn't know what he was going to do when he found what he was looking for, but he knew he had to do something.

"How'd you fit all of those in that?" Eli asked while nodding toward her gray Toyota Corolla.

"Be surprised how much I can fit into that old thing. It carried my whole life back from New York so I could work on Daddy's case."

As of late, Liza was experimenting with letting her hair grow natural, and this morning the sun shone from behind, illuminating her perfectly picked orb of an Afro. She looked like a seventies album cover with her white tank top, bell-bottom jeans, and tattoos. Eli loved a natural woman.

"Hope I didn't come too early," Liza said.

"Nope. Been up for a minute. Coffee's brewing."

After a handful of trips, the fifteen boxes sat piled in Eli's place, and Eli poured the coffee as Liza joined him at the table.

"How's Ty?"

"I saw him yesterday. Now that the adrenaline has worn off, he's pretty sore. All he kept saying was 'They did me like Rodney.'"

Liza shook her head and dabbed the corner of her eye.

"He's got a knot on his head, bruises on his back, and the worst part is he can't breathe without pain because of a bruised rib. Going to be a bit before he's able to play sax again."

Liza was now crying. Eli got up, searching for a tissue, but he had to settle for a cocktail napkin embossed with The Roz's logo. He remained standing and leaned back against the counter with his arms folded.

"I will find them. Trust me, I'm going to get who did this."

"What are you talking about? You can't go after the police."

"He's right. They did him like Rodney. The only thing is there was no camera. If there hadn't been somebody recording what they did to Rodney King, those cops would still be out in the streets with their badges and clubs instead of waiting for a trial right now."

"You know they're moving the trial from LA to Simi Valley?" asked Liza. "Those white cops are going to get themselves a jury of their peers."

Eli shook his head and clenched his jaw.

"You know it's all connected, don't you?"

"What's that?"

"These boxes. They even share the same last name—Rodney King and Moses King. There is a system-wide problem with how justice is administered. Its starts with the cops on the street and is finished by the DAs in the courtroom."

"It's all absurd," Eli chimed in. "What we saw them doing to Rodney on video, what happened to Ty, and what they did to Moses—which, by the way, I still can't figure. How does someone get convicted because of a dream?"

"While you're out there chasing the police, I'll be here trying to unravel that last one. Problem is, figuring out the absurdity is the easy part. Trying to unravel the tangled knot of absurdity— that's going to take some doing. The system is designed to get convictions, not undo them."

Eli returned to the table for his coffee. "I know you can do it. It's just going to require a bit of creativity on your part." After a sip, he raised his mug to Liza. "Here's to creativity in the face of absurdity."

"I can't thank you enough for letting me keep these here, though you have less space in this room than I do in my car. How is this going to work for you? I can still find another place—"

"I'm good," Eli said. "With everything I need to do at The Roz, I'm barely here. You and your boxes are not in my way. Stop by whenever to get what you need."

Eli retrieved a key from a kitchen drawer.

"Here, you can just let yourself in."

"Thank you, but it feels like I'm imposing."

"Trust me, it's all good. Who knows, maybe we can connect the dots—from Rodney King to Moses King."

Liza raised her coffee mug to Eli, and as they drank, her eyes told him she had a question. He thought she might have smelled the whiskey wafting from his coffee.

"I need to ask you about something."

He braced himself.

"This." She stood and, with her arms held out, gestured around. "I don't understand the absurdity of this. None of this makes sense. No bathroom or bedroom. Eli, monks under a vow of poverty live better than this."

He emptied his mug. The whiskey numbed his tongue and bit the back of his throat.

"Eli, I'm not leaving until you tell me your secret."

THE SECRET PLACE

Liza wanted to know his secret, and deep down, Eli wanted to share.

He left her behind at the table, walked to the center of the room, and shoved one box aside, revealing a barely perceptible handle. After he'd purchased The Roz with this adjoining storage room at the back of the building, he'd discovered this door and the belowground room by accident one day while sweeping. Best he could figure, it was a relic left over from the days of Prohibition.

Eli pulled, and the hatch door creaked open, revealing the dark cavern beneath.

"Eli, what in the world . . ." Liza's voice trailed off as she stood, hand covering her mouth.

"Like I told you, when it comes to my place, there's more than meets the eye."

Eli sat down at the opening. "Now don't get your hopes up. This is not the hidden bunker of a wealthy comic book superhero. Quite the opposite." He descended the ladder and pulled the string to the ceiling light. Looking up, he said, "Welcome to my secret."

Liza was now standing at the opening as she peered down on him, her hand still covering her mouth.

Eli could tell that she had no category for what she was experiencing, and he didn't blame her. He wasn't sure how she would react, but when he coaxed her, Liza knelt down and maneuvered her body as he had. As she descended the ladder, he steadied her as best he could with his hands around her waist until her feet touched the ground.

Eli waited as her eyes surveyed the room.

His mind made a case for why this was a mistake, but his heart silenced those arguments with an even stronger longing to be seen and known by this daughter of Africa. He knew that his living conditions would be difficult for Liza to understand, but he was tired of hiding the reality of his life.

Her eyes settled on the small army cot with its pillow, folded blanket, and adjacent space heater.

"Eli, this is where you sleep?"

Eli remained silent.

She made her way to the small bathroom, which was shoehorned into a corner.

"And this is your . . ."

Eli nodded.

"And this is—"

"My father's library. He died when I was a teen."

"You've never told me about him. What was his name?"

"Father—Myriel—he wasn't my real father. He was . . ." He'd almost said murdered. He wanted to tell her how he'd witnessed the gruesome death of the only father he'd ever known, but now was not the time. So he just said, "He was a good man, a man of the cloth, who saved my life."

He followed Liza from the bathroom past his jump rope and heavy bag. She ran her hands along the ends of the bookshelves and turned left down the farthest aisle of his library.

Eli held his breath. On the bottom shelf next to Liza's feet were Slager's journals.

"Have you read all of these?" Liza asked, motioning toward the rows of books sitting on the shelves.

"More times than I can count."

"All of them?"

"Every single one."

Eli wasn't about to share his evening ritual of mind, body, and spirit—how he first exhausted his mind, then his body, and then prayed for God to have mercy on his soul for the things he'd done and the things he was about to do.

"Eli, I don't know what to say. This is beautiful and terrifying at the same time. On the one hand, I'm amazed at how you did all of this, how you got all of this down here, but this isn't normal. I'm worried about you. How do you . . . why do you live like this?"

Eli didn't know the answer. What had initially been motivated by fear and grief had become a necessity. That was the sad and painful reality of the last few years.

Antoinette was dead.

And Eli didn't know how to live.

HUNTSVILLE

"Ms. Liza, I can't believe it. You drove all the way here from Denver?"

Liza was doing her best to appear competent and put together, but inside, she was a mess. After leaving Eli's place, she'd hopped on I-25 and headed for Huntsville, the home of her new client, Moses King.

The drive gave her time to think, mostly about Eli. She knew he was grieving, but seeing his underground quarters had opened her eyes to the depth of his brokenness and pain. Months ago she'd vowed in her heart to wait for him. Once he healed, Liza believed, Eli would be the man for her and Journey. Though she had yet to tell anyone, Liza loved Eli, and while she knew his heart still belonged to Antoinette, she saw that as a good thing. If Eli had loved once, that meant he could love again. But now she wasn't sure.

Visiting Moses in prison also had her thinking about her father. She used to visit Langston at least once a month and usually more frequently, making additional trips if it was Journey's birthday or if she wanted to share with him her conviction that she was going to get him out. She now felt guilty for the false hope she had given him.

Liza stopped only for gas and made the drive to Huntsville in fifteen hours, arriving just as her dashboard clock turned to three AM. Parked in a gas station parking lot, she slept in her car until the sun warmed her face. After brushing her teeth, touching up her mascara, and changing into her lawyer-like pantsuit in the Quick Mart bathroom, she was ready.

Huntsville revolved around the business of housing and executing those condemned to die in the friendship state. In law school she'd read about the effects of the prison industry on the lives of those who lived in towns like these—how when a prisoner was executed, the whole town took part and benefited. It wasn't just the lawyers, prison guards, and wardens who were involved; everyone, from the motel owners to the restaurant managers, made their living and paid their bills by living next to the Death House.

"Ms. Liza, feels like Christmas. Not only did you drive down here, but you're my lawyer too."

The stale smell of the visiting room reminded Liza of the last time she'd visited her father and they'd held hands across the cold metal table, the rattle of his handcuffs echoing off the walls. Today, Moses wasn't wearing handcuffs, but leg restraints still secured his ankles.

Liza had yet to say a word, but holding back the tears required her full attention. She pretended she needed something in her briefcase to buy herself some time to find her composure.

"Your father said you would help me, and here you are."

At that, her tears fell with the ease of a spring thunderstorm upon her cheeks.

"Oh, Ms. Liza. I'm sorry. I didn't mean to make you cry."

The grandfatherly tone in his voice put her at ease. Moses reached out to her with slender dark fingers attached to wiry arms and an even more wirelike body.

"It's no accident that you're here. Even though I told you not to come down here, I knew you would. I've been fasting for this moment."

Moses removed his metal-framed glasses and wiped his eyes with the palms of his hands and then, when that wasn't enough, used the sleeve of his dark-green jumpsuit. The dark skin of his bald head reflected the flutter of the fluorescent lights.

"You read my letters. Did you have time to read my case files? Did you see how all they had was her dream, and did you see how—"

Liza held up her hands. She had found her lawyer self.

"Mr. King—"

"Ms. Liza, please call me Moses."

As much as she'd wanted to keep this first meeting professional, Liza knew her tears had already broken that barrier. "How about Mr. Moses?"

His smile signaled that they'd agreed.

"Yes, I've read your letters, and while I have obtained and secured your files, I haven't had the chance to wade through them."

Out of habit, Liza looked at the clock and checked for a guard who might interrupt their meeting, as one always had with her father, but then she remembered that this was a lawyer-client visit and they had as much time as they needed.

"Mr. Moses, I'm not supposed to be here, let alone be acting as your counsel. To be honest, your case doesn't meet the criteria of the organization I work for, as you are not facing death or even life behind bars."

"At my age, my sentence might as well be a death sentence."

"I understand, but that doesn't change the fact that we can't take your case."

His shoulders slumped.

"Ms. Liza, did you drive all the way down here just to tell me you couldn't take my case?"

"I can't make any promises. But if there's a chance that I can help, I need one thing from you."

"Anything. I have nothing to hide. I'll even take a lie detector test if you need to know for sure that I had nothing to do with this."

"The confession. You said that you received a letter of confession in the mail. Do you have it?"

Moses smiled.

"Don't go anywhere without it, not even the shower."

Moses checked for the guards and bent over like he was tying his shoes. Instead, he unrolled the cuff of his pant leg and retrieved a small ziplock bag like the ones used for individual doses of medications. Inside was the letter, folded tight with creased edges.

He unzipped the plastic bag.

"Not to be too disgusting, but this little bag has been in some unmentionable places. I've done all I could to protect this, but the letter is clean. I promise you."

Liza glanced for the guards and then gave him a nod.

With great care, as if he were handling the only copy of a priceless ancient manuscript, he worked the letter out of the plastic baggy and onto the table.

Liza palmed the small square and, after another glance for the guards, put it in her briefcase.

She stayed for another thirty minutes, recognizing that times like these were a precious break from the monotony of prison life. They talked about Langston and how life had changed on the outside. Moses dreamed about how he would move in with his mother and care for her in her advanced years.

"Please, be careful with that letter. It's the only proof I have. It's the only thing that can get me out of here."

"Mr. Moses, I'll do what I can."

"Ms. Liza, that's more than I can ask for."

LC

Liza slid the key into the lock on Eli's door like she was trying to avoid waking a newborn baby. She'd peeked in at The Roz and seen that Eli was still serving last call, but she was still trying to be quiet, because Eli's home felt more like a cemetery chapel.

With the door closed behind her, Liza entered the room with new understanding. The above room was an inner sanctum of sorts—the kitchen table with its two chairs, Antoinette's orange scarf draped on one of them, an unlit candle sitting center table. This was the altar of this strange religion of the dead, and Eli was the monk who lived below, the caretaker of this shrine to a woman, a marriage that still existed in Eli's heart. Even with the boxes from the Moses King case stacked neatly in a corner, they still felt like an intrusion upon this shrine, a desecration.

Eli had told her she could drop by anytime, but midnight felt like she was pushing things. After meeting with Moses in Huntsville, she'd driven straight back to Denver even faster than she'd left.

She was tired and needed to rest, but the letter of confession had her searching the files for a name—Levar Calhoun. Calhoun was in prison for assault on multiple women, and in the letter he claimed that because of a spiritual awakening, he'd come to grips with the reality of God and wanted to clear his conscious. Calhoun said he was no longer comfortable with Moses King doing time for a crime he had committed.

"We weren't friends, just drinking buddies," Moses told Liza. "We all knew each other back in the day, nothing deeper than sharing a blunt and a buzz together from time to time."

Now this former drinking buddy wanted to help Moses by writing a get-out-of-jail-free card.

The letter was promising, but Liza felt it wasn't enough. The DA would argue that Calhoun was just a friend trying to help a friend. She planned on visiting Calhoun to assess whether he would hold up on the stand under cross-examination. But before she did, she wanted more. That's why she was at Eli's shrine in the middle of the night, going through the boxes from Moses King's case.

Liza needed something to add credence to the confession. She didn't know exactly what she was looking for but hoped she would recognize it when she saw it.

She fingered her way through the first box and stopped to fan the pages of a composition notebook containing notes from Moses's prior attorney. Her eyes burned from the lack of sleep, but she was determined to find something.

A knock at the door captured her attention, and before she could stand up from underneath the lapful of files, the door opened.

It was Eli.

"Why'd you knock on the front door of your own place?"

"Saw your car and didn't want to startle you."

"Sorry I'm still here. I was hoping to get in and out before you closed things up."

"No worries, I said you could stop by anytime."

"I know, I know, but I don't want to overstay my welcome in the first couple of days."

"So what are you looking for?" Eli said as he grabbed a chair from the kitchenette and sat down next to her.

Liza told him about her trip to Huntsville and back and her meeting with Moses King. She showed him the letter of confession and told him how, after meeting Moses face-to-face, she was convinced he was telling the truth.

"I'm still stuck on the fact that you've been to Texas and back."

"I know. It was kinda crazy and I really need to get some sleep, but what I need more is to find out if Levar Calhoun is anywhere in these files."

"Well, let's do this." Eli picked up his chair and moved to the other side of the stack of boxes. "I'll start down here, and we'll meet in the middle. I know I don't have a law degree, but I can read. Tell me what I'm looking for."

"Eli, you don't have to. There's at least a dozen boxes to go. This is my cause, not yours."

"Liza, I'm good. I've got a few minutes."

It was then that Liza noticed the bottle of wine he'd set on the table when he retrieved his chair.

"Eli, I'm so sorry, I can leave. I don't want to intrude on your time with *her*."

Eli retrieved two glasses and poured them both a glass.

"I'm in," Eli said. "Teach me how to do this."

They worked in tandem, each taking a box, scanning each page of every folder and notebook and unfolding every scrap of paper.

"I can't get over the redundancy in these forms, the constant retelling of what happened at each appeal hearing," Eli remarked. "Best I can tell, the prosecution's case boils down to this: Moses had opportunity to commit the crime because he lived in the same apartment building, next door to the victim. As neighbors, they, along with others, would hang out at times,

even go out together and drink. Moses wasn't a suspect immediately, but they started taking a closer look after the victim
said she could identify him. That was it. There's nothing in here
about corroborating evidence. At trial, the prosecution only presented two witnesses, the detective and the victim. She literally
said that after she had her dream, she knew who did it. That was
it. I still don't get how that can happen."

"For jurors—and detectives, for that matter—there's nothing more powerful than eyewitness testimony, especially if that
witness is the actual victim. She was there; who can fault them
for believing her? I blame the detective for not backing up her
testimony with cold, hard facts."

Eli nodded.

"But what's good for the goose . . ." Liza took a sip. "What's
better than the eyewitness testimony of the victim? The confession of the real perpetrator, right here in black and white." Liza
lifted the handwritten letter that Moses had given her, signed by
Levar Calhoun.

Another half hour passed, and the bottle of wine sat empty
between them when Liza stopped and buried her face in her
hands in disgust. "You've got to be kidding me. Eli, get this.
There was an assault kit performed on the victim. Years later,
Moses petitioned the court to have the DNA tested, hoping it
would show that he was not a match."

"What did they find?"

"What *didn't* they find is the question," Liza said. "When
they went to retrieve the evidence bag that was marked DO NOT
DESTROY, what do you think they found? That's right—it was
gone, destroyed. Just like what happened with Daddy."

Eli's eyes comforted her, and though she was slowing down,
she moved on to another box.

"Might this be what we're looking for?" Eli handed her a
notebook.

Liza's heart leapt, as it was the scribblings of the lead detective on the case. Eli's thumb marked a spot midway down the page: *Interview LC again, something doesn't seem right.*

"Eli, this is it. He was an early suspect. This connects Calhoun to the case!"

After a brief high five, Eli stood, opened the hatch leading to his underground apartment, and disappeared down the ladder.

Liza packed up the boxes and arranged them back in the corner. She grabbed her purse and briefcase containing the letter of confession from Levar Calhoun and the note from the detective about investigating someone with the same initials *LC*.

Eli reemerged, wearing dark-gray sweatpants and a hoodie with binoculars around his neck.

"Eli, you look like a burglar or something."

"Takes one to catch one," Eli quipped as he headed out the door.

NO CHASER

Eli walked past The Roz and headed west on Welton Street toward Sonny Lawson Park. He passed M&D's with its *Smoked All Night, Served All Day* message painted on the window. The smell of smoked chicken and brisket wafted from the storefront restaurant, and Eli made a note to stop in for lunch later that day. Now it was only three in the morning, not even breakfast time.

He'd have to explain his abrupt departure and mysterious outfit to Liza, but at the moment, watching the police assigned to Five Points had his focus. What they'd done to Tyrone had Eli on tilt, and he was more determined than ever.

When the weather was warm enough, Sonny Lawson Park was a local hangout for Denver's homeless and low-rent drug dealers, the kind who were more of a threat to themselves than to others because they consumed more of their product than they sold. Eli felt a kinship with them as he reached in his pocket and fingered his flask of whiskey, which he'd filled from The Roz's top shelf. He slipped into an alley across from the park and sat in a dark corner created by the back wall of a store and a dark-green dumpster. The smell was far from pleasant, but here he had a full view of any activities in the park.

He watched Sonny Lawson Park because he'd heard that it was a frequent patrol destination for bored police with time to kill while the city slept. The park provided them with late-night entertainment as they rolled the homeless for cigarettes and the dope dealers for any cash they had, which around the first of the month could be significant, with Social Security, veterans, and disability checks having arrived.

Eli figured that the sorts of cops who would steal from those at that park would also be the kind who would use a young man's saxophone for batting practice. He estimated that at the most, there were twenty-five officers assigned to Five Points. A simple but time-consuming process of observation and elimination should yield results.

He leaned back against the wall, trusting that the darkness concealed him, and waited. With his binoculars at the ready, he let his mind drift back to his conversation with Liza. He was still in disbelief over the fact that she'd driven all the way to Huntsville and back and was still going with no sleep. Eli desperately needed sleep himself. Running the bar by day and into the night and then spying on the police until dawn was taking its toll.

"This is it—this is what I needed in order to feel confident going to see Calhoun down in Cañon City," Liza had said.

Eli hoped she was right. Liza needed success after feeling like she'd failed her father.

He slid the half-empty flask into his pocket and closed his eyes. That's when he noticed how quiet things were. During the day, the park was abuzz with activity. By night, it was usually an all-out ruckus of shouts, fights, and stumbling addicts looking for their next score. Tonight the loudest noise came from Eli's stomach as it anticipated the smoked white-meat chicken combo with corn bread that he was going to get from M&D's in a few hours.

Eli scanned the park with the binoculars. The dealers were not in their usual spot under the bleachers by the softball field, and there weren't the usual huddles of homeless beneath the trees.

The park was bare, deserted.

Even if the police had come through before Eli arrived, they would have just emptied pockets. They never cleared the entire park.

Eli wasn't sure what to make of it, but it was clear that his stakeout was a lost cause. He headed home for some needed sleep.

Turning right out of the alley and heading east on Welton Street, he approached Freeman's Furniture Store. Mr. Freeman was a good man, and the community was good to him. It was a running joke that every butt in Five Points sat on a Freeman couch at least one time a day.

As Eli was about to pass by the large plate-glass display window, a beam from a flashlight inside the store caught his eye as it swept toward the back of the store. He ducked down and watched two silhouettes as they made their way through the back of the store and then, without hesitation, kicked in the door that led to Mr. Freeman's office.

With the closest pay phone at least a block away, a 911 call couldn't happen soon enough to make any difference. Eli contemplated banging on the window with his binoculars in an attempt to scare the apparent robbers away.

The screech of brakes and tires on pavement interrupted his plan as a police car came to a stop with its front wheels on the sidewalk between Eli and The Roz. An officer jumped out of the car and shouted for Eli to put his hands in the air.

Eli raised his hands with the calculation of a sloth. The officer crouched behind an open door. Eli knew what this looked like. A burglary was in process and he was outside peering in, dressed all in black, carrying binoculars.

Something didn't feel right, though. The officer crouched behind his open door, but there were no emergency lights flashing atop his car. Even the headlights were dark.

"Slowly," the officer demanded. "Now put your hands behind your head. Slowly."

The dark barrel of a gun aimed Eli's way, serving as an exclamation point to the order. Eli complied.

"Now turn around."

Eli again complied.

The officer closed his car door.

As far as Eli was concerned, he had only one option.

He darted for the darkness of the park.

If he heard a gunshot, he would zigzag and duck. Until then, he would run straight as fast as he could toward the largest tree in the center of Sonny Lawson Park.

No shots fired.

No commands rang out.

Not even the sound of footsteps chasing him disturbed the night.

At the large evergreen tree, Eli peeked over his shoulder to see how close the officer was, but he was still standing next to his car, gun at his side, staring at Eli.

Eli stopped.

He was grateful that he had his hoodie pulled low and that he'd never looked up and showed his face.

However, Eli had seen the police officer's face and had another one to put on his list.

While he didn't know why the officer had failed to pursue him, Eli turned and kept on running.

ONTO SOMETHING

Eli ran out of precaution. For all he knew, the cop had called for backup and the cavalry was on the way.

Upon exiting the park, Eli continued north in a sort of zig-zag pattern through the neighborhood, moving farther away from The Roz. He kept mostly to alleys and hugged buildings until he crossed Brighton Boulevard to the railroad tracks. He spotted an abandoned freight car and ducked underneath.

He lay there not so much to catch his breath as to let the adrenaline ease its way out of his body. It always caught him off guard how quick his fight-or-flight response kicked in at the sight of a police officer. He remembered how, when he was a young boy, a blue uniform made him as antsy as a gazelle on the Serengeti. As a man in his late thirties, he would have hoped to have grown out of this reflex, but he was a Black man in Five Points. The concrete jungle still lived in his blood, and his shackle-free ankles weren't willing to take a chance. So he ran.

Eli lay on his back between the steel wheels long enough for his heart to reach its resting rate and for him to plot his path home. Then he took a peek inside the freight car. There were two men curled up in their respective corners with a collective pile of belongings between them. A pair of grease-stained khakis and a white Colorado Rockies T-shirt were within arm's reach. Eli removed and tossed his hoodie and sweatpants onto the pile of items. Neither of the men moved or showed awareness of his presence.

By the time he arrived home, he'd traveled at least ten blocks to go the two blocks from Freeman's Furniture to his place. When he slipped in his door, he half hoped Liza was still there as he eyed the neatly stacked boxes for Moses's case. But then again, how would he explain to her what was going on? Why he'd left dressed in black like some sort of cat burglar and returned looking like he'd just changed the engine on a car?

Thankfully, Liza was gone, and he didn't have to explain anything.

He grabbed a glass of water and sat down at the kitchenette table. There was a reason the officer hadn't given chase, and he needed to figure out why.

There had been a burglary in process.

The cop had slid up on the scene without sirens or lights.

He'd trained his gun on Eli, who was in fact dressed the way one might expect a night prowler to be dressed, and yet when Eli ran, nothing.

This had to be the first time in the history of Five Points that a son of Africa had run from the police and the police did not give chase.

Eli was sure he was onto something, but in order to figure out what it was, he knew one thing: he needed a different disguise.

SICK AND TIRED

"Boss, I'm not doing well," Liza rasped into the phone, hoping Garrett would find it believable.

Sensing he was convinced, she continued.

"Headache, slight fever, feeling the chills coming on. I can't make it in today."

While Liza wasn't sick, she was tired after the round-trip drive to Huntsville and the early-morning search with Eli through King's files.

She'd made it home in time for breakfast with Journey before taking her to school. On the drive to Park Hill Middle School, Liza told her daughter all about the trip to Huntsville and the man who knew her grandfather.

"Are you going to get him out before they kill him too?"

It pained Liza that Journey had to experience such harsh realities at her young age. Eighth graders shouldn't have to carry with them the wrongful execution of their grandfather.

"No, baby, they don't want to kill him like Grandpa, but I still want to get him out. Also, let's keep this a secret between us. I don't want to upset Grandma with the idea that I'm trying to help someone who also knew Grandpa."

Though her eyes were ablaze from lack of sleep, Liza returned home once more and reread the detective notes Eli had found. Levar Calhoun had been an early suspect in the case, but after the victim had her dream and ID'd Moses, they'd failed to pursue him further.

"Is there anything I can do to help you with the Dexter Diaz case? I don't want us to fall behind," Garrett said, after hearing she wasn't coming into the office.

"No, I'm on top of it. I should be able to work on it today in between shivers and doses of Mom's chicken noodle soup."

"Well, if you need help, let me know ASAP. We need a game plan for getting the false confession thrown out, and the sooner we file our motion, the better."

"No worries, boss. I'm on it."

Liza hung up the phone, only to see her mother watching with a wry smile on her face.

"Chicken noodle soup, eh? I'll get right on it."

Liza couldn't remember the last time she'd seen anything resembling happiness in her mom. Liza could fool Garrett, but Elizabeth Brown was another story.

"Now that you mention it, soup sounds perfect with some of those butter rolls you used to make." Liza gave her a mom a wry smile of her own. "And if you don't mind, pick up Journey after school? I need to run an errand, but I'll be home for dinner."

She shoved the files into her attaché case and grabbed her keys as she headed out the door.

Liza had a date with a violent and vile man.

THE CONFESSOR

"Pretty lady, you can just call me Levar."

Liza wasn't sure what she'd expected evil to look like, but a short, overweight Black man with horn-rimmed glasses and male-pattern baldness was not it. His ruddy, misshapen, pockmarked nose announced years of drugs and alcohol abuse.

"Mr. Calhoun, for our conversation, I think it best that we stick with last names," Liza responded.

His eyes shifted from the left to the right side of her chest and back to her lips. Liza was grateful that she'd wore an unflattering beige pantsuit with a shirt buttoned to the top.

"Ms. Brown, for my purposes, I'm going to need your first name if we're going to continue."

Levar Calhoun knew why she was there and that she needed him more than he needed her. Liza weighed her options as she eyed the fogged plexiglass that separated them.

He deserved to be on the other side of that glass. While she believed there were serious flaws in the criminal justice system, she was grateful when it captured, convicted, and locked up men like this. Calhoun had kidnapped and assaulted both a mother and her daughter just two miles away from the crime for which Moses King had been arrested. The system that had wrongly incarcerated Liza's father also, for the good of society, kept men like this off the streets.

She decided to acquiesce.

"Liza," she said. "Liza Brown."

"Now, sweetheart, that wasn't too difficult, was it?"

His smile turned her stomach.

"Now, let's get to know each other a bit. Is there a Mr. Brown in your life?"

She had given an inch, but a mile was out of the question. This man had reached out to Moses King for a reason. He had his own set of motivations and desires. There was no way he was trying to help Moses out of the goodness of his heart, so she took a chance.

Liza hung up the phone, stood up, and walked away.

Three steps.

Five.

Ten more.

Calhoun tapped on the glass with the receiver of the phone.

Liza turned, stepped back into view, and waited.

After Calhoun's eyes traveled the length of her body, he crossed his hands over his chest and mouthed, "I'm sorry, sweetheart."

Liza didn't budge.

"I'm sorry, Liza."

Her feet remained planted.

"Ms. Liza Brown."

She returned to the booth, sat, and picked up the receiver.

"Mr. Calhoun, I'm not here to play games. Moses King is doing your time, over twenty years for you—"

"How is my old buddy Mo? I haven't seen him in a minute. He holding up okay?"

Liza retrieved the folder and held up the letter.

"Did you write this?"

"C'mon, pretty thing, why you got to be like this? Can't you just take your time—"

"Time! You want to talk about time? Every minute we waste here is a minute of freedom lost by Moses King. I'm only going to ask once more: Did you write this?"

"Pretty thing, I like you. You're a strong one."

"Mr. Calhoun." Liza stared him down.

Finally, he nodded. "Yes, I wrote that."

"Care to tell me why?"

"Sweetheart, you ever meet God?" Calhoun gazed into the distance. "I haven't, but I know I will. I know that someday I'm gonna stand before the Almighty." His eyes settled back on her chest. "No, I'm not saying I've had some religious awakening or that I met Jesus. No. All I'm saying is that I know I'm going to be judged someday, and I'm hoping that if I help Moses by telling the truth about what I did, well, then, maybe the thermostat for my room in hell won't be on its highest setting."

Liza waited for his eyes to return to hers.

"Are you willing to tell the truth to a judge about your assault on the victim?"

"Oh, hell no! I don't know where you got that."

"You said right here that you want certain things to come to light. Are you or are you not willing to help Moses?"

"I'll help Moses, but what happened between me and her, that was consensual. Do I look like a guy who has to force himself on a woman? Shh . . . no. I beat her, but the rest, that was real."

Liza returned the letter to her bag. Even if Calhoun wasn't willing to confess to everything, what he was saying was enough to put him at the scene of the crime.

"Mr. Calhoun, I hope you are a man of your word."

"Sweetheart, there are a lot of things I'm not, but that I am."

"Well, I intend to give you a chance to prove it."

Liza stood. She now had enough to get Moses a new trial.

RESERVATIONS

It was like opening night all over again.

"We are going to have to take reservations for our reservations," Eli said to a petite golden-haired woman with light olive skin—Antoinette's sister.

Savoy was there to see Tyrone, her son, return to the stage.

It had been three weeks since they'd carried him into The Roz, unconscious and bleeding. His bruises and scabs were almost healed, and everyone wanted him to know they loved him.

"So, how is he doing?" Eli asked.

"Depends on if we're talking about his body or his heart. What they did to him was unconscionable. Keep thinking that if there were someone with a video camera, then maybe we could make them cops pay like they're getting ready to do out there in LA."

"Yeah, seems like the only way people are going to believe us is if we travel with our own camera crews, filming every encounter with the police." Eli shook his head.

"They didn't beat him as bad as Rodney, but Tyrone deserves justice too. He didn't want to, but I made him go to that police station. All they did was take our statement and ask him if he was sure that it was a cop who did that to him. Even accused him of being high on drugs."

Eli thought about the officer he'd encountered outside Freeman's Furniture Store. He wanted to get back out there, but he was lying low for the time being, trying to figure out his next move.

"So he's angry. It's going to be a while before we get over that, if ever," Savoy said.

Eli excused himself as he took a trip down the bar, making sure everyone had a drink. Then he returned to Savoy at the end of the bar.

"So, what about you? How are things?" she asked.

"This bar is driving me crazy," Eli snapped. "I can't keep up. This is what I wanted, but it's far from what I expected. The ice maker keeps going out, the beer tap system is spitting out foam, and—"

"Eli, you know I'm not asking about The Roz." Savoy placed her hand on his shoulder. "You need to come out of that hole and start living again. You know that's what she wanted."

"Savoy, let's not do this now."

"Eli, there's never a good time. You know I promised her I'd look out for you. Make sure you—"

"Savoy, I can't do this now."

"I understand it's difficult, but remember the promise you made to her. She knew you needed to love. You told Antoinette you would allow yourself to love again. I promised her I would remind you often."

Eli knew Savoy meant well. He also knew Antoinette was right—he needed to love. Unfortunately, it was also love that he was desperately avoiding. It was love that had created the heights from which he had fallen, and he had determined he would never fall that far again.

Liza appeared, rescuing him from Savoy.

"Hey, boss, are we ready?"
Eli nodded, and Liza made her way to the stage.
Savoy squeezed his arm.
"Eli, all I'm trying to say is that Liza is a good woman, and *boss*, I think you're ready."

THE TY PIPER

Eli slipped into the back room as Liza took the stage.

"Good evening, everybody, and welcome to The Roz. Are you ready to have a good time?"

The crowd responded with hoots, hollers, and applause.

Eli kept one ear on Liza as he retrieved a black saxophone case from underneath the desk. Over the past few weeks, Eli had collected donations from patrons to replace Tyrone's saxophone, and tonight they were presenting him with the finest sax ever played at The Roz.

Eli peeked out of the office and spotted Tyrone on the other side of the room.

"We all know why we're here tonight. Tyrone, our main man, our rising star, is back in the house!"

The crowd stood in ovation, and the band provided walk-up music as Tyrone took the stage. He was wearing his black suit, the last of the two Eli had purchased for him.

"Tyrone, take it in, feel the love. We love you. Welcome back home!" Liza said as she stepped to the side. The applause of the crowd drowned out even the drummer's feverish welcome.

Liza motioned for the crowd to take a seat as she stepped back to the mic.

"Tyrone, we want you to know that we are with you and how sorry we are for what happened to you."

"Sorry and angry," a man shouted from the balcony.

"That's right, Ty, we love you," hollered another.

Liza waited a few moments, then continued. "We have a surprise for you. A welcome-home gift of sorts."

Eli now joined them onstage and took the microphone.

"Tyrone, you think you're here tonight to serve as bandleader for Liza's set, but all these people came out because we want to hear you. We know your ribs are still a little sore, but we were hoping you'd play at least one song—and that you'd play it with the shiny new horn that's in this case."

Eli held the case as Tyrone unlatched and opened it. Tyrone's eyes welled as he took in the glint of the brass.

Eli handed him a new reed. "Get it wet, because we want to hear what this axe can do."

Tyrone took the reed, and Liza took the mic.

"Tyrone, this is a gift from everyone in this room. We all chipped in."

"Wow. Just wow." Tyrone spoke without the mic, but all could still hear him. "I never thought I'd hold a horn like this. This is big-time."

"You're big-time," someone shouted.

"My man, thank you. All of you, thank you. Thank you."

There was gratitude in his voice but fire in his eyes.

"Ya'll, this means a lot, and I'm extremely grateful, but . . ." His voice cracked.

"It's okay, Ty. We're here for you."

"I'm not okay. We are not okay." The strength in his voice returned. "I appreciate this welcome-home gift, ya'll, but I never left. This has always been my home."

The room was silent. Eli spotted Savoy as she clasped her hands in an attempt to give her son strength.

"I know out where you now live that the houses are bigger and the crime is less, but we need you here. We need you more than you need the suburbs. You are here tonight to welcome me home, but when are you all going to stop visiting and come back home yourself?"

Tyrone slipped the neck strap over his head and clipped on the back of the saxophone.

"I'll play you a song tonight, best I can with my sore mouth and broken heart, because this ain't working for all of us. We all look the same, but we aren't the same. Like I said, it's good to be home, but I never left. I'm not the one who drives in on a Friday or Saturday night for some good music and then leaves just as fast as you arrived. What do they call Five Points? The heart of Denver's Black community? I'm here to tell you that our heart is in bad shape. For those of us who are still here, it's struggling. We need you here more than for a few hours on the weekend."

Eli put his hand on Tyrone's shoulder.

"Uncle, you came back, and look at what you did. You lost your wife, and we all know that you still are not healed, but you came back."

Tyrone's anger had now turned to hurt. Tears filled his eyes.

"I can't go back to the way things were. I'll play you a song because this is what I do, but I'm playing on the same stage where they laid my limp body after some of Five Points' finest beat me unconscious.

"I'll play you a song on this stage, but I need you to join me out in the streets too. Don't just use those streets to drive in and out of here. We about to do something, and we're going to need all of you in here to be out there."

Tyrone turned to Eli and bowed his head into his chest. Eli wrapped his arms around him. Two Black men, two different generations, joined in pain, on the stage of The Roz.

The room was still silent.

When Eli opened his eyes, he first saw Liza.

"Tyrone, look."

Liza stood facing Tyrone, her right fist in the air.

"Tyrone, they hear you."

Eli turned Tyrone toward Liza and the rest of the room.

Every person was on their feet, fists in the air in solidarity.

"Brother, we are still here. The heart is still strong," the man from the balcony boomed.

"Play your song," Eli whispered in Tyrone's ear. "Play your song, and I promise you, we will all follow."

Tyrone nodded to the band, and the drummer counted off the beat. As the groove settled and everyone took their seats, he stepped to the microphone.

"I got a new song for you. A song for us." Tyrone raised his fist into the air. "It's a song called 'Reckoning.'"

WHAT'S NEXT

"That's right, man. Be gentle. Hold it like a baby," Eli shouted as both he and Liza watched Tyrone gently tuck his new saxophone into the case. After snapping it shut and hoisting the strap to his shoulder, Tyrone made his way to the bar.

"Ty, I've seen nothing like what happened tonight," said Liza.

"I can't thank y'all enough for this. I didn't know how I was going to get another outside of making payments on some secondhand horn at the pawnshop."

"You deserve it," Eli said. "But not just what's in that case, Tyrone. You deserve the support and trust of the people that were here tonight. You've earned it."

"Yeah, we were just talking. You were special on that new sax, but something special happened among us, Ty, and it was because of you," Liza said.

Tyrone thanked her with a hug.

"What you said tonight wasn't easy, but it was necessary. I meant what I said. We will follow you," Eli said. "When they laid you on that stage, unconscious, you got their attention, but tonight you captured their hearts. They are ready to follow you."

"I hope so, but now I have to figure out where to take them once I get them back in the streets."

"Just follow your heart, Tyrone, because that's why we're following you," Liza said.

Eli's mind shifted to how Tyrone was going to make his way home. He lived only a few blocks away, but that was enough for the cops to take another inning of batting practice with his new sax.

"You need someone to walk with you?" Eli asked.

"I'm good. Mom's waiting outside in the car, but thanks for looking out for a brother."

Eli gave him a nod as Liza said goodbye with one last hug.

Then Eli and Liza turned back toward each other. They were the last two left in the bar. Eli poured, wishing they could do this more, but with her singing at The Roz only on Friday and Saturday nights, he'd take what he could get.

After a few silent sips, Eli went first.

"You know you're the one who started this. Tonight was not the beginning of something but a continuation of what you did for Langston. We all watched in awe when you recruited the guys from his old barbershop and formed them into a silent group of relentless sign-holding protesters that followed the governor. Everywhere he went, Black men holding *Or ELSE* signs greeted him. Governor Stash received the message loud and clear that he needed to do something *or else* there would be hell to pay."

Liza raised an eyebrow in reflection.

"Tyrone is just taking the baton from you and running his leg of this never-ending race." Eli raised a glass. "Cheers to you."

"Cheers to Langston Brown," Liza added.

Eli admired her deeply—the ways she loved her father and mother, her commitment to giving Journey the best childhood she could, and the way she had embraced a life she never would have chosen for herself. Eli wanted what she had, but he felt stuck between the deferred dreams of his past and the emptiness of his future. He'd call it quits if he could, but he no longer had the courage to end his life, nor the will to change it.

"So catch me up. What's the latest on Moses King?"

"Well, I went to see Calhoun to get a read on what I'm dealing with."

Eli now raised an eyebrow.

"What's he like?"

"Vile. Disgusting. Constantly undressed me with his eyes. But I got what I was looking for."

"Did he say he did it?"

"Mostly. He copped to the fact that he beat her but said everything else was consensual."

"Is that enough?"

"It's enough to put him at the scene of the crime."

"That's great. All you have to do now is show the letter to the DA and—"

"Ha." Liza laughed. "I wish it were that easy. This is not a collegial search for truth, especially not with DA Taylor. If it were, they would have pursued Calhoun in the beginning. No, we still have a battle ahead of us."

"So, how do you force Taylor's hand?"

"Well," Liza asked. "Ever hear of habeas?"

HABEAS WHO?

"Habeas what? Slow down, my juris doctorate friend." Eli said.

"Habeas corpus. It's Latin for *bring me the body.*"

"That's morbid, but then again, Latin is a dead language."

"Very funny, my bartender friend. Why don't you fill up this glass, and I'll explain things to you."

Eli obliged and watched as she took a sip, leaving another lipstick print on the glass.

"So back in the day, if you got arrested, an officer of the court could ask the judge to order the jailer to bring the body, habeas corpus—bring the prisoner to the courtroom so things could get sorted out."

"I'm following. So how does that help Moses?"

"Well, first, habeas corpus still applies today and it will force them to bring him back to Colorado. Down there in Huntsville, he's all alone, but if we can get him back here, then he'll be able to see his family again. Especially his mom; she's not doing well healthwise."

"That sounds like a win right there, but I'm guessing there's more."

"Yes, a writ of habeas corpus is about presenting evidence that was not presented at trial. It's about previously unknown evidence."

"So you're going to argue that the letter of confession from Calhoun is new evidence that now needs to be considered by the court."

Liza nodded.

"Seems like a slam dunk. You file the motion and show the judge an actual confession by the guy who really did it." Eli leaned forward with emphasis. "Then Moses is free. How could they not let him out once they see that letter?"

"I wish it were that easy. Habeas is all about getting a new trial. If the judge grants the request, then what he's saying is that Moses can have a new trial with the additional evidence added to the old evidence."

"This is crazy," Eli said. "I get the need for process, but it seems like it's twice as hard to prove someone innocent than it was to prove them guilty."

"All while people like Moses and my daddy waste away in a six-by-nothing closet of a cell."

"But we have a written confession by the real perpetrator, who is in prison for a similar crime that happened just minutes away from the one Moses was wrongly convicted for, and he's willing to testify in court. Our chances are good with this one."

Eli caught himself. He was speaking in the plural, including himself in Liza's fight. Truth be told, he believed in Liza the way everyone believed in Tyrone. Her heart was good, and she made him want to follow. He enjoyed supporting the dreams of a strong Black woman. He'd always said that Antoinette was the brains and he was the brawn, and he was feeling the same way about Liza. She was smart, and he knew she was going to do for Moses what she'd almost done for her father. Allowing her to store the boxes at his place made him feel like he was helping her ready her sling to fight the giant that he knew she would decapitate.

"I hope so, but I don't know, because . . ."

"What's got you worried?"

"Self-doubt, past failure, lots of things."

"Like what?"

"Eli, I read the trial transcripts. This case is as absurd as it sounds. Moses was literally convicted on a dream. The only evidence presented, outside of the fact that he was her next-door neighbor, was the victim's testimony. She said, and I quote, 'After I had that dream, I had no doubt who did this to me.'" Liza shook her head, but not in disapproval. "I get it—jurors are predisposed to believe victims even when everything in their story doesn't add up. It was the system that failed Moses. No one, not the detective nor the DA, went the extra mile to corroborate her testimony with actual evidence. That's why we need this new angle. Habeas is our way to get over this mountain, but . . ." Liza trailed off in thought.

"What really has you worried?"

"The biggest obstacle we are facing is him."

"Who?"

"Judge Morris."

Eli sat back in disbelief.

Judge Morris was the same appeals court judge who had ultimately been responsible for Liza's father's execution.

BLUE HAT PLAYA

"When are you going to clean up your own trash?"

It was like a Wild West stare-down. In moments like this, Denver felt like the frontier town that it was.

Eli stood on one side of Welton Street with work gloves on and a plastic bag full of trash, not from The Roz but from the new club across the street.

Eli eyed the new club's owner as he stepped out of his BMW adorned with oversized rims. The man adjusted the brim on his blue ball cap, checking himself in the reflection of the tinted windows. His gold chain was thick and looped just above his navel.

"I said, when are you going to clean up your own mess?" Eli was now annoyed at being ignored.

They'd spoken only one other time. When the man put up a GRAND OPENING sign, Eli had gone over to welcome him to the neighborhood. He hadn't liked his new neighbor from the moment he introduced himself as "Chance—but my friends call me White Chocolate."

Chance finally turned and acknowledged Eli. "Playa, why you comin' at me all hard?"

Eli never could figure why some children of Europe wanted nothing to do with the children of Africa and then others wanted to be just like them, or at least a caricature of what it meant to be like them.

"Time for you to pull your own weight on this block." Eli's voice was calm but just shy of a shout. "We're all here trying to make a living, but ever since you showed up, we all have to take care of our own stuff and yours too."

"Man, it was a late night. Place was hoppin', feel me? I'm lucky to even be here at this early hour."

Eli looked at his watch. It was one PM.

"Plus, man, you don't even know if that's my trash."

Eli had spent the last half hour picking up coupons and promotional cups with Chance's name on them, and he wasn't in the mood.

"I'm not saying that we can control the people that come to our clubs," he said. "I'm sure my people drop as many roaches on your side of the street as yours do on mine. All I'm asking is that you—"

"Playa, please. I ain't picking up no trash." Chance leaned back on his car and lit a cigarette. "But why don't you come over here and let me give you a few bucks for your janitorial services."

Chance's condescending comment reminded Eli of his admiration for the way Father Myriel handled young men. Whenever there was a beef in the streets, Eli's mentor would bring the two boys together and ask them, "Do you want to settle this with words or with gloves? Try words, but if they don't work, let's lace them up in the ring and find some resolution."

Eli had always thought it odd that a priest would condone violence, but there was wisdom in his approach. Father Myriel believed in turning the other cheek, but he also understood that when disagreements festered unresolved, it was only a matter of time before there was an explosion. On more than a few occasions, Eli had gone a few rounds in the ring with a would-be foe only for them to end up friends in the streets.

Did he want to settle this with words or with gloves? At the moment, Eli would give anything to meet Chance in the ring, where he could knock the blue hat off his head and the smugness off of his face. He looked at the work gloves on his hands. They weren't boxing gloves, but they would do.

"You coming old-school?" Chance asked. "I know you need the money, because ain't you heard? Jazz is dead. Those old heads ain't going to pay your bills much longer, cuz they're going to be dead too. The future is over here. Let me break you off some now, cuz man your sidewalk looks good, and I could use a man of your talents on my side of the street too."

Eli was halfway across Welton Street headed straight for Mr. White Chocolate. His right fist clenched tight.

Eli had to hand it to Chance. Most guys would have squared up by now in recognition of the threat coming their way. But not this man. All he did was take another puff from his cigarette and rest his hand on his waistband. At first, Eli thought it was the outline of a large belt buckle, but then he saw it, the distinct imprint of a gun.

Eli kept walking until he was within jabbing distance.

Chance lifted his shirt, revealing the brushed silver nine-millimeter with rosewood grip inserts.

Eli sidestepped him and lifted the trash bag to chest level and dropped it on the hood of the BMW.

"Man, you are a fool." Chance jumped to attention. "If that dented . . . no, scratched . . . no"—he stuttered—"no, if that even leaves a nick, I'm definitely going to shoot you."

Eli leaned in, his mouth next to Chance's ear.

"All I'm asking is for you to take care of your own trash."

Eli turned his back on Chance and walked back toward The Roz.

"Man, you don't know what you just started."

Eli never looked back. That night, however, he went a few extra rounds with the heavy bag.

ICU

"Why didn't you tell me you were in here?"

Eli was at St. Joseph Hospital, sitting at the bedside of the woman who'd raised him—Sister Francis.

"Oh, it's no big deal."

After Father Myriel died, it was Sister Francis who'd taken Eli in and done her best to help him heal from the trauma of seeing his mentor murdered.

"No big deal? Sister, the nurse said you had a stroke."

"Yeah, but it was just a little one." She smiled and winked a blue eye. "Doctor said it was a TIA—transient ischemic attack. That's big talk for a small thing."

"Didn't sound small from what Sister Phoebe said. You couldn't walk or talk. It was like you were paralyzed."

"Well, do I look paralyzed to you? I'll be out of here in no time. Doctor says all I need to do is take some aspirin to thin my blood so I don't get more rogue blood clots clogging up my brain."

Her once-brunette hair was now a dull gray and tucked, as usual, behind her ears. The hospital blanket hugged her body, revealing a tiny form. Eli moved the oxygen tube that lay on the bed and sat down beside her, taking her hand as he did so.

"Sister, I can't lose you. You're all I have now."

"Eli, don't worry about me. In no time, I'll be back at the Sacred Heart, feeding the deer, chopping wood, and leading morning prayers."

"That's what I'm worried about," Eli said, squeezing her hand. "You need to slow down."

"Oh, stop fussing. Enough about me. How are things for you?"

Eli knew what she was asking. It'd been more than four and a half years. Was he ready to move on after the death of Antoinette? Did he remember the promises he'd made his late wife?

"Things at The Roz are good. A little too good, to be honest. I can't keep up with the management duties, inventory, staffing, food and beverage costs—"

"What about her?"

Eli considered pretending he didn't know Sister Francis was talking about Liza, but doing so would only prolong the inevitable conversation.

"Liza's busy with the new innocence project. Fighting for others as she fought for her father. Actually, she's working on an interesting case."

If he kept talking, maybe he wouldn't have to answer the real question about why he hadn't pursued Liza for more than friendship.

"His name is Moses King. Get this. There was a woman, his next-door neighbor, who was attacked, and at first she said she couldn't identify her attacker. However, the next day she tells the police she had a dream and in her dream she saw it was Moses who did it. Can you believe that? That was the only evidence directly against Moses that was presented at his trial. The prosecution put her on the stand, and she said she knew it was Moses who assaulted her because of her *dream*." His voice caught. The emotion he felt for a man he'd never met caught Eli by surprise.

Eli studied Sister Francis's face. The wrinkles that branched from the corners of her eyes seemed deeper than the last time he'd seen her just a few months ago. He loved this woman, this daughter of Europe, who'd once said she felt God had put her on the planet just to love and raise him.

Her eyes were closed, so Eli decided to slip out and let her rest. He crept off the edge of the bed and kissed her hand as he eased it under the blanket.

"What's her name?"

"Sister?"

"The woman who had the dream, what is her name?"

FIRE IN THE HOUSE

Eli stopped by the chapel on the first floor of St. Joseph Hospital and lit a candle for Sister Francis. With Father Myriel and Antoinette gone, he couldn't bear losing her. So he prayed.

From there, Eli headed north on foot toward Five Points. Small single-level brick homes lined each block. Mature trees stood tall in the front yards, their leaves now on the ground, crunching beneath Eli's feet.

While there was much at The Roz to occupy Eli's mind, all he could think about was Sister Francis's question: "What is her name?"

The absurdity of the story baffled Eli. Decades of Moses's life had been lost because of this woman's testimony that she knew who her perpetrator was because of a dream. If he was honest, he felt disdain for her, not compassion. How could somebody do that to another human being?

What is her name? Sister Francis's simple question made it impossible for him to ignore the fact that if the woman had a name, then she too had a story. Eli now felt his disdain shift to himself for not regarding this nameless woman with the empathy and compassion she also deserved.

One night, she'd lain down in the comfort of her own bed, in the sanctuary of her own home, only to be awakened by a presence bent on harming her, pummeling her and gouging her blind. How did one process that absurdity, that brutality? She had closed her eyes in the darkness, and because of what Calhoun had done, darkness was now all she could see.

When the attack was over and Calhoun had left, she'd had to navigate her apartment, find the phone, and call 911 all by touch. When help arrived, she'd had to trust that they were the good guys and not the one who'd left her wounded and traumatized. She couldn't identify the man for the police because the first thing he'd taken from her was her sight. Eventually, once her body would no longer cooperate, she'd had to succumb to sleep again, only to relive her attack in a dream and to wake up to darkness again.

The relief she must have felt when somehow her dream revealed to her the familiar face of her neighbor, Moses King. Finally, she was able to know, able to understand, able to see again. Comfort surely descended like light into her darkness when she realized that she—despite her darkness—could still see a face. That she could still identify the person who'd done this to her. In her darkness, she had one less fear to face in her uncertain future.

Where was she? Was she too living in a hole?

Has she moved on from the trauma of her life? Or was she, like Eli, stuck in the prison of her past?

* * *

What is her name?

Eli didn't remember seeing a name in the files that he'd read up to this point, and he intended to ask Liza next time he saw her. Today, however, Eli knocked on the firehouse door.

The same door he'd knocked on when he was a child.

In middle school, he and a friend had been passing the playground as they walked home from school when they saw an odd sight: a child of Europe in Five Points. He was a grown man, midthirties, wearing jeans with a black leather jacket and work boots. A wallet chain hung from a belt loop on the front of his pants.

The man climbed up the tallest slide and slid down. His chain clanked and scraped the metal as he yelled, "Whee!"

Eli and his friend erupted in laughter as they pointed at the man and his glee. But their laughter turned to terror as the man stood, reached in his pocket, and flashed a knife, freezing their every nerve. The man charged in their direction as they ran. Instinctively, they both headed to the firehouse half a block from The Roz, across the street from where Eli now lived.

The man had cackled with joy as he gave chase. Eli and his friend bypassed at least a dozen homes, hoping the firehouse was the best place to find sanctuary and rescue. They pounded on the iron door to the firehouse until it felt like their knuckles would bust open. No one answered, but when they turned, they saw the man running away out of fear of the heroes inside.

Today, the neighborhood heroes were home, and Eli's childhood friend and petrified running partner answered the door.

"Eli!" boomed Chief Barrinton.

"What up, Bear?"

They clapped hands and bumped shoulders and then let out a simultaneous "Whee!"

Bear was a giant in stature and heart. The neighborhood kids loved him, and much to his wife's chagrin, the women loved him even more. But Bear was a good man and an even better husband.

"You look like you've been spending more time with potato chips than sit-ups, because you're getting a dicky-do!" Eli jabbed.

"What in the hay is a dicky-do?"

Eli pointed at Bear's midsection. "It's when your belly pokes out more than your dicky do!"

Bear erupted, the bass echoing past Welton Street.

"Man, I'm glad you stopped by. I know we're only across the street from each other, but seems like I never see you."

"Well, if you'd stop by The Roz more, you would. You know first glass is always on me."

"I know, man, been meaning to, but me and the fellas have been over at Chance's Place. Man, it's poppin' hard over there. Did you see who he had in last week? There was barely room to stand because Public Enemy was in the house."

Eli tried not to grimace. Bear must have noticed.

"Eli, I'm sorry, wasn't meaning no disrespect."

"None taken. It's all good."

Eli's clenched fist said otherwise. He was still hot over the trash and the gun and the arrogance of a man who had the gall to offer him a job as his janitor.

Eli was grateful when Bear pulled him back.

"So, man, what brings you by?"

"So back in the day, there was this lady who got attacked over in Park Hill. The guy left her in real bad shape, blinded her."

It was a long shot, but Eli figured when the nameless victim called 911, perhaps the firehouse paramedics had responded to such calls along with the police.

"Man, are you some sort of detective now? Does this have anything to do with Ms. Lawyer Brown? We've been seeing her come and go from your place on the regular—"

"No . . . yes." Eli's voice now echoed as he paused. "Yes. This has something to do with a case that Liza's working on, but no to what you're insinuating."

"If you say so, but just so you know, me and the fellas think you two should be a thing."

Eli flashed his wedding ring and waited for his friend to return to the topic at hand.

"Yeah, we respond on calls like that, but that one was before my time here."

"But what about the old-timers? Could you ask around and see if anyone remembers anything, knows where she might be?"

"This is a young man's game, but there are still a few OGs floating around biding their time until retirement. Most of them got those cush assignments at the airport helping people who twist their ankles stepping off the escalator and waiting for a plane to crash. I'll see what I can do."

They bumped shoulders again.

"And don't forget, man," Eli said. "Move your hips more than you eat those chips—that's how you get rid of that dicky-do."

Eli walked the half block to The Roz, and as he unlocked the door, Chance's blue hat caught his eye. Chance was standing in the doorway of his club, hand on his waistband.

Eli knew who the real public enemy was, and it was going to take more than a knock on the firehouse door to get rid of him.

FORBIDDEN AND LOST

"You what?"

The marker hit the wall, this time leaving a dent.

"You went and saw him? In Huntsville? I thought we had an understanding."

Garrett and Liza were alone in the conference room.

"He has proof," Liza said, grateful that the others had left before she told Garrett about her visit with Moses. "Someone else has confessed. Look for yourself." She offered the letter. "I also visited Levar Calhoun. He verified that he indeed is confessing to the crime. He's even willing to testify."

Liza expected another projectile, but Garrett's hands were now empty.

The strength of his reaction had caught her off guard. She'd figured he'd be disappointed but not outright incensed like a teakettle on full whistle.

"This is new evidence, the stuff of habeas. This is how we get a retrial." She decided not to tell him she had already filed the petition and that Moses King was on his way back to Colorado.

"Sixty-five times," Garrett said with great measure.

Liza sat and was grateful that Garrett followed her lead and did the same.

"Dexter Diaz was just a kid. They locked him in that room, deprived him of his mother. Grown men with badges intimidated him, but that kid stood strong and sixty-five times proclaimed his innocence until they finally broke him."

Garrett was right. Dexter deserved her best but wasn't getting even half of her worst.

"Liza, you're the lead on Dexter's case. What have you done for him? Moses is alive and will remain alive. And when he does his time, he'll be free, but Dexter does not have that hope."

"But I don't understand. Why can't we do both?"

Garrett sat back in his seat and sighed.

"Maybe this was a mistake. Liza, I can't control you, but I can remove you."

"I promise you, you didn't make a mistake putting me in charge of Dexter's case. I will come though—"

Garrett interrupted. "I know you can do a good job, but that's not what I'm talking about."

Liza folded her arms.

"I'm starting to wonder if it was a mistake to hire you in the first place. All of this is too personal for you. Fighting for the innocence of your father as a passion project is different than doing it as a full-time job. Liza, this is not your fault, but it was my mistake."

Liza wanted to plead her case and convince him he was wrong, but his words triggered an avalanche of doubt, wiping away the words that she could use to mount a defense.

Garrett retrieved the marker from the floor and tossed it on the table. "Only time will tell," he said as he walked out of the room. "But hear me. Dexter Diaz is our focus. We cannot and will not take King's case too."

* * *

It was now late evening, and Eli was sitting on the floor with Liza, combing through the boxes again. The room was an organized mess, with box lids strewn to the corners and manila folders fanned like decks of cards on imaginary poker tables.

"Why does everyone I love have to be in some sort of prison?"

Liza was in a high state of focus and frenzy. The last time Eli had seen her in this state was the month of her father's execution. For the last hour they'd surveyed hundreds, perhaps thousands, of pages, looking for anything that might help with Moses's habeas petition. Eli read every word of every page, though he wasn't sure what he was looking for.

"I mean, think about it. First there was my father, God rest his soul."

Eli put down his folder, grateful for the break.

"And then there's my mother. She didn't actually go to prison, but every day Daddy did was a day she did. She's done some hard time."

"Now there's Moses King and Dexter Diaz," Eli continued for her.

She sat, legs crossed and back straight.

"It's like their conviction is your conviction, their sentence is your sentence, their time is your time," Eli went on. "Liza, you've carried a lot—"

"And then there's you! I mean, Eli, look at you. You sleep underground in a self-imposed dungeon. Right beneath us is your bed, books, and bathroom." Liza slapped the floor. "I get it, but I don't get it." Her eyes watered. "I didn't sign up for any of this, but I can't just walk away."

"Do you really want to walk away?" Eli asked on behalf of the entire group of imprisoned people in Liza's life. "If you could leave, would you?" He asked this second question for himself.

"I don't know. At this point in my life, what else am I qualified to do?"

Eli picked up the last folder that Liza had discarded. It contained more detective legal pad sheets of paper ripped along the top perforation and stapled.

"I don't want to walk away from any of this. But I don't know how I'm going to get through it all either. Moses King is innocent, I know it. We have Calhoun's confession, but Garrett won't bend the rules. And Dexter Diaz, I get it. His family is hoping against hope that someone will do something, and I'm that someone who needs to get my act together for him. Eli, I haven't even gone to visit him or his family. What kind of lawyer am I? He deserves justice too."

Eli was about to respond. But then, on the next page of the detective's notes, he read:

CC had a dream.

He skimmed the last few pages, and while there was no more mention of Calhoun or a follow-up interview, the detective had written on the last page:

CC says Moses did it.

Eli felt like he'd discovered a long-lost treasure as he showed it to Liza.

"Yeah, I've got that in my notes too. That's proof that once they focused on King, they forgot about Calhoun." Liza flipped through her legal pad.

All Eli could see were the initials *CC*. It wasn't the woman's name, but he felt one step closer to knowing who she was. "Why is she only listed here as CC?"

"I've been looking for her full name as well. They're usually pretty good at protecting victims in court documents, for obvious reasons, but there's often one folder with the highly sensitive information," Liza said. "If we find nothing here, I'll ask Moses."

Eli was about to ask if it was necessary to find the woman's full name before the habeas hearing, but a hard knock at the door interrupted them.

Eli answered, and Savoy stepped in. Panic filled her face.
"Eli, he's gone."
"Who?"
"Tyrone!"

PART II

We don't see any American dream.
We've experienced only the American nightmare.

—Malcolm X

IT'S A RACKET

Denver's City and County Building was a majestic crescent-shaped structure on Bannock Street that filled the entire block between Fourteenth and Colfax. Throughout the year it housed the city's mayor, city council, and courtrooms, but during the holiday season it transformed into Denver's premier festive attraction.

With barely a month before Thanksgiving, the transformation was well under way. Unlit red-and-green strands of lights already adorned the stately columns. Wreaths dotted the top edge of the building, and the massive front steps now held platforms that would support Santa, snowmen, and a nativity, complete with a light-complected baby Jesus. Beginning on Black Friday, thousands would flock here for pictures and to take part in the Parade of Lights. Tonight there were a few hundred people gathered not to sing carols but to chant in protest.

Eli arrived not knowing what to expect. After failing to reach his nephew through his pager, he'd found Tyrone's roommate, who said that Tyrone was already at the county building and that everyone else was on their way to the courthouse to demand change. Not knowing what that meant, Eli ran. Was Tyrone under arrest and in the jail? Was he about to do something he'd regret?

"Free Jamal," a man shouted through a bullhorn.

"Free us all!" the crowd responded in unison.

Eli made his way through the crowd of brown faces toward the steps. He needed to find Tyrone.

"Free Jamal!"

"Free us all!"

The man with the bullhorn was a short, wide-shouldered child of Africa with tenor in his voice. After one last "Free Jamal," he raised his hand, and the crowd quieted; he handed the bullhorn to the man standing next to him.

It was Tyrone. As he lifted the bullhorn to his mouth, his back straightened and his jaw clenched.

"We are here in the middle of the night because that's when they do their deeds."

"That's right. Cockroaches," a woman's voice from the back of the crowd said.

"It's a racket," Tyrone began. "They treat us like Denver's ATM. And by *they*, I mean all of them who sit up in this place and have their meetings—the mayor, city council, the judges, the prosecutors, and the police. *They* are in this together."

"You writing this down?" shouted a young woman holding a *Free Jamal* sign.

A small collection of reporters were on hand from the *Post* and *Rocky Mountain News*; spotting a video camera, Eli guessed a local television news crew was here as well. He also spotted Roberta Messay, the lead investigative reporter for the Weekly Word, Fredricka's paper.

"Break it down for them," the woman shouted to Tyrone.

"Here's how the racket works: City hall wants money but knows that no one will go for their raising our taxes, especially those in Cherry Creek. But they still going to get the money, so they call in Mr. Chief of Police and tell him to raise some revenue. Then you know what he does?"

"Tell 'em!"

"Mr. Police Chief sends all his officers down to Cherry Creek and starts handing out tickets to those fine white folks who can afford it."

Laughter erupted.

"No, that isn't what happens. They come to Five Points, and while we're sleeping, they write tickets for you name it—parking too far from the curb, expired tags, cracked windshield . . . man, this is Colorado; who doesn't have a cracked windshield!"

More laughter.

"And what happens when we can't pay? The judges in there put a warrant out for our arrest. Raise your hand if you got papers over a parking ticket."

Virtually every hand was in the air. It was times like this that Eli was grateful he didn't have a car.

"Then what happens?" Tyrone continued. "Good citizens like our friend Jamal come over here to the courthouse to square things up, and they bust him for jaywalking *and*, because he has a warrant, they arrest him.

"Ya'll"—Tyrone's voice cracked—"all he owes is a buck fifty, but when he came down here the first time to get on a payment plan, they wouldn't take his money. They said all or nothing, so they got nothing."

Tyrone paused and made eye contact with Eli. His bruises were still visible.

Reckoning.

When Tyrone had played his latest original song on his new saxophone at The Roz, there was a forthrightness in the melody and a frenzy at the break. Tyrone was talented and could play anything, but that night not only was his talent on display, his heart was evident too. Pain and passion combined, and all knew it wouldn't be long before something like this happened. A moment of reckoning was only a matter of time. At the conclusion of the song, the packed house had stood, not in applause but in silence. Men and women—all children of Africa—with fists in the air.

As Tyrone's eyes met his uncle's, it was as if he needed to hear Eli say it again: *If you lead, we will follow.*

Eli nodded. Tyrone again lifted the bullhorn to his mouth.

"We are done. We've had enough. Them in there"—Tyrone was pointing at the City and County Building—"they are no longer our pimp!"

The applause and cheers were building.

Tyrone turned to the reporters.

"Let it be known that we in Five Points, Black folk in this city—we refuse to be the whore they slap around whenever they like so they can take our money."

"Free Jamal!"

"Free us all!"

Eli looked at the reporters, all of them, including Roberta Messay, heads bent as they scribbled their stories. Fredricka had arrived. She looked at Tyrone and then at Eli. Eli knew she wanted the journals, but he wondered if she would settle for an exclusive with Tyrone. Most likely not.

Eli turned his attention back to his young nephew.

"Let's go." Tyrone stepped down. The crowd fell in line behind him as they headed across Bannock toward Broadway.

The familiar feeling of loss crowded his feelings of pride. First Father Myriel, Antoinette, then Liza . . . Sister Francis wasn't doing well, and now Tyrone. It looked like he was leaving too, trading his saxophone for the bullhorn.

Eli turned back toward the nativity and the other reminders of the impending holiday season.

How could he face the losses of tomorrow if he had yet to face the losses of his past?

LOSER

"Chica, where have you been?"

Liza was sitting across the table from Dexter Diaz at another small-town Colorado prison virtually identical to Stratling.

His Hispanic brown skin was smooth on his arms and cheeks, but acne reddened his forehead. A hodgepodge of tattoos adorned his arms and neck.

"Mr. Diaz. I'm Liza Brown, and I'm here from Project Joseph. As you know, we have reviewed your petition, and we believe you are innocent. We want to help—"

"I said, where have you been?"

"Mr. Diaz, we are doing our—"

"I sent that application months ago, and yeah, I got your letter saying you were going to take my case." He leaned back, legs spread. "That white man came here and visited for a minute, but I ain't heard nothing since. What took you so long?"

Dexter's voice was deep, and his accent was thick.

"Mr. Diaz, I'm sorry. We receive countless requests for help and can only take on a few clients who meet our strict standards. Thankfully, you do, and that's why I'm here. Please know that I appreciate your patience—"

"Thankfully?" His volume was just shy of a yell, but Liza felt it in her chest. "Lady, I got nothing to be thankful for. I've been in this place for half my life, much of that in solitary. Thankfully?" Dexter leaned forward. "I haven't been patient. I'm not patient. I don't plan on ever being patient. I need you to get me out of here *now*." He pressed his finger on the table and then pointed it at Liza. "Got that, chica?"

Liza kept her composure.

"Mr. Diaz, I understand how you feel, and I'm sorry, but I'd hoped you and I could at least review your case. I'd like to explain our strategy to you and get your feedback."

"You want feedback from me? Chica, you the lawyer; why you here to ask me for advice?"

Liza was on her heels. She was there to help him, but he was attacking her. She took control.

"If you don't mind, Mr. Diaz, I'll speak to you with respect, and I expect the same from you. I also need to you to dispense with *chica* and call me Ms. Brown, or Liza would be fine too."

Dexter's left eye twitched, giving motion to his teardrop tattoo. Liza tried to remember what the teardrop represented. Did it have something to do with time served in prison? Or did it represent the number of people he'd attempted to kill? Murdered?

The thought sickened Liza. How could she help a man who was actively violent?

Dexter blinked.

"Ms. Brown. Liza Brown, I got a question." Dexter leaned back and spread his legs again. "How did I end up with you?"

"I don't follow, Mr.—"

"Talk about my luck. The one innocence project that wants to take my case is the one that sends me the lady who couldn't even help her own father? Your papi got the needle, but you think you can help me?"

"Mr. Diaz, I don't work alone. You have a team of people all working for your good."

"Then why do I need you? Why don't you get my team in here?"

Liza packed her bag.

"At least you look good." Dexter sucked his teeth. "Tell you what, you can stay on my team just because of that. I see those tattoos peaking out from under your blouse. How about this, chica? If you show me yours, I'll show you mine."

Liza stood.

"Good day, Mr. Diaz."

RAISED BY WOLVES

"Eli, I can't do it."

Liza had stopped by Eli's home long enough to trade one brief-case full of files for another. As she left, Eli walked her to her car.

"He was rude, vile." She turned her eyes up as if looking for a more precise word. "Ungrateful. I know he's supposed to be innocent, but he sure didn't act that way."

She looked back at Eli.

"He even had a teardrop tattoo. Doesn't that mean that he hurt somebody?"

Eli considered telling her it could also mean that Dexter was in mourning or, even worse, might symbolize that he was a victim. Life was not safe for a child in adult prison. There was a fair chance that he'd been violated and marked with the teardrop as someone's property.

Eli wanted to draw her attention to the fact that Dexter had been only a kid when he was put in prison with full-grown adults and that he had not had the benefit of good home training. He wanted to remind her she was the one who'd presented Dexter's case to the project because she believed he was worthy of their time. But Liza was venting, so he fought the urge to offer explanation, suggestion, or rebuttal.

Instead, Eli said nothing.

Antoinette had once told him that all she needed in times like this was to share her fears and frustration with someone who was safe. Sharing her feelings wasn't an indicator that she was incapable and in need of help. She just needed Eli to listen, and—by doing so—he validated her feelings.

Eli remembered a book in his library about a boy who'd been raised by wolves. By the time other humans discovered him, he could only be described as feral. Even as an adult, he possessed two natures and had a hard time fitting in with society. He was uncivilized in that setting, but with the creatures who raised him, he would have been acting civilly.

Eli thought about how his own life would have been different if he had been raised by a wolf instead of fierce lambs like Father Myriel and Sister Francis. His basic instinct was fight, not flight, especially when his fear turned to anger, and he was plenty angry at what was happening in Five Points—Chance's arrogance, the police, Tyrone's beating, and now Jamal. Liza was correct when she said he was in prison, trapped. Reopening The Roz wasn't the healing balm of Gilead he had wanted for his broken heart. And, if he was honest, he was angry with Liza for pursuing her dream and leaving him behind.

Before Father Myriel, he too had been feral, running with whatever pack would take him in. And now, without Antoinette and with Liza engaged with Project Joseph, all he had was his anger to keep him company. That and the drinking. The things he was thinking about doing were out of bounds by most standards. In his depression, after Antoinette's death, he'd wanted nothing more than to take his own life, but now his anger had turned outward. As a lone wolf, he hunted, fearful of what he might do if he ever caught his prey.

"And he would not stop calling me *chica*. He's nothing like Moses King, and he's definitely not Daddy. Sitting with

Dexter was like being in the room again with that disgusting Calhoun."

Liza reached through the passenger door window and placed her purse and briefcase on the seat. Eli made his way to the driver's side and met her with an opened door.

"Maybe Garrett was right. Maybe I'm not cut out to do this as an actual job. I became a lawyer to help my father, not because this is what I wanted to do with my life."

Liza wrapped her arms around his waist and squeezed.

"Thank you, Eli."

"Of course. A lady's hand should never touch a door when a gentleman is present."

"I'm not talking about the door." Liza smiled. "I'm grateful for this talk. You have helped me more than you can imagine."

Liza sat and swung her boots into the car. Eli closed the door.

She reached out her hand for Eli's. "Again, thank you."

Then she let go and sped away.

Antoinette was right.

Without someone to love, Eli was just uncivilized.

WHITE CANE FIELDS

The nib of her cane was sharp, hewn by the concrete that scraped with each radar sweep. She moved with speed, aided by broad strokes that delivered their findings to her fingertips for interpretation. Her feet trusted her fingers—the only thing she trusted these days.

Smooth and steady.

Measured and on a mission.

Today her goal was simple: go to the grocery store and return home as soon as possible.

Snow was coming. She could smell it the same way she did the rain in the spring. This substance she'd once loved was now her nemesis, because snow meant ice and ice meant that she had to stay at home. The one place she didn't want to be.

In her bag were eggs, milk, and cherry cigars. The trip home from the grocery store took less time because she'd already scanned the memorized route and removed any obstacles so she could make better time coming than going.

Her greatest hurdles were not the cracks in the sidewalk or even the winter ice, but people. She'd lost track of the number of times people—not kids but grown adults—would hear the scrape of her cane and yet stand dead still in her path until she ran into them. It made no sense why they wouldn't move or say something or whistle. It was as if they thought she was the one with the extra sense to detect their presence. So while she had surveyed the route for stones and wood, she couldn't detect a person with rocks for brains and petrified common sense who had blocked the path in the last twenty minutes since she'd passed by.

As she neared the open field on her right, she shifted her cane to her left hand along with the plastic bag and reached her right hand into her coat pocket, gripping the cold metal. It was here that she had smelled the faint odor of marijuana when she had passed by the first time, and she wasn't taking any chances that the partaker wasn't coming out of his stupor, hungry for who knew what.

Three cars passed on her left, and based on the sound of their exhaust, she was pretty sure they were a Honda, a Volkswagen, and some version of Detroit steel. After another block, she was in the open stairwell of her apartment building.

Folding her cane and slipping it into the pocket of her coat, she made her way up the three flights, skipping steps and stopping briefly on each landing to click her tongue and listen for any anomalies in the echo that would signal the presence of a person.

At her door, she stopped.

Inhaling deeply through her nose, she tried the doorknob and found it still locked, as she had left it. Another deep breath, this time through her mouth. Satisfied, she slid her key first into the chamber on her reinforced iron screen door, then into the double locks on the interior door.

Inside, with both doors locked behind her, she set the milk and eggs at her feet and stood with absolute stillness.

Like a deer on full alert, she waited.

Mrs. Gilette, her neighbor, was watching *Jeopardy*. She heard the voice of Alex Trebek, a buzzer and a wrong answer, but nothing else invaded her ears.

A deep breath through her mouth for taste. Nothing.

In through her nose. The lingering residue of her last cherry cigar in the ashtray.

She removed the knife from her pocket, the handle now warmed by her grip, and made her way through her small, one-bedroom apartment room by room, inch by inch.

Claudette Cooper would never to be caught off guard again.

FRIEND OR FOE

This time, Eli was ready.

"Beautiful morning, beautiful day." Fredricka made her entrance.

Eli, with his wedding ring on his finger and resolve in his heart, came out from behind the bar and met her center floor.

The Roz was warm from the morning sun that silhouetted her blond hair. Fredricka greeted him with an even warmer hug and a soft kiss on his cheek.

"Mind if I grab a cup of coffee?" Before Eli responded, Fredricka retrieved a mug from behind the bar and poured her own cup.

"Mind if we have a chat?" Eli chose a window table in full view of any passersby, and Fredricka sat across from him and leaned forward.

"You seem uptight this morning," she continued.

"Freddie, this needs to stop. You. Everything." Bluntness was his tactic. "Popping in like this. I know what you want, and it's not going to—"

"Eli, do you really know what I want? If you do, then you could make things easier for both of us."

Eli raised his left hand for her to see his gold wedding band.

"Is this really what you wanted to talk about, my stopping by too often?" she asked. "Done. Your wish, my command."

Fredricka took a sip, leaving red lipstick imprinted on the white mug.

"I appreciate that. Thank you for understanding." Eli nodded. "I know we had something, but that was a long time ago. We were kids. That was before Antoinette, before she . . ." He still found it difficult to speak the truth about her death. "And yes, after she passed, there was that one night . . . but Freddie, that should never have happened. I was vulnerable, and I was—"

"Weak." She was leaning forward, her tone compassionate. "Eli, I understand, because I was weak too. That's how I am with you. You don't fault me for trying again, do you? You have always been the one that got away."

"And I hope you understand that not only am I asking you to no longer stop by, I'm asking you to stop, period. It was weakness that brought us together, not strength. I need you to let go."

Fredricka leaned back and stared out the window. After a deep breath, her lips pursed. "I hear you. I will stop. Promise."

Eli believed her.

She finished her coffee, and he decided to change the subject.

"I saw you and your reporter the other night at the protest."

The crowd that night had raised enough money to cover Jamal's bail but not enough to pay his fines and late fees. It was only a matter of time before the court issued another warrant.

"Freddie, things aren't right here in the Points," Eli said. "What they're protesting about is true. The harassment is real. Tickets, illegal stops, even beatings. I'm trying not to be paranoid, but sometimes I think they're actually looking for me. Wonder if I'm responsible for some of what's happening."

"Well, if they knew what I do, then you'd be the most wanted Black man in Denver." Fredricka leaned forward again. "You know that don't you?" There was now ice in her tone. "Mr. Stone, now that you don't want me to want you, why should I be the only one who knows your little secret?"

"Freddie."

Eli was rarely on the receiving side of Fredricka's threats. Before starting her own paper, she'd climbed the ranks at both the *Denver Post* and *Rocky Mountain News* because she wouldn't take no for an answer. She knew she was Robert Bly's "golden hair woman," the one powerful men would surrender their strength to for the fantasy of what might be. But when that advantage failed, she was cutthroat. She'd risen from intern to editor because unsuspecting men saw her as the blonde who needed to stick with reporting on society and fashion. They did so at their own peril. Now Eli was about to find out what happened when Fredricka no longer saw you as an item of desire but as an obstacle in need of bulldozing.

"What did you think, that you could wave me away like a fly? What do they say about a woman scorned?"

"I told you in confidence." To help Liza with Langston's case, he'd reached out to Fredricka and told her how he had been present when Slager leapt to his death. He should have known. "Freddie, you wouldn't."

"No, your Freddie would not, but Fredricka, Denver's relentless and ruthless exposer of truth, most definitely would." Fredricka stood and straightened her pencil skirt. "Mr. Stone, when we were kids, you kicked me to the curb and moved on, but this time it will not be that easy. There's only one thing that I want more than you."

She picked up her purse.

"The journals. I no longer want a peek. I want them. All of them."

Her sunglasses were in place. Eli could see his reflection.

"I appreciate this little chat we've had, and now that we have defined our relationship, Mr. Stone, you are standing between me and what I want. Which, as you know, is not a safe place to be."

As Fredricka turned and walked into the morning sun, one thing was clear to Eli.

Fredricka was no longer feeling weak in his presence.

IT'S A MEANINGFUL LIFE

Moses loved writing letters, and Liza had a growing stack of them in her desk drawer, the latest in her hands.

Ms. Liza,

> *Thank you for bringing my body back to Colorado. With Thanksgiving fast approaching, my mother is especially grateful. She's already come to see me twice. Huntsville was hard on her because she doesn't have a car reliable enough for the trip from Denver to Texas. Even though the drive here to Cañon City is only a couple of hours, I still worry about her getting stranded on the side of the road. There's no way she could walk to a nearby town for help, though sometimes my aunt comes with her.*
>
> *Anyway, Ms. Liza, I'm writing because I feel like we need to talk about something important: we need to be on the same page as to what success and failure look like for us.*

Liza wasn't in a philosophical mood; survival was her focus. On the desk in front of her sat two legal pads in a stack. Her growing list of notes on Dexter Diaz was on top. The team was relying on her to lead, and while Dexter had appalled her during their meeting, she was still determined to move forward. The bottom legal pad contained her notes for Moses and his habeas petition. His body was due in court, and she wanted to be ready.

My guess is that you feel you failed your father because you could not secure his freedom before they took his life. While we haven't known each other long, I sense that even though you did your best, you still feel you could and should have done more.

Ms. Liza, you didn't fail Langston. Quite the opposite. You loved him fiercely, organized for him with determination, and fought with grit. After they murdered him, you took your fight all the way to the statehouse and made sure they cleared his name. You made the most of the hand they dealt you. You did not reach your goal, but—ask anyone—you did not fail.

Yes, I have an extreme dislike for this place and hope that you will get me out of here soon. I pray you will be by my side when I walk through the doors. I dream of sitting down at my mother's table again for Thanksgiving and would love for you to be there too. But Liza, I've had a lot of time to think about success, given that I can't have a career or own a house or take fancy vacations. To be honest, I didn't have those things before I got here—mostly worked odd jobs to make ends meet—but I did have dreams of being my own boss someday; was going to get a truck and start my own handyman business. I've had to come to terms with the fact that in this place a "successful" life is no longer possible for me. In here, I work, but it doesn't amount to much more than keeping me occupied as the minutes of my life tick away. I have, however, found meaning, value, and significance despite my circumstances, and I choose daily to find joy in all things. To pass the time, I've even resorted to reading the dictionary.

If I'm honest, I didn't reach out to you hoping you could restore me to a successful life. No, Ms. Liza, I contacted you out of jealousy. I loved Langston, but I was also envious that he had you. Outside of my mother, I feel abandoned by everyone in my life. The police, judges, even my own lawyers have moved on and all but forgotten that I exist. Your father, however, never felt alone in this fight because he had you. It's hard enough to go through this as an inno-cent man, but it's soul crushing to not have anyone who actually believes in you enough to jump in the ring with you. All I've wanted is what you gave your father.

Because of you, I feel seen and heard. When we go to court, I want you to know that in my mind we have already won. If you do for me what you did for your father, regardless of the outcome—even if I die in here—you will have succeeded.

All I've wanted these last twenty-eight years is someone to fight for me.

Sincerely,
Moses

Liza laid the letter on the desk, set aside Dexter Diaz's legal pad, and scanned her notes for Moses's case. She was in the ring with gloves and mouthpiece in place. She was ready for a battle, but when she fought, only one outcome would satisfy her—winning.

FREEMAN'S FURNITURE

Eli left his place, turned left, and walked the half block alongside the east side of The Roz. The once-boarded-up windows now gave sight to floors he'd sanded, the bar top that he'd restored, and the stage he'd rebuilt, all with his own hands. For Eli, renovating The Roz had been an act of desperation that he'd hoped would distract him from the loss of Antoinette. It had worked for a while, but sometimes it felt like he missed her more now than he had when he started.

The second and third floors of The Roz were still in their abandoned state, and he still had plans to turn them into artists' studios or a halfway house or some kind of affordable housing. Perhaps taking on a new project would distract him again, at least for the time being, from his genuine desire to join Antoinette in death.

He stopped at the five-point intersection with the front door to The Roz at his back and surveyed the familiar surroundings. The historic intersection was a testament to the entrepreneurial spirit of the children of Africa with its beauty shops, restaurants, music venues, and real estate and law offices. To his right down Welton Street, he could see the spinning barber pole at the shop where Liza's father had cut hair and held court. Across the street was the local branch of Unity Bank, where Shemekia Turner kept everyone's money safe and, as the bank's only Black president, made loans to people like Eli, who didn't technically qualify by the bank's rigorous standards but needed a break. Eli was proud to be counted among the business owners of Five Points. He admired each one except for the recent addition to the neighborhood. Thankfully, the man with the blue hat was nowhere to be seen.

Eli had time before the first delivery arrived, so he headed west on Welton Street toward Sonny Lawson Park. After the break-in, he thought he'd check in on Mr. Freeman to see how he was doing.

Eli stopped and peered through the same window through which he'd seen the men kicking in the back office door. This morning, standing in the middle of the sofa section was Mr. Freeman, a tall, lanky child of Africa in his seventies. When he spotted Eli, his eyes lit up and he trotted over to unlock the door.

"Eli, I ain't no rollin' stone. How are you doing?"

"Not bad, Mr. Freeman," Eli said as they clasped hands.

"Come on in, young man. I'm not open yet, still have another hour, but I'll sell you a couch any time o' day. What you looking for today—sectional, sofa, or you need a love seat for you and that fine Liza Brown?"

Eli loved this about Mr. Freeman. He was always on his game, always selling. Eli wondered how he stayed motivated, opening the same door day after day for decades with the regularity of Big Ben. Eli had been at it less than a year and was already wondering if he had what it took.

"No, Mr. Freeman, I need nothing today, but when I do—"

"But when you do, you know I'll come through." Freeman sang the jingle from his KDKO radio spot that all of Five Points had learned to sing even before they learned "Amazing Grace" in church.

"That's right, Mr. Freeman, that's right."

"Well then, what can I do you for?"

"I just thought I'd stop by to see how you're doing. We all heard about the break-in the other night."

Mr. Freeman took off his glasses and took in a deep sigh.

"I'm dumbfounded, Eli. This is the first time in almost forty years that something like this has happened. First time."

He shook his head.

"They came in through the back door, busted it all up with a crowbar or something, and then made their way to my office back there." Mr. Freeman pointed with the hand holding his glasses. "They must have karate kicked it or something. Made a real mess of things."

Eli could see the splintered doorjamb from where they were standing.

"Don't know why they did that. They must not have tried the doorknob. That door was unlocked—all they had to do was walk in—but now I have to get that fixed too. Eli, they robbed me blind. Took all I had."

"Did the alarm sound?"

Eli knew the answer; he'd been there, standing out front watching, but had wondered how the burglars could get in without triggering the security system.

"Shoot, I don't have nothing like that." Mr. Freeman put his glasses on again. "Eli, I trust my people. I trust everyone until they give me a reason not to."

None of this made sense to Eli. Why hadn't the burglars been deterred by the officer who stood out front of the store in clear view? Why had the officer arrived without sirens or lights? That night, before Eli ran, the officer had shouted for him to freeze as he stepped out of his car with his gun drawn. The burglars must have heard him from inside, and yet they'd still robbed the place.

"What are the police saying? Any leads?"

"Damnedest thing, Eli. They called, woke me up, and told me what happened. When I got here, the cop was sitting out there in his car. Told me they probably wouldn't catch whoever did it and that I should call my insurance company to file a claim. He had the entire report ready for me. Handed it to me and left. Never even got out of his car."

"Mr. Freeman, I don't know what to make of that either. Did you get the officer's name? I wouldn't mind talking to him about how I keep my place secure."

"Yeah"—Mr. Freeman motioned toward the office—"his name is on the report."

Eli followed him to the office, and while Mr. Freeman retrieved the report from his desk, Eli inspected the door.

"Says here that his name is Winston." Mr. Freeman handed the report to Eli.

In the bottom right corner was a scribbled but legible signature in the box marked OFFICER: *Mark Winston*. Eli now had a name for the man in blue who'd failed to give chase that night.

Handing the report back to Mr. Freeman, Eli asked, "You say they robbed you blind? How much did they get?"

"All of it. Eli, they took everything. See for yourself."

Mr. Freeman pointed to the corner. As Eli approached the desk, he now understood what Mr. Freeman was getting at. Eli knelt down to look; a square patch of the floor was missing. Someone had actually cut a section out of the floor.

"What happened here?"

"That is where my safe used to be. They ripped it out of the floor and made off with all that was inside."

After promising Mr. Freeman he would return the next time he needed a couch, armoire, or anything furniture related, Eli left and began walking back toward The Roz, passing the spot where he'd raised his hands in surrender to Officer Winston before making his escape. Across the street at Sonny Lawson Park, life had returned to normal. The homeless were awake and huddled next to the basketball court, where two teens, late for school, were trying to settle which one was going to be next up in the NBA draft. The drug dealers wouldn't show up until later.

Eli spotted the tree that had given him shelter.

Officer Mark Winston. Was this Slager's partner in crime? Was this the cop responsible for the increased harassment in the neighborhood and for what had happened to Tyrone?

In the gutter along the street was a discarded flyer from Chance's Place advertising another hip-hop performer Eli had never heard of. He snatched it off the ground and crumpled it into a tight ball, then crossed the street. Chance's car was not out front, but Eli still pounded on the front door out of frustration and then pulled on the handle of the locked door. He squeezed the wadded-up flyer even tighter as he backpedaled a few steps. Out of sheer frustration, he threw the ball of paper at the door, wishing it had the heft of a shot put, capable of denting his target.

The elevated pulse of his heart throbbed in his ears as he crossed Welton Street and unlocked the door to The Roz, though he wasn't going to stay long. Yes, he had work to do—there was always something—but that would have to wait along with the deliveryman.

After grabbing a bottle of rum—his finest, he didn't care—he locked up and turned right toward home.

There was a note on his door. *I got something on that lady you were asking about.*

Eli glanced across the street. Chief Barrinton would also have to wait.

Inside his home, he put the note and bottle on the table and pulled open the hatch.

Slager's journals.

Items he wasn't supposed to have. When Eli confronted the man he suspected of murdering his mentor and framing Liza's father, Slager had leapt from the balcony of his luxury condo instead of facing the facts of what he'd done. Eli had spotted the journals and, on a hunch, packed them in a suitcase as he left the dead detective's apartment. They had been more than he'd expected, full of notes about cases and rough drafts of detective novels in which Slager veiled his misdeeds. Eli had read them multiple times, but now he had a name. He flipped through the journals and selected the ones he thought might contain information on his new target, Officer Winston. Perhaps Slager had written something that would connect the two of them.

He put them in a duffel bag and made his way back up the ladder.

Since opening The Roz, he had felt in his heart like there were two pit bulls battling for his future, and he wasn't sure which one he wanted to win. Just a few months ago he hadn't wanted to live, and he had the scar to prove it. Now Eli was too angry to die.

He tucked the bottle of rum in his bag and headed out the door.

Eli knew what he needed.

He needed Antoinette.

THE BLACK ANGEL

Eli was at Riverside Cemetery, five steps past the grave of Clara Brown, the Black angel of Denver. He recalled the time when Father Myriel had brought him and a few other neighborhood boys here to tell them her story.

"Clara was born into slavery," Father Myriel said. "When she was thirty-five, her first owner died, and you know what happened? They separated and sold her whole family. Her husband Richard went to the Deep South, and she wasn't sure where her three children ended up. A man by the name of George Brown purchased Clara to look after his family. That's where she got the last name. For the next twenty years, she raised her new master's children while wondering about the fate of her own family."

Father Myriel shook his head. Eli and the other boys stood in a half circle around the grave, facing the headstone that announced the year of Clara's freedom, 1857, and the year of her death, 1885.

"Mrs. Brown died at eighty-three," Father Myriel said. "So, who can do the math for me? How many years did she live after her enslavement?"

"Twenty-eight years," a boy answered.

"That's right, only twenty-eight years of freedom, not count-ing eternity," said Father Myriel. "And let me tell you what she did with her few and final years."

As always, Eli's mentor's words transfixed him.

"She headed west, working as a domestic for those caught up in the gold rush, and eventually she ended up right here in Denver. Some people think she was the first daughter of Africa to arrive in Colorado. She moved to the mountains and worked as a cook and midwife and started the first laundry service in the area."

"What's a midwife?" asked the same boy who had calculated the math.

"That's a woman who assists in the birth of a child, like a doctor, but without the training." After the boy nodded his understanding, Father Myriel had continued telling Clara's story. "Get this. She saved thousands of dollars, bought sixteen lots of land in Denver, seven houses in Central City, and a few mines as well. Despite a system that afforded her no justice, sus-picious fires that destroyed some of her property, and the every-day struggles that go along with being a daughter of Africa in Colorado, she still amassed a fortune."

Eli was now at Antoinette's headstone, where he sat down with his back resting on her name. He unzipped his duffel bag and removed the journals, then placed them on the grass next to him. After he took a deep swig from the bottle of rum, Father Myriel's voice continued in his head.

"She used her money to establish churches of all denomina-tions, including the one I oversee, and resettled a myriad people in the Mile High City, not just children of Africa but Europe too. She sent countless young women to college."

Young Eli had raised his hand, and Father Myriel acknowl-edged him with a nod.

"Did she ever find her family?"

"Eli, she never stopped looking. For years she wrote letters in search of her loved ones. Eventually, she discovered that her husband Richard and her daughter Margaret had both died. And while there was no trace of her son, Richard Jr., she eventually reunited with her daughter Eliza."

They all stood in silence a few more beats until Father Myriel drove his point home.

"That's what she did with those twenty-eight years. This former slave built an empire here in Colorado and then gave it all away." Father Myriel had gestured with both hands toward the ground where they stood. "This lady loved, cared for, and built our city, and—get this—she died without a penny to her name. Denver owes what it has become to her, because without her, we would not be who we are."

Eli's tears flowed freely as the rum lightened his head and brought the anchor of his emotions out of the depths of his heart. Clara was Denver's Black angel, but Antoinette was Eli's. As much as the city and Black folk had needed Clara, this Black man, this child of Africa, needed Antoinette.

The midday sun broke through the clouds and onto Eli's face while the warmth of the rum kept him company. He took another swig and held the liquid gold in his mouth as he flipped through the journals, looking for any mention of Officer Winston. As Eli swallowed the sweet mix of molasses and alcohol, he felt solidarity with the slaves who'd first brewed the concoction to anesthetize their trapped existence.

"Baby, there's nothing here. Nothing," he said aloud.

He stuffed the journals into the bag and threw it aside.

Even after another draw on the bottle, it frustrated him that his medicine of choice wasn't calming him as he'd hoped it would.

"I know The Roz was our dream, but I don't know if I can keep this up. The constant upkeep of the building, staff schedules, and then . . ." He could feel his forehead and ears getting warm. "Then there's that fox across the street acting like he owns the place. Our young folk aren't just letting him bring that filth to our community—they're going there packing his place."

Eli corked the bottle in dissatisfaction. His tongue was now numb to the spices that teased his taste buds.

"I'm going to lose Tyrone, like I lost Liza. Like I lost you."

Eli's eyelids sagged along with his shoulders.

His vision blurred, causing the rows of headstones to look like miniature mountain ranges as the fog rolled through his mind. Eli lay flat on his stomach, the grass and the dirt keeping him from the angel who owned his heart. Was there any difference between him and the people Liza was trying to save? Eli, like them, was imprisoned with little hope of freedom. Despair, anger, and a deep sadness closed his eyes, and as he faded into sleep beneath the midday sun, he knew something needed to change.

CLOSING TIME

Eli knew what he had to do and figured tonight was as good a night as any to do it.

Each time Liza and Tyrone took the stage together, something special happened, and this Friday evening was no different. The Roz was packed, and while it was almost midnight, no one left, because the crowd knew that the final set was the "fire set" that always left those in attendance wanting more. It was this part of the night that had everyone bragging at the late service on Sunday morning that "you should have been there."

Eli rang the bell announcing the final call and served everyone their last drinks as the band made its way back to the stage. Liza and Tyrone stood in the wings, finalizing the set list. Eli slipped back to join them. He was determined to follow through on the decision he'd made after his visit to Antoinette's grave. Something had to change.

Liza and Tyrone turned and shifted, making room for him in their conversation. Eli squared with his nephew and placed both hands on his shoulders.

"Tyrone, I want you to know that you're an amazing talent and an even better man. You can accomplish whatever you set your mind to."

Eli then turned to Liza and placed his right arm around her shoulders with a side hug. "I don't know how I could have made it this far without you. Liza, there's no way I can repay you for all you've done for The Roz and for me."

"Eli, what—"

"Uncle, why are you being so serious? Feels like you're eulogizing us or something."

"I just . . ." He put his hands on both their shoulders. "If you don't mind, before you take the stage, I'd like to say a few words."

"Stage is all yours, boss. But Eli, are you okay?" Liza asked.

"Hopefully, I will be." Eli couldn't look her in the eye, and he turned to the band as they finished their preparations onstage.

* * *

Before taking the stage, Eli paused and glanced at the tattoo on his forearm, a symbol from Ghana of a bird flying forward while looking backward. It was supposed to be a reminder of the value of honoring the past while living one's life. As he liked to explain, "We can't know where we're going as a people if we don't know where we've come from." Tonight, the symbol felt like an omen. Eli was the bird flying blindly into the future, because all he could see was his past. If he had headed its warning, he might have been able to do something, but it was too late. A crash was inevitable.

Eli climbed the three steps and approached the microphone at center stage. He scanned the crowd, took a deep breath, and interrupted the conversations that were taking place.

"How are you all doing tonight?"

Applause and shouts of affirmation greeted him.

"I know you want to hear some more music, so I won't be long, but I need to make a quick announcement."

Eli glanced toward Liza. As their eyes met, he hoped she'd be able to forgive him for blindsiding her . . . and everyone else in the room.

"You all know my story. That this"—Eli gestured up and around the room—"was our dream."

Eli found his wedding ring with the thumb of his left hand.

"We—me and Antoinette. It was our dream to save enough money to buy the building and open it again. We felt that here in Denver, we as a people needed a place to come and relax and to not have to be more than just ourselves."

His mouth turned dry, and his voice cracked. For anyone in the front row, his eyes betrayed the fact that he was holding back tears. Every glass sat undisturbed, and all conversation had ceased.

"Little did we know it would be the insurance money from her death that would make our dream possible. She would have loved to see this, to be here with me and with all of you."

The room was full of reminders that he'd tried to forget his pain. The floors he'd refinished, the banister he'd sanded and polished. From the stage he'd built, he could see the closed door of the storage room that doubled as his office. On his desk were bills that went unpaid, not due to lack of funds but lack of will, next to a late notice from the IRS and an unfinished workers' comp claim for a cook who had sliced his finger during meal prep.

"We love you, Eli."

"I . . . I love you too," he replied.

Eli took another quick glance at Liza.

"I love all of you. More than you know, which is why this is difficult, but you all know that I'm not doing well. Haven't been since Antoinette . . ." Eli trailed off as he looked up from the people to the back of the bar, where another bottle, this time vodka, was missing from its spot.

"The holidays are coming, and I can't do this anymore. I'm done. All of this didn't help me forget, and right now all this place does is remind me she's not here.

"I'm sorry, everyone, but this is goodbye."

Liza was now standing next to him with tears also streaming down her cheeks. She was about to say something, but Eli raised his hands in protest and leaned into the microphone.

"This last set is it. After tonight, The Roz is closed. For good."

ELI DESCENDS

It was rage that threw Eli down the ladder.

After Eli announced he was closing The Roz, he left before anyone could convince him otherwise. Eli couldn't face the waves of questions he had no answers to.

What was he going to do now? What was going to happen to the place? Why now, after so much time and financial investment in renovating the building, was he giving up and walking away? In the balcony, he'd seen Shemekia Turner, president of Unity Bank, and he knew she wanted to know how he planned to pay off the loan. He didn't have answers, but he understood what he would not do anymore. So he left . . . mostly so he wouldn't have to face Liza.

As she approached him onstage, he'd felt her shock for The Roz and concern for him, but he wasn't ready for her consolation. So Eli hopped off the front of the stage and bolted for the door.

Now in his makeshift basement apartment, a cavern left over from the days of Prohibition, Eli looked up through the open hatch and screamed. It was a howl, guttural and primal. The muscles and ligaments in his neck stretched the skin, and his heart throbbed first in his forehead and then his ears.

Eli was on a familiar edge: the liminal space between sanity and despair that had beckoned him as a child after the death of Father Myriel and enveloped him in darkness when Antoinette died. The last time he stepped into the darkness, it had stolen his sense of humanity. Time wasn't past or future, just now. Food became optional and his very life undesirable.

When he moved into this underground space, it had been for his own safety. A sanctuary where he could tend to what kept him on the sane side of life. Eli remembered his mantra, the three words he spoke every night as he descended the ladder into this sacred space: *Mind. Body. Spirit.*

As sweat soaked through his shirt and his heart rate leveled, he repeated the words, taking a breath between each of them.

Mind.

Body.

Spirit.

Eli pulled the string on the single lightbulb in the ceiling and surveyed the room. In front of him and across the room was the bathroom he had piped and wired himself. He knew it would draw a citation from even a blind city inspector. To his left was his bed, a cot from the surplus store, where his rest was interrupted by his dreams of the woman he loved, the woman he'd lost. The heavy bag that received his anger and his rage hung still. To his right were three rows of bookshelves overflowing with his mentor's library.

Mind. Body. Spirit.

He approached the tall shelves containing the books he'd read, memorized, and used to console himself at the loss of his mentor, the closest thing he'd ever had to a father.

Eli removed his sweat-soaked shirt like a snake shedding its skin. Repeating his mantra usually soothed his spirit, but now it felt like it was betraying him.

"Mind!"

Eli grabbed his head and swayed on his feet.

"I feel like I'm losing my mind. I'm sick of this. All of it." The guttural tone was back. "I'm done with everything. The phone calls and the staff, the repairs and the taxes and the bills and picking up the trash."

Eli stood and made his way down to the last row of books. Upon reaching the end, he reached up and—as usual—pulled at the corner of one of the bookshelves until it tipped, spilling its contents onto the floor.

"Body!"

Eli stepped right to the next bookshelf and, with clenched fist, worked the books like the heavy bag. At first the spines resisted, but with each punch they soon gave way, splitting, cracking, and bursting.

"I want out of my body. Why can't I do it? Why can't I die? God, why . . ."

The corner to his right was a monument to his failed attempts at joining Antoinette in death. The stool he'd once stood on with a rope around his neck. The sword he'd once used to pierce his chest below his rib cage before Liza saved him just moments from what he'd hoped would be his last heartbeat.

Again, Eli reached high, grabbed the top corner of another shelf, and pulled it down. He stepped over the books at his feet and tilted another and then another as he worked his way down the row until he stood next to the stool and sword.

"Spirit." He was no longer yelling.

Tears soaked his beard as he picked up the stool and smashed it against the cement wall until the legs gave way and lay at his feet. The sword he snapped with his knee.

"My spirit is—"

A distant memory interrupted. An Ash Wednesday long ago with candles that filled the darkened sanctuary as he sat on the platform. Father Myriel was preparing the congregation to receive the body and the blood by quoting the words of the carpenter from Nazareth.

Eli improvised on those ancient words. "My spirit is *not* willing and my flesh is weak," he said as he pulled and tipped the final shelf, dumping the last of his books at his feet.

Eli squatted and sat back on his heals.

"All I want is my wife back. Do you hear me? That's all I want."

He pressed his palms into his eyes to hold back the flood of tears that continued to flow. After several minutes of silent weeping, he uncovered and opened his eyes, surveying the path of destruction. The tilted shelves served as makeshift lean-tos with the scattered piles of his library underneath their protection.

Eli's eyes finally came to rest on the book at the top of the pile strewn closest to him. It was a copy of Martin Luther King Jr.'s last book, the book he'd released a year before he was assassinated. The black-and-white picture on the cover depicted a dozen people walking along a road next to a field. Children of Africa and Europe, side by side, carrying American flags.

Above the picture, the title taunted Eli—*Where Do We Go From Here: Chaos or Community?*

He stood, head still throbbing from the pulse of his heart. Stepping over and around the mess he'd made, he reached the ladder that led out of his room, only to grab for the handle on the hatch door to slam it shut and lock himself inside.

He had no desire to read or pray or even to collapse on his cot. His eyes were on the heavy bag as he raised his fists and lowered his chin.

Where would he go from here?

Eli had made his choice.

Chaos.

RUBBIN' IT IN

"How much?"

Eli had hoped to slip in and out of The Roz without seeing anyone, let alone Chance on his side of the street. No such luck. Chance spotted him as he departed, yelling at him from the dirty sidewalk outside his club.

Eli had stopped into The Roz primarily to meet with the deliveryman. After apologizing for having him make the trip, Eli had canceled all future deliveries.

"For how long, Mr. Stone?" the man had asked.

"For good. I'm not reopening."

"Do you mind if I just say 'indefinite hiatus' for paperwork purposes? You know, just in case . . ."

Eli's expression offered no reply.

He had also called the Denver Rescue Mission to donate all the frozen food in the walk-in. The person on the other end noted that the homeless were about to "dine like kings. Steak and lobster! Are you sure, Mr. Stone? Wait till they find out we're having a surf-and-turf night!"

Before leaving, he had turned his attention to the wall of spirits behind the bar. These Eli was donating to himself. At the rate he was going, he'd be lucky if the thirty bottles of rum, bourbon, whiskey, cognac, and tequila lasted him through New Year's. He decided to ration the hard stuff and grabbed two bottles of wine, a red and white.

As he locked the front door, that's when Chance approached. "I said, how much?"

Eli stood for a moment taking in Chance's reflection in the glass. He wore his usual baggy shorts, this time white, even though it was after Labor Day; a Broncos jersey; and, of course, a blue hat tilted to the side. For Chance's sake, Eli decided not to turn around.

"Man, I could do something with this place."

Eli shouldn't have been surprised that news had traveled, but it stung, more than a little bit, that someone had run and told this man, of all people, about his decision to close The Roz.

"Been dreaming about it ever since I took over across the street. You know, I'd have to remodel the inside—no offense, my brotha, but let's just say our tastes aren't the same. Would have to bring things from the fifties to the nineties; the new millennium is just around the corner. The bones are good, but it needs some serious upgrades if we're going to party like it's 1999."

Chance added a snap as punctuation.

Eli had restored The Roz just how he and Antoinette had dreamed. "Vintage and with a sense of classic elegance," was how Antoinette had put it. "A place where you'd feel comfortable for a causal first-time date or celebrating your silver anniversary." Eli inwardly lamented what Chance would do with the building. The Roz was historic and needed someone who respected what it stood for.

"Not going to lie, my man, but I saw this coming. Didn't expect you to just up and quit, but it was only a matter of time before you realized you weren't cut out for this business."

Eli's jaw clenched, his fist even tighter around the necks of the wine bottles.

"So, what do you say? Let me take the old girl off your hands. Don't even have to have your people call my people. We can figure things out down and dirty and save on lawyers. You can't carry that note much longer. Surprised Shemekia hasn't already run over here to give you the business."

Chance was right. Shemekia was another person he was trying to avoid. She'd risked her reputation and job to push the loan through committee for Eli. Eli owed her an explanation. She deserved it.

"And the offer still stands. You can even work for me. Like I said, I could use someone with your talents."

Eli's fists squeezed the necks of the wine bottles even tighter. He hoped for a brief moment that they would give way, leaving him with two sharp-edged glass stubs to use against the man whose words sliced his back. When they didn't, Eli took one last look at Chance's confident and cocky face reflected in the glass of the front door and turned toward home.

Eli would deal with Chance, just not today.

WITH ALL DUE RESPECT

"They're going to keep mi hijo forever."

Liza was meeting with Dexter Diaz's mother. When Dorothy invited her to the house, Liza hadn't known that his four siblings and nieces and nephews would also join them.

Liza sat in a recliner with a legal pad and pen. Across from her on the couch sat Dexter's mom and his two sisters, while his two brothers stood on the side, one resting his knee on the armrest. The children wandered in and out of the small west-side living room, taking turns sitting on their grandmother's lap.

"Ma'am, I hoped that I could hear from you what happened at the police station."

Liza was familiar with the crime. Kathy McCarver, a beloved special needs teacher, had been found dead in her front yard on New Year's morning. "When I first saw her laying there, I thought she was passed out after a night of partying," a neighbor had said at trial. "I called her name and started to approach her, but a giant dog ran out of the opened front door and stood guard over her body. I kept my distance, but I could see blood frozen in her blond hair."

Police said the assault began in the house, where the attacker beat Kathy with her own shoe, and ended outside. A softball-sized rock was the ultimate murder weapon. Initially, the prime suspect was Kathy's boyfriend, who was sleeping inside and said he heard nothing because they were both inebriated after a night of partying. However, he had an unexplained injury on his hand, and suspicion only increased when he began talking about "someone else living inside him." A background search revealed multiple run-ins with the law.

"Ma'am—"

"Please, call me Dorothy. You are fighting for my son, mi hijo. That makes you family."

Liza looked around the room at Dexter's family. Both sisters held tissues in their hands. One brother stood with his hands in his pockets, while the oldest folded his arms and let them rest on his stomach. All eyes felt kind.

"Yes, ma'am—Dorothy," Liza corrected herself. "While I understand what happened to Ms. McCarver, I was—"

At the mention of the dead woman's name, everyone in the room, including the children, bowed their heads and crossed themselves as if in church. Liza bowed her head before continuing.

"What I don't understand is how the police turned their attention to Dexter."

All eyes were on Dorothy.

"Mrs. Brown," she said, but then corrected herself after glancing at Liza's ring finger, "I mean Miss Brown."

"Please, call me Liza. We're family, right?"

"Yes, Liza. I wasn't always a good mother for my children, but that's no reason for them to let him die in there."

One of her daughters offered a tissue, while the other put a hand on her mom's shoulder as they huddled on the couch.

The older brother cleared his voice and spoke with the tenderness of a priest.

"Our mom struggled when we were young, and we had to

take care of each other for a while. With most of us working and going to school, that left no one to look after Dexter."

"Dex, he started smoking weed and running with the bangers. You've seen his record, so you know he picked up a few charges. He wasn't a bad kid, we were all just trying to . . ." He glanced at his mother. Her head was now bowed, not in respect but in shame.

"Anyways," he continued, "a few days after the murder, one of Dexter's friends came by and asked if he wanted to ride around in his new car. Dexter went, not knowing that the kid's new Lexus was actually Miss McCarver's."

Liza waited as again they bowed and crossed themselves.

"So that explains why they picked him up to question him, but why did he speak to the police at the station? He was only fourteen but had experience with them. And Dorothy, you were there with him."

"They tricked me," Dexter's mom boomed, startling the children now sitting at her feet. "I was in the room with him while they were talking to him about the car, but then one detective said he needed me to go with him to fill out some paperwork." Her volume now was barely above a whisper. "While I was gone, they started pressing him about the murder. They tricked him too, told him they had evidence."

Liza had yet to watch the video of the interrogation, but she remembered how Garrett said Dexter had caved after denying involvement sixty-five times.

"They wouldn't let me back in the room."

"What was the evidence they said they had against him?" Liza asked.

"Liza, our little Dex was gullible because of his age, and also because he didn't go to school much. He wasn't always the brightest when it came to book stuff." The older brother was now speaking. "They told him they had all kinds of finger and boot prints, and—get this—they even told him they had hair prints. What's a hair print?"

Dorothy took the lead in telling the narrative once again. "So by the time they let me back in the room, he'd already confessed. When I sat down next to him, he whispered to me, 'No les creas. No lo hice.'"

"Don't believe them. I didn't do it," one of Dexter's sisters translated for Liza.

Liza thanked her with a nod as she scribbled on her legal pad.

"Señorita Liza, can I ask a question?" asked the young niece sitting on the floor in front of her.

"Yes, dear, of course."

"Are you going to get our tió out of jail?"

Liza thought about the many times Journey had asked her the same question about Langston. About the many times she'd said yes with absolute certainty, only to have failed.

"Because Abuela says they want to keep him until he's dead."

Liza didn't know what to say as everyone in the room bowed their heads and made the sign of the cross.

COURTESY CALL

"We're moving forward on habeas," Liza said.

DA Frank Taylor cocked his head to the side like he was unsure what she was talking about.

"The Moses King case," Liza clarified.

The district attorney's office was majestic. Perched in a corner suite of the City and County Building and furnished with a desk, credenza, and conference table all in matching cherrywood, it was larger than most of the apartments that could be seen through the east-facing windows. It surprised most DAs that they'd have to downgrade their office if they ran for mayor. Taylor sat at his desk wearing a full suit and tie while Liza sat, legs crossed, in a curiously low chair that forced her to look up at the man.

At the mention of Moses King, the politeness drained from his steel-blue eyes and his smile disappeared, hiding his bleached white teeth. Liza had seen him only on TV, but now, in person, she could verify what everyone suspected—his perfect salt-and-pepper hair was as fake as the Rolex on his wrist.

"Listen, Ms. Brown, I took this appointment out of deference to your father. You and your family have been through a lot, and had I been DA at the time, I like to think things would have been different and your father would still be alive. But you can't be serious. There's no way you think that King is actually—"

"Mr. Taylor, I'm not here for permission or even advice on what I can and cannot do," Liza asserted herself. "Before we meet in court, I thought it only proper to confer with you first with the hope that we can come to an agreement. I'm here to request that you revisit the case, trusting that if you knew what I now do, then you'll do the right thing."

"Not going to happen," he said, now removing his glasses and leaning back in his chair. "That case was solid and will stand up."

"With all due respect, Mr. Taylor, you don't actually think a dream that took place a day and a half after the assault counts as solid evidence. I couldn't believe it. That was all you had on Moses. No physical evidence, no—"

"Listen here, Ms. Brown. I know you're now on a vigilante mission to review every case because you think that if it happened to your father, 'there must be more.'" Taylor made quotes as he spoke the final phrase. "Isn't that what you said to the *Denver Post*? Well, I'm here to tell you that there isn't any more, and there is no way I'm going to let you drag that poor woman back into court. She's been through enough."

Liza had thought about what this might mean for the victim and hated the idea of traumatizing her again with a new trial.

"Mr. Taylor, on that we agree, and we can avoid causing her more undue harm if you would just be reasonable."

"Habeas requires fresh evidence. What do you have that makes you think you can convince a judge of the need for a new trial?"

"How about a confession from the actual perpetrator, Levar Calhoun?"

"You have got to be kidding me. Calhoun?"

"Before you were DA, you put him in prison for an almost identical crime that happened less than a five-minute drive from our case. We've got an affidavit from him confessing to the crime for which Moses is in prison."

Liza was speaking as assistant director of Project Joseph, even though she knew she was on her own. She slid the paper across the desk and watched as Taylor put his glasses on and read.

"Calhoun says that what happened was consensual. No chance this'll hold up."

"On the contrary," Liza shot back. "And besides that confession, we've also discovered a note from the detective on the case that shows Calhoun was an early suspect."

Taylor shook his head.

"Ms. Brown, do you really want to do this? If you win this, then there's a new trial, and a new trial means that poor woman has to go through this again. She's been through enough."

"Don't put this on me. Moses King has been through enough too. By the time he gets out, he'll have lost the most productive years of his life. No, Mr. Taylor, this is on you. If you do the right thing, I'll even let you look like the hero in the eyes of the media and your constituents."

Taylor stood up and ceremoniously fastened the top button on his suit coat.

"Ms. Brown, I'll take my chances in court."

Liza remained seated for a moment. She had one more item to talk to Taylor about, but her time was up.

Dexter Diaz would have to wait.

THE HARD TRUTH

"I'm sorry I couldn't make it down to see you. Would have rather had this conversation with you face-to-face."

Liza was sitting in her office at the project with the door closed. She spoke barely above a whisper for fear of Garrett catching wind that she was still on Moses's case.

While she'd never seen the phones inmates used at Stratling, she imagined they were like the ones in the movies: a row of handsets with people lined up shoulder to shoulder trying to block out other conversations and hear the person on the other end of the line, warnings posted in front of them that their conversations were subject to recording.

"Ms. Liza, that's all right. I know you're working hard, and I appreciate you taking my call."

Liza scribbled a reminder note to complete the paperwork required to allow for lawyer-client phone calls in the future without prying ears that could leak information to DA Taylor.

"So, Ms. Liza, how are things going? I can't wait for you to tell that judge about Calhoun and his confession. Been waiting a long time for this whole mess to get straightened out."

Liza's excitement was growing as well, but first she needed to be honest with her client.

"Moses, there's something I need to tell you."

She paused as she searched for the right words. Moses jumped in.

"Ain't nothing you going to tell me that's worse than when they said I was guilty. Shoot straight with me. Did Calhoun back out?"

"No, it's not that. It's just that even with Calhoun, this is not a slam dunk.

"First, while we have a signed affidavit from Calhoun, he takes responsibility for the beating but distances himself from the assault. It's a start, but it's not as clean as we first thought. Plus, the two of you used to be drinking buddies. The DA is most definitely going to argue that this is a case of Calhoun helping an old friend out of a jam."

You have five minutes remaining in your phone call. An electronic voice interrupted their conversation. But then there was a click, followed by momentary silence.

"Are you still there?"

"Yes, Ms. Liza, that's just the sound of the little birdies that like to listen in on the line."

While Liza was concerned about DA Taylor hearing what she had to say, she also needed to make sure that Moses understood the true nature of his case.

"I met with the DA to see if he'd be willing to do the right thing, but he has no interest. So it looks like we're going to court. But . . ." Liza trailed off for a moment, then remembered that their phone call would end soon. Her experience had taught her that five minutes unusually meant three.

"But I haven't given you the bad news yet. Moses, it's just me. All you have is me. I did my best to convince the project to take your case, but Professor Garrett is not budging, because, Moses, you don't fit our criteria. We have limited resources, and compared to others, you technically still have hope. I know it sounds harsh, but you are only serving forty-eight years. Compared to others like my daddy, you still have a chance to get out with life to live." She took a breath and then continued. "So I need you to know that I do not have permission to work your case. I'm doing this on my own. We don't have any money or resources. It's just me."

"Ms. Liza—"

"And I just passed the bar. I'm barely a lawyer, Moses. I've never stood before an actual judge and argued anything. Moses, this is real. Your life is on the line. And to make things worse, we're appearing before the same judge that denied Daddy a new trial."

You have one minute remaining in your call.

After a long pause and another click, Moses spoke. "So you're saying it's just you and me?"

"Yes," she said. "Just us."

"Ms. Liza, that was good enough for my friend Langston Brown, and it's good enough for me."

Your call is now complete.

WHEREFORE ART THOU, ELI?

That night after Eli made his announcement and left, Liza had been the one to console the crowd, apologize for the news, and remind them of Eli's grief. Not knowing when or if she'd ever sing again, Liza, along with Tyrone and the band, gave them everything she had.

"This might be it," she told them. "We don't know if The Roz will ever see another day, so let's all stay to the end, if this is the end. Then we all can say we were there for The Roz's last hurrah, and it was amazing."

She sang past two in the morning, and no one left as they all savored the moment. They would have gone until dawn, but Liza's voice gave out. As the band played one last song, she made her way around the room to hug and thank everyone for their love and support. When the last person left, she set the alarm, turned the OPEN sign to the side that read CLOSED, and locked the door.

Today, Liza drove past the front door of The Roz, where the CLOSED sign in the window hadn't shifted since she'd flipped it, and parked in front of Eli's place.

The street was empty and quiet except for a homeless man stumbling past the fire station across the street and settling on the sidewalk to sleep off his stupor.

Liza grabbed her purse along with some files from Moses's case and stepped out into the cold air. Her breath rose in front of her face as she found the key to Eli's place on her key chain.

"Eli!" Liza shouted as she unlocked the door. "Eli, are you in here?"

After closing down The Roz for the last time, she'd come here to check on Eli, hoping he would talk. She'd known he was underground in his room and could hear her, because when she pulled on the hatch door, it was locked from the inside.

Today, though, she pulled, and the door opened.

"Eli, it's me."

Liza put down her purse and files and sat with her legs hanging down in the opening next to the ladder.

"Eli, can we talk? We . . . I need to know that you're okay."

Silence met her words.

"Eli, I'm coming down."

She descended into the darkness. The only light available to her eyes was the one that came through the opening from upstairs. It was enough for her to see two things. Her breath—it was as cold down here as it was outside—and Eli's sword. She had seen it before and been alarmed by the bloodstains on the blade. Today it lay next to a broken stool, snapped in half.

"Eli?"

Liza searched for the pull string for the room's light. By the time she found it, she had half prepared herself to have its light reveal Eli's dead body. To find that he'd finally succeeded and joined Antoinette like his heart wanted to.

Liza gasped when the light flashed on. It was like a tornado had whirled from each corner of the small room. The neat rows of bookcases had been replaced by a pick-up sticks mess of tilted shelves arched over mounds of books.

"Eli, what have you done?"

Liza's eyes darted around the room, searching like a light-house lamp. His army cot was in place, an unfolded blanket draped across the bottom. In one corner stood a record player with three LPs cued and ready to go. The heavy bag lay strewn on the floor with a broken chain. Liza checked the bathroom and shower; Eli was nowhere to be found.

Liza turned her attention to the pile of books and shelves.

"Eli?"

He couldn't be under there, could he? No, there was no way he would have pulled all of that down on himself. But what if someone had attacked Eli and covered him up underneath?

Liza poked around the piles of shelves and books. It made little sense to her that someone could have overpowered Eli in his own place. She knew he had secrets, but what were the odds that there was someone who was out to get him and would murder him in such a fashion? No, what she was witnessing was the physical expression of Eli's despair. This was a visual manifestation of his pain.

After one last visual sweep, Liza turned off the light and made her way back up the ladder. She closed the hatch and exchanged the files she'd brought with her for new ones. She was frustrated and worried not only with Eli but with herself. Why had she allowed her heart to commit itself to such a broken and unavailable man? First Journey's father and now Eli. Her head told her it was time to give up hope, but her heart reminded her that Eli had been there for her in her darkest moments and that she must do the same for him, if he would let her.

Liza's eyes took in the two kitchen chairs, one draped with Antoinette's orange scarf and the table covered with empty wine, rum, and whiskey bottles.

Liza removed a notepad and pen from her purse. She had finally read through all the files in King's case and had found

again in his direction, she hadn't made the connection that the homeless man passed out across the street was the man she was looking for.

So far, no one had registered that Eli was the newest homeless man in the neighborhood. Not his friend Chief Barrinton, nor any of the guys at the firehouse. Not Mr. Freeman when they crossed paths on the sidewalk, not Shemekia when she unlocked the bank doors for business. Not even Chance when he arrived and walked past the trash on his side of the street.

Since his run-in with Officer Winston, Eli had been looking for something other than sweats and a hoodie to wear when stalking the local police. Already convinced that children of Africa were invisible in America and Denver in particular, he'd decided to take shelter with the residents of the streets, another unseen population.

Hanging out with the homeless was also providing him with unexpected intel on the activities and habits of the local officers. He'd learned from the cadre that lived at Sonny Lawson Park that there were seventeen regular officers assigned to the neighborhood and that only a handful seemed to be up to nefarious activities, such as stealing from the homeless around the first of the month when they were flush with cash from their government checks. Eli had also discovered that a favorite pastime of the area officers was playing a game they called "Who's doin' who?" The dark fields just north of the runways of Stapleton Airport were a favorite place for couples to park in order to save the expense of getting a hotel room. Apparently, the police had also discovered it was a favorite spot for the rich and powerful men of the city to park with their mistress or favorite lady of the night. The police, besides rolling homeless vets on the streets, liked to catch unsuspecting couples in the act and demand a donation in exchange for not putting their mug shots on the morning news.

The night before, Eli had witnessed the corruption firsthand as he lay in the park with binoculars in hand. Two neighborhood teens hopped off the bus and cut through the park toward home. As soon as the bus was out of sight, a patrol car sped over the curb and headed straight for the young men. They froze due to the spotlights in their eyes. A familiar voice ordered them to the ground, faces in the grass. It was Winston. Eli tightened his grip on the binoculars, preparing to wield them if the officer lifted a hand against the adolescents.

Eli watched as Winston rifled through the teens' backpacks and frisked them as they lay still, hands behind their head. He could hear Winston speaking but was too far away to make out any words. He remained still, doing his best to look like what Winston believed him to be: just a lump of drunkenness sleeping off a stupor underneath a far-off tree.

Winston barked another indiscernible order as he picked up the teens' basketball and punted it over the softball fence toward second base. He got back in his car and left as the two boys put their belongings back in their bags and went to retrieve the ball.

Eli believed that cops who would engage in these sorts of activities might also be the type to be involved with robberies like the one at Freeman's Furniture and to beat up young men like Tyrone. Officer Winston was at the top of his list of potential ringleaders.

Eli felt at ease with those who didn't have a home. After his parents died, he'd run from every foster family that social services had convinced to take him in, and it was on the streets that he'd found solace among those who were abandoned or on the run or both. It wasn't until he was picked up and put in the care of the local Catholic Charities that things had started to changed. That was when he'd met Father Myriel.

"You're free to run," Myriel would tell him. "But if you stay, I promise to help you, and little by little, it will get better."

Eli believed this kind man of the cloth because he'd seen him on the streets handing out sandwiches and hot chocolate. Father Myriel was one of the few people everyone trusted. While Eli never lost the desire to run, his desire to learn life from this man grew stronger as they talked philosophy and theology and together went to the streets with food, socks, and coats. Now that he was on the run again, it only made sense to him to find cover with the people and in the place where it had all started.

Green cargo pants, boots, a heavy coat, and an oversize hat with a scarf wrapped across his lower jaw allowed him to move freely again. He wanted to investigate a rumor that the police were rotating their extracurricular activities between Five Points and the Broadway business district two miles away.

Eli held his breath as Liza passed in front of him, again glancing in his direction not even fifty feet away. She made her way to The Roz, unlocked the front door, and turned on the lights. This was the ultimate proof of concept that he needed. If Liza didn't recognize him, then neither would an officer who had seen him only for a moment in the dark.

Eli was ready to resume his hunt.

STRENGTH TO LOVE

Liza locked the door behind her, turned on the lights, and dropped her purse, briefcase, and armful of files on the nearest table.

The first time she'd walked through the doors of The Roz, she'd been desperate and willing to do anything to help her father. To her left was the bar, where Eli had poured her a drink that afternoon and listened to her woes—the same bar where they'd later sat for hours processing, dreaming, and commiserating together. This was where her heart had learned to feel again, where she'd started be believe that she and Eli might someday find a future together.

A familiar desperation filled her heart for Moses King and Dexter Diaz—two men, one with gray hairs multiplying and the other barely old enough to grow a mustache, both in need of help. Liza had come here to do what she knew how to do: work hard, hoping to catch a break.

Liza filled the silent space with song. The click of her boots kept time as she made her way behind the bar and started a pot of coffee and then headed to the back room to turn on the heat.

Liza removed her coat and moved her briefcase and files to the stools along the front of the bar. First, she placed a legal pad with the name *Dexter Diaz* underlined and circled at the top on the far right of the bar and said out loud, "Trust me, I will get to you." She had the law students doing research at the law library and would meet with them tomorrow.

Today was about Moses King.

Starting on the far left side of the bar, she laid out the artifacts of his case. A stack of letters from Moses, including the first one, in which he'd written, *I was convicted on a dream . . . I'm innocent . . . I have proof, the best kind.* Then the affidavit from Levar Calhoun admitting to consensual sex with the victim and beating her blind. Next, the detective's note from the case files proving that they were aware of Calhoun and should have done their due diligence. Fanned out across the middle of the bar were pictures of the crime scene, the apartment, and the victim, Claudette Cooper.

She poured a cup of coffee and, with the mug warming her hands, sat down at the bar and surveyed the case.

On a fresh yellow legal pad, she wrote *Habeas.* Over the next couple of hours, she outlined the facts of Moses's case and refined her argument and presentation. The sunset painted the sky as she moved from the bar to a low-top table. When darkness descended, Liza took a break, turned off the coffee warmer, and rinsed the now empty pot. She was grateful to find a bottle of moscato in the cooler and poured a glass. With the wine in her right hand and a legal pad tucked under the same arm, she grabbed a barstool with her left and made her way to the stage.

The stool served as her podium as she faced the empty room and made her case.

"Your Honor, we are here because of a gross miscarriage of justice . . ."

In less than a week, she would stand before the same judge who'd dangled freedom in front of her father only to allow him to die. A judge who had since remained silent, even though

DNA evidence had exonerated Langston and the state legislature had issued an official apology. Liza was surprised at how quickly he'd granted her requested hearing for Moses, but apparently even Judge Morris was aware that after what had happened with her father, another high-profile debacle would bring unwanted scrutiny his way.

"Your Honor, it is imperative that you right this wrong . . ."

She took a sip of her wine and jotted down a note as she worked to refine her talking points, knowing that with this judge, anything short of perfection was not enough. She had to be better than perfect to even have a shot.

A knock on the window behind her startled her back to the moment. She turned and saw Tyrone waving.

"Yo, sis, I hope you're not in here working on something new without me?" he said as Liza opened The Roz's front door. After a hug, they made their way to the stage and sat on the edge.

"Oh, I'm not working on anything musical, but what about you? Still keeping your chops sharp on that new axe?" Liza asked. "We didn't buy you a new horn for you to just lay it down in surrender."

"No worries, no surrender here."

They sat a few moments as they both scanned the room where people had come to hear them do what they loved to do.

"Ty, have you seen him?" Liza asked.

"No, I was hoping you had. Last time he disappeared like this was right after Auntie passed. We knew he was in their old house, but there was no way in. When he finally came out, he was a shell of himself. Had lost so much weight I almost didn't recognize him. But he was also on a mission to open this place. Fixing up The Roz saved his life. Liza, I'm worried, because I don't know what will save him this time. If all of this wasn't enough to heal his broken heart, then I don't know . . ." Tyrone's voice trailed off as he looked toward the balcony.

"They had something special, Eli and Antoinette, didn't they?"

"Like Cliff and Claire with a blue-collar flare."

"Would have liked to have met her. Sounds like she was a special woman."

"True that. Auntie was one of a kind. But to be honest, all of us kinda thought you and Eli would get together. You were cut from the same cloth as Auntie—that no-nonsense-Black-woman strength and elegance."

Liza almost agreed out loud that she too saw her and Eli together. That was the desire of her heart, but overcoming Eli's brokenness and despair felt like trying to climb Pikes Peak barefoot in a blizzard. She was glad when Tyrone changed the subject.

"So what's all of this?" Tyrone referred to her stacks of files and yellow legal pads.

"This is the stuff of nightmares. Twenty-eight years and counting for something he had nothing to do with. I'm trying to get my act together for the hearing next week."

"Your father would be proud—still keeping up the fight."

Fighting was all Liza had done with her adult life. She could barely remember a time when her jaw wasn't set and her neck wasn't taut. At some level, she understood Eli, and she almost wished she had the courage to check out and disappear like he had.

"So what about your friend's case?" Liza asked. "Sorry, I haven't been able to keep up. Is he out of jail?"

"Jamal is out, but for who knows how long? I know you're busy with all of this, but he needs a lawyer too. This is all about parking tickets. They stop us, harass us, and then cite us for anything and everything here in Five Points. We're all driving cars barely worth a few hundred dollars, but we owe thousands in fines and late fees. We can't afford that. Their focus is on the young people because they don't think we'll do anything. So, like I said, I know you're busy with all of this, but we could use you to be our street lawyer too."

Tyrone was right, but how could she help him and Moses, Dexter and Eli? There wasn't enough room on her shoulders for another fight.

"So we going to do something," Tyrone announced. "Tonight, we are going to start making some noise. Going to cause a racket that matches the racket they are running."

Tyrone stood up and grabbed his coat.

"What does that mean?"

"Fire with fire. Remember how you turned up the heat on them for your daddy? We're going to make sure they feel the heat everywhere. Time the entire city feels what we feeling."

Tyrone's talk about fighting fire with fire and turning up the heat on the whole city felt familiar. Liza identified with that kind of rage, but something in the way Tyrone said it made Liza feel uncomfortable.

"Ty, we stood on this stage together and saw a roomful of Black folk with their fists in the air, ready to support you. You called us to action and we're ready to follow you, but you have to let us know where we're going. We need to know what you're planning and that the destination is right and worthy."

Tyrone checked his pager.

"Listen," Tyrone said, standing up. "What I know is that what we've been doing ain't working. Singing 'We Shall Overcome' still has us overrun and overlooked. We need a fresh approach. Something that doesn't have us lying unconscious in the street with no recourse."

"But, Ty—"

"Do you know Mom took me down to the department, and we filed a report about what happened to me? Do you know what they said? 'We'll look into it.' That was it. Haven't heard a thing since. 'Look into it' means 'We'll make sure nothing happens.' So we're going to make sure people can't ignore us, that's all. They will have to see us."

Liza understood. She too had felt the dismissive swipe of the arm of justice, but she didn't want Tyrone to doing something he'd regret.

"My friend is waiting, and I need to go." He zipped his coat.

"I'm worried about you."

They hugged.

"Don't be. We're going be wise like serpents, but believe me, we are going to make this city feel our pain."

As Tyrone left, Liza returned to the stage next to the stool. As she surveyed the empty seats, it felt like her singing dreams had died a second death. Eli was gone, and Tyrone was out doing who knew what. She couldn't imagine going to other clubs and begging for stage time, and she sure would not join a cover band and spend her Saturday nights singing at weddings.

Liza returned the stool to its place by the bar and washed the empty wineglass. She gathered the files and both legal pads, Moses's and Dexter's, and placed them next to each other in her briefcase. Moving from right to left along the bar, she stacked the evidence for her habeas petition.

Finally, she picked up the letters she'd received from Moses. He was still writing to her just about every other day. Every so often, the letters contained a legal strategy or a memory he thought might be helpful to his case. More often he sought to encourage her, but the letter that arrived this morning also had a request.

Ms. Liza,

I am grateful that you are on my case. You are risking a lot, but they'll see you were right to follow your convictions.

Next week, when you plead my case, it will be an honor to be the first person you've officially represented. You are going to be magnificent. That was a word Langston used a lot when he talked about you.

I do have a favor to ask.

I'm not sure if I'm going to get to see Levar before the trial. Most likely, they'll keep us separated. My worry is that he probably thinks I'm feeling some kind of way about him for what he did.

Liza, I hold no ill will toward him for what he's done to me. I understand he was operating out of fear and I forgave him a long time ago.

Will you please tell him that? Before he enters the courtroom and takes the stand to admit what he's done, please tell him I harbor no anger and that I offer him peace.

With hope,
Moses

THE NUTS

Eli eyed Liza as she hugged Tyrone and locked the door behind him as he stepped out onto the street.

Tyrone paused for a moment and checked his pager, perhaps wondering the same thing Eli was: *Where are the police tonight?* Eli decided he would follow Tyrone and make sure he made it home without incident.

"Yo, T," a voice shouted.

Eli looked to his right and saw a young man wearing a hoodie. After looking all five ways, the young man jogged across the intersection with a duffel bag in his left hand. He dapped and bumped shoulders with Tyrone, and without words they headed south on Washington Street. Inside The Roz, Liza had returned to the stage, and even from this distance Eli could see the concern on her face as the two young men walked away.

Eli's plan of stalking the police after he secretly escorted Tyrone home dropped from his mind. Tonight, his eyes would be on his nephew wherever Tyrone went. He waited until the two young men had walked the length of The Roz, and after they'd passed the front door to his place, he got up and followed. Liza was still inside The Roz, gathering her belongings.

Eli lagged, and as Tyrone and his companion made their way deeper into the neighborhood and away from traffic, he could hear their voices, though he couldn't make out what they were saying. Five minutes later they reached Colfax, and as they turned right, Eli could see that Tyrone was now carrying the duffel bag.

Eli jogged to the corner, afraid of losing the two young men in the evening crowd of prostitutes, cross-dressers, hustlers, and an influx of men from the suburbs exiting the peep shows now in search of more than just a peek.

By the time Eli reached the corner, Tyrone and the man had already crossed Colfax and were now turning left down Pearl Street into Capitol Hill. Capitol Hill was a neighborhood that enjoyed the shadow of the gold-domed statehouse by day and the absence of police harassment by night, even though plenty of illicit activities that started on Colfax were consummated in the darkness of this neighborhood's side streets.

After a few more blocks, the men navigated Speer Boulevard and drifted into a quiet neighborhood inhabited by urban-dwelling children of Europe. Eli worried. Two young men and a homeless guy, all three children of Africa, were sure to look out of place.

As if by prearrangement, the two men Eli was following split. Tyrone continued walking while his friend ducked low next to a fence. Eli glimpsed his face. It was Maurice, one of the men who had carried Tyrone's unconscious body into The Roz.

Eli immediately slowed to a drunken walk, hoping that Maurice would see no threat in the presence of a tipsy homeless man over a block away. Eli staggered and fell down, mumbling.

Maurice paused for a moment but then turned toward Tyrone and waved a signal.

Tyrone was standing in the street next to a parked car. It looked as if he placed something under the windshield wiper.

He knelt down by the left front tire, removed a tire iron from the bag, and, one by one, removed the lug nuts from the wheel.

Maurice whistled a quick note, and Tyrone responded with a whistle of his own. In less than a minute, they were off and running. Eli followed and, as they turned right at the corner, sprinted to keep pace while keeping to the shadows. When he arrived at the corner, they were now two blocks away, turning left at another intersection. Eli cut through the ally, hoping he could run full speed unseen. At the end of the next block, he stopped and looked around the corner just in time to see Tyrone and Maurice slow to a brisk walk.

The home values increased exponentially as they reached North Cherry Creek, and Tyrone and Maurice split again. This time, Tyrone was on lookout. Maurice approached a car and carried out the same routine. First, what looked like a note was placed on the windshield, and then the car's lug nuts were removed. Maurice was considerably slower than Tyrone in completing the operation, but after a few whistles, they were off and running again.

This time, Eli let them go. When they were out of sight, he approached the car. If the owner were to drive away without noticing the missing hardware, their tire would fall off when they executed their first turn out of the neighborhood.

Eli removed the folded xeroxed paper from the windshield and read.

Dear citizen of the City and County of Denver,

This is a note to inform you to check your nuts.
As long as you allow the Denver Police to harass and terrorize us in Five Points, we will do the same to you.
Use your power, or ELSE.

NO REST FOR THE WEARY

Claudette reached her hand into the lukewarm water and pulled the drain on the kitchen sink. The scent of Palmolive rose as the water gurgled down the drain. She dried a plate, glass, and two pots, placed them in a cabinet, and moved a plastic container with leftover spaghetti into the refrigerator.

Jay Leno's monologue was ending as she took five steps to the chair in the living room. Using the remote that sat on the side table, she turned off the TV as a commercial about cat litter began.

She used to love this time of day. As her mother would say, "Claudette, the nighttime is the beginning of the day, not the end. The Word says that when days were created, 'there was evening and then there was morning.' We start each day with sleep. It's a sign of trust."

Ever since the attack, all Claudette had known was that nighttime and trust were no longer synonymous. In her world, even though all light switches were permanently in the off position and darkness was her sole reality, the rest she needed was as real as a child's fairy tale.

Four more steps to the front door of her apartment. She unlocked the dead bolt and opened the door as far as the chain would allow. Her nose took a quick sniff of the cool air as she

172

felt for the knob and dead bolt on the wrought-iron screen door. Both were in the vertical position, as she had left them. Closing the inside door, she reset the dead bolt and knob lock and double-checked that the chain was still in place and secure. Next came the window. It didn't matter that she was on the third floor with no balcony. She pulled on the frame, making sure it didn't budge.

After seven steps back toward the kitchen, she stopped in the hallway. Leaning on the wall was a rolling pin wrapped in tissue paper. Claudette slipped down to her knees and, facing the front door, crawled backward, unrolling the tissue paper like a wedding runner down the center aisle of a church. Multiple pieces taped together stretched the length of the fifteen-foot-long hall. Was the paper pink or blue for a baby shower or red and green for Christmas? Claudette didn't know. But as she pressed the weight of her hand onto the paper, a slight crackle broke the silence. She knew it might provide the warning she needed this time.

The king-sized bed filled most of the small bedroom, leaving narrow paths on three sides. Claudette slid the rolling pin underneath the bed near the headboard.

Six steps to the bathroom, where she washed her face and brushed her teeth. Retracing her steps back to her bedroom, Claudette felt the bedspread for the pile of blankets and pillows arranged underneath to resemble a human form. Then she dropped to her knees.

Her right hand found the warm handle of the knife in her pocket. After removing it, she lay down, her back to the floor. A few shimmies to her right and she was underneath the bed with the rolling pin within reach above her head and her blade resting to her right.

Only then did Claudette take a deep breath, hoping to find at least the illusion of rest.

BETTER LATE THAN NEVER

Liza was late, and the unhappiness on Garrett's face was apparent as she walked into the conference room. The team was gathered to discuss Dexter Diaz's case.

She'd prepared for the meeting the night before, and then, after a few hours' sleep, she'd left her house early before sunrise. It had been a while since she'd had a face-to-face with Moses, so she'd made the two-hour drive to Stratling Correctional Facility. She'd known that in order to make it to Stratling and back to Denver on time for the meeting, things would have to go perfectly; however, they had not.

Return traffic on I-25 from Colorado Springs to Denver had spoiled her plan to arrive by ten forty-five for the eleven AM meeting she was to facilitate. The influx of people from California was something the state of Colorado wasn't excited about nor ready for. While some locals welcomed and others decried the granola politics, everyone despised the traffic the Californians brought and their lack of ability to drive in the snow. So Liza was late, and Garrett's look, along with his accompanying sigh, signaled that he was still considering whether she was up for the task of leading Dexter's appeal.

She apologized for her lateness as she unpacked her brief-case, but her mind was still on Moses.

"Why aren't you angry?" Liza had asked Moses a couple of hours prior.

His even-keel demeanor, along with the note he'd sent asking her to extend forgiveness to Calhoun on his behalf, had her rattled. They were about to enter a street fight, and she needed Moses in the right state of mind. Prepping her arguments on behalf of Moses at The Roz the night before had left her in a rage over the injustice this man had endured.

"Twenty-eight years. That's longer than Daddy was in this hellhole, and you are asking me to . . ." Liza held up the letter Moses had written about forgiving Calhoun. "Moses, when I get him on that stand, I intend to grill him like a side of beef. Calhoun has let you rot in here for almost three decades, but first you want me to tell him you hold no ill will?" She returned the letter to the table. "Moses, this is your last chance. I double-checked—we don't even have DNA to test, because they destroyed the evidence."

The night before, Liza had read again how the bedsheets and victim's garments had been sealed in an evidence bag marked DO NOT DESTROY and how—after seven years of fighting—Moses had finally won the right to test the items to prove his innocence, only to discover they had been "discarded in the dumpster." She knew the devastation of learning such news, because the same thing had happened to her father.

"Yeah, Ms. Liza, that hurt real bad. Convinced the court to allow me to test the evidence, and because they said I had to pay for it myself, all the fellas in here pooled their money and gave it to me, no strings attached. Can you believe that? They gave a thousand dollars to help me. When I found out that the police threw the evidence in the trash, that broke me. But what can you do?"

"We can win this habeas petition, and that starts with going after Calhoun. Then, when we get you out of here, we'll make them pay for every year, every month, every second of your life they wasted. Moses, getting you out is just the beginning. We must hold them accountable."

"In here I can't afford to let my feelings get the best of me. If I did, I'd end up hurting someone or even myself. So when it comes to anger and revenge, guess I'm grateful that I've got you for that."

That was two hours ago, but now she was here in the conference room, twenty minutes late. Liza took charge of the silent room.

"We can win this case, and we will, but it's going to take all of us."

Liza had believed in Dexter's case when she first read about what had happened to him, and while his demeanor had put her off at their first meeting, she continued to believe in his case. This man had been a fourteen-year-old boy who was tricked and convicted, and he was now serving life.

"They stacked the deck against our client, and as is always true with these cases, finding grounds for a new trial won't be easy, but we can and we will."

One intern said what everyone was thinking. "I don't see how we overcome the mountain of evidence against him."

"Before we can climb the mountain, Jennifer, we have to face it," Liza said as she stood and wrote on the whiteboard. "First, there's the fact that he was in the victim's stolen car two days after the murder. Then there's the taped confession. Most people, including judges, don't understand why someone would admit to a crime they didn't commit, especially murder. On top of all of that, there's the fact that he's Hispanic, and witnesses say they saw multiple Hispanic teens running from the scene."

They all stared at the board, and then the same intern interjected.

"So, why do we believe he didn't do it?"

Liza understood the sentiment. Dexter was far from a choir boy. At the time of his arrest, he'd already racked up charges of vandalism, truancy, and petty theft.

"Our justice system entitles every person to a vigorous defense, and that's what we will give him," Garrett interjected.

While Liza believed that in principle, her heart felt differently. She did this for people like her father, like Moses—good people crushed by the worst of the world. She sympathized with Dexter the boy, but Dexter the man presented a challenge. While Garrett was in this for the love of the law and the Constitution, Liza's love was more complicated. She needed to satisfy both the law and her heart.

"Let's start with what possible new evidence we can present that was not previously available," Liza continued. "As I read through the transcripts, I wasn't able to see that there was any DNA evidence presented at trial. Can you confirm?" Liza turned toward the second intern, Megan.

Both interns searched their notes.

"No, we don't think so."

Liza wrote *DNA* on the board.

"I'm thinking that this is our path over the mountain. Megan and Jennifer, I need you to reread everything and verify that there was nothing presented along these lines. And once you double-check, I need to you check a third time.

"And Janet, two things: Could you check recent case law on DNA evidence? Don't want to get caught off guard by what we don't know. Also, would you please call the DPD evidence room and find out what evidence was preserved?"

After losing the evidence in Langston's and Moses's cases, she didn't want to get her hopes up.

"And Dr. Garrett"—she smiled—"I need you to tap your vast network of relationships. If we get back before a jury, we're going to need an expert who can help us explain how and why false confessions happen in the first place."

"I'll see what I can do. There are few people who owe me favors." Garrett smiled back.

"We'll meet back here next week. Same day, same time."

Everyone left, but Garrett remained seated.

Liza felt his attention.

"Ms. Brown, I've been waiting for you to bring the fire. Glad you finally showed up."

UNFORCED ENTRY

When Liza turned ten, Langston and Elizabeth had taken her to Celebrity Sports Center to play video games and go bowling. Between spares and bites of cake, Langston had struck up a conversation with the white couple bowling next to them. The man said that he was a Realtor and offered a card to Langston, saying, "If you're looking to get out of the Points, I've sold more than my fair share of homes there in Dark Hill."

Dark Hill was a euphemism for the neighborhood a mile east of Five Points. When redlining kept Black people from moving to the suburbs, Park Hill was as far as they could dream. The man's slur was the end of Liza's party as Langston told her to finish her cake and change her shoes. He then took the man's card, crumpled it, and threw it down the alley toward the pins. If the crumpled card had been as heavy as the man's words, it would have struck and shattered the pins. It was one thing to know that white people called Park Hill "Dark Hill," but it was almost unbearable for Liza's father to actually hear it.

"We must fight our subjugation even when it comes to the language they use about us," Langston said on the drive home. It was the first time Liza had heard the word *subjugation*, and when she looked it up in the dictionary, she agreed with her father.

Liza now sat in her car at the scene of the crime, an apartment building in Park Hill. It was here that Claudette Cooper had experienced a most horrific subjugation, and because of her dream and a flawed system of justice, Moses King also bore the weight of the subjugated. Langston's words echoed in Liza's memory, and she was ready to fight.

She stepped out of the car and made her way through the gate into the courtyard of the U-shaped complex. Three stories above and to her left was Claudette's old apartment.

After the strategy session for Dexter Diaz, Liza had shot out the door and headed here with the hope of seeing things with her own eyes before she picked Journey up from school. She was looking for anything that might help her as she prepared to square off with DA Taylor.

The complex held no more than fifty apartments, each with a front door that opened to a walkway and a railing that overlooked the shared courtyard. The perfect place for parents to monitor their children and each other.

Levar Calhoun was adamant that, outside of his beating Claudette Cooper, what had happened was consensual. One question that lingered for Liza had to do with how Calhoun had gotten into Claudette's apartment, given that it was on the third floor and there were no signs of forced entry. There were no balconies or ladders on the backside of the building that Calhoun could have scaled to make entry. She worried that this might somehow be a sticking point, despite the fact that he was confessing to everything else.

Checking her notes, she made her way up to the third floor. The third apartment on the left was 305, where Moses had lived, and the next was Claudette's place, 307.

Each door had two locks, one on the knob and the other a dead bolt above. She was snapping a picture with a disposable camera when a voice from below called out to her.

"Can I help you?"

Liza looked down to see an elderly Black woman looking up from the center of the courtyard.

"Are you looking for someone?" the woman continued.

"Hello, ma'am. Um, no, but maybe you could help me." She raised a finger and made her way to the stairs. The woman met her at the bottom of the stairwell.

"Ma'am, my name is Liza Brown, and I'm—"

"Langston's baby girl." The woman smiled and wrapped her arms around Liza. "Look at you. Liza, we sure are proud of you. The way you made the entire city—the governor, the mayor, all of them—admit what they did. How are you doing, baby?"

"Did you know Daddy?"

"Your daddy and your mother too. Went to East High School together back in the day. Never believed he did it. Never. He was a good man. How's Elizabeth doing? We prayed for her too."

"Mom is hanging in there, considering."

"Well, you tell her that Mrs. Williams said hi. Janice Williams."

Liza nodded. "Mrs. Williams, perhaps you could help me. I'm working on another case—"

"Claudette and Moses?"

"Yes, Mrs. Williams. I'm representing Mr. King."

"What happened to Claudie was wrong and horrible. Someone needs to pay, but we all know Moses didn't do it either. I just think Claudette got confused or something, bless her heart."

"I don't think Moses did it either, and we think we know who did."

"Really . . ."

"Yes, you'll see it on the news soon, but someone has confessed to the crime, a man by the name of Levar—"

"Nasty, nasty man. Lived around the way, used to come around here cattin'. When he did, all of us parents brought our kids inside."

"Mrs. Williams, what I'm trying to figure out is how someone like Calhoun might have gotten into Claudette's apartment that night. She was up there on the third floor, and each door has double locks."

"Locks!" Mrs. Williams laughed. "Here in this place, we're family. We didn't lock our doors. Do now, but didn't back then."

MOTHER-DAUGHTER TIME

"Sorry I wasn't here when you woke up this morning," Liza said to Journey.

Or when you went to bed last night, she thought to herself.

Moving back home after the death of her father had provided stability. Liza was grateful for her mother, who was more than willing to pick up slack by cooking meals for Journey and taking her to school, but Liza couldn't shake the guilty feeling that those tasks were her job.

Liza felt like she was failing her daughter as a mom, and tonight was her way of trying to make up for her shortcomings.

After visiting Claudette and Moses's apartment building, she'd picked up Journey from school, apologized for her absence in the morning, and announced, "Grandma is playing bingo, and we are having a spa-and-movie night."

Journey's smile said it all.

While Journey finished her homework, Liza prepared the living room with tubs to soak their feet, nail polish, and makeup for fun. Pizza, popcorn, and a copy of *Beauty and the Beast* from Blockbuster would round out the evening.

As the sun set, Journey was lying on her back with Noxzema on her face and cucumber slices covering her eyes.

Liza was supposed to be doing the same, but she couldn't help but prop herself up with her elbow and behold her daughter.

"You'll see, you're going to blink and she'll be in college," Elizabeth had told her when she was born. And she was right, as Liza could see the little girl fading in favor of the woman she was becoming. From the moment she was born, it had been clear from her eyebrows, lips, and tight-coiled hair that she was definitely a Brown. But it was Journey's charm and wit along with her skin tone, a shade between Liza's chestnut and the mahogany of Johntell Jones's, that made it clear who her father was, wherever he might be.

"Where did you go this morning?" Journey asked.

Liza told her the truth. "Stratling. I woke up early to drive down to the prison."

Journey adjusted and pressed on the vegetables covering her eyes, ensuring that they were in place. "I miss Papa."

Liza knew Journey was thinking about visits with Langston, sometimes through scratched plexiglass, other times slipping underneath his arms for hugs when there were chains on his wrists.

A tear rolled out from beneath the cucumber and into Journey's hair just above her ear.

"Me too, baby, me too," Liza said as she placed her hand on the top of her daughter's head and moved closer. "So his name is Moses, and guess what? He knew Papa. They were friends."

Journey sat up and sat with crossed legs, cucumbers now in her hands. "Did he do it? Are you going to get him out?"

"I'm trying real hard."

"How?" Journey was stuttering this time. It was as if she'd seen this movie before and knew that Liza's hard work would need to be supplemented by a miracle. "How are you getting him out?"

Liza gave Journey a thumbnail sketch of the case. It felt like good practice. If she could explain her points to an eighth grader, then hopefully the absurdity of a man doing time because a victim had a dream would be clear to all.

"Yes," Journey said as she pumped her fist. "You even have a confession from the real guy. They have to let him out."

Liza hoped so, but she knew from experience not to get her hopes up, especially with this judge.

"Are they trying to kill him like Papa?"

Twenty years left in a forty-eight-year sentence for a man in his mid-fifties.

"No, they're not trying to kill him. But they are trying to take his life."

Liza was up early the next morning, and so was Elizabeth. They shared a pot of coffee and talked about bingo and why some beauties seemed to fall for the beasts and where Eli might be hiding out. Elizabeth sat at the kitchen table while Liza stood at the counter and assembled Journey's lunch—a peanut butter and jelly sandwich, a bag of chips, a juice box, and cucumber slices left over from the night before.

The morning news anchor with her too-cheerful-for-the-morning voice caught their attention from the television: "Denver residents are upset and say they want police to do something immediately."

At the word *residents*, Liza looked at her mother, and they both said in unison, "You mean . . . white people!" They laughed. Since Langston's execution, Liza couldn't remember the last time she'd seen her mother smile.

Langston used to say, "Pay attention to these talking heads. Whenever they talk about Black or brown folk, they use the word 'community'—the Asian community, the Hispanic community, the Black community—but when they talk about white folk, they call them 'residents' and 'citizens.'"

This morning was no different as the anchor pitched the coverage to a reporter in the field standing next to a car.

"Yes, we are standing here in North Cherry Creek, where citizens are up in arms."

"Ya mean—" Liza started.

"—white people!" Elizabeth finished.

"Over the last few days, someone has been removing the lug nuts from people's cars and leaving warning notes on their windshields. I'm standing here with Jerry, one of the local residents of this quiet neighborhood."

Jerry, a red-haired, red-faced man, stepped into the frame.

"Bingo," Elizabeth said.

"You were a victim of these acts of vandalism. What do you make of it?"

"I'm mad. I'm just trying to go to work and make a living, and now I have to deal with this. Whoever is doing this needs to stop, the police need to do something, and if they don't, then we will. We have a neighborhood watch meeting tonight. We'll do something."

The reporter jumped in. "We can hear the frustration in your voice, and I'm sure police will catch the lug-nut culprits."

As the reporter pitched things back to the newsroom, Liza thought of Tyrone. He'd been acting coy when he left The Roz. What had been in that duffel bag his friend carried that night?

"So what have you been working on at the project? Any promising cases?" Elizabeth asked.

Liza wanted to tell her about Moses and how he knew Langston and that she was going to court in a few days to argue her first case and that things looked encouraging. That they even had a confession in hand. But she didn't want to ruin the laugh they'd just shared. Instead, she told her mother about Dexter and his sixty-five denials and the hope for a DNA test.

"I remember when that happened, you were back in New York. What they did to that schoolteacher was horrible."

Liza almost crossed herself out of reverence for the dead woman.

"But you know what always got me?"

Liza closed the lunch box and licked the peanut butter off the knife before placing it in the sink as her mother continued.

"The boyfriend. I don't care how drunk he was. How does a man sleep in a cold house with the front door open while his woman fights for her life in the living room and dies in the front yard? Don't make no sense."

Liza nodded her head, but with all of her focus on Moses, she hadn't finished reading through the case files for Dexter. She hadn't formulated an idea about an alternative suspect in the case.

"If you ask me," her mom concluded, "that's one citizen of Denver that needs some extra attention."

THE BOYFRIEND

This time Liza showed up unannounced. Because of how their last meeting had gone, she was sure DA Taylor would have avoided her if he'd had a chance.

"So, are you here to concede before court tomorrow? I knew you'd eventually come around—"

"No concession when we have a confession," Liza shot back.

Taylor rolled his eyes.

"Tomorrow is about Moses King. Today I'm here about Dexter Diaz."

"What? We caught that kid red-handed. Was riding around in the dead teacher's car." Taylor added a smirk for effect.

"And that's all he's guilty of—taking a joyride with the wrong friend."

"All he's guilty of? Have you seen his juvenile record? This was not that kid's first rodeo. And allow me to reiterate: that wrong friend was driving the car of the murdered teacher. Looks like you and that innocence project need a better screening process."

Liza was proud of her two boxes marked NOW and LATER, but if the DA ever caught wind of it, he would mock her and Project Joseph before every judge and media outlet in the city.

"What about the boyfriend?"

The look on Taylor's eyes turned from green to yellow like he had arrived at an intersection he'd long forgotten.

"The boyfriend who, when the police arrived, and as his girlfriend lay dead in the snow in the front yard, was found sleeping inside."

"They were both inebriated from a night of club-hopping on New Year's Eve."

"So drunk that he slept through the attack that began in the living room? She must have screamed, don't you think? So drunk that he slept for hours with the front door open and cold air pouring into the house? That's the story you're selling?"

After her conversation with her mother, Liza had spent the day at The Roz, poring over Dexter's file. She was up to speed.

"We looked into him."

"Including his criminal record? Talk about a rap sheet— only his offenses were not part of a juvenile file. No, he was a full-grown adult. Your detectives barely gave him the once-over and instead focused on Dexter Diaz. Why?"

She didn't wait for an answer.

"What did he say when the detectives questioned him? Let me see if I can remember . . . oh yeah, 'There may be someone else inside me.' But you cleared him from your list of suspects?"

"Ms. Brown, you've got nothing. Neighbors saw a group of Hispanic boys running from the scene."

"It's a Hispanic neighborhood. For all we know, that was Lincoln High School's cross-country team. Did you even look into that?"

"Ms. Brown—"

"Didn't you find it suspicious that the boyfriend had a wound on his hand? Talk about red-handed. You didn't even test the evidence for blood type, let alone his DNA."

"They lived together. He was her boyfriend. Of course his DNA would be at the scene."

"Even on the bloody rock? The victim died from cold exposure but had been bludgeoned with a rock from the front yard."

Taylor looked up at the ceiling and cracked his neck.

"What do you think we're going to find when we test that rock?" Liza stood. "This is the second time I've given you the opportunity to do what's right."

She was bluffing. Her team wasn't yet sure whether or not the rock had been preserved along with the rest of the evidence. However, by the look on DA Taylor's face, he believed she had pocket aces.

FRONT OF THE RAIL

For a moment, the rail transfixed Liza. The waist-high polished wood barrier separated the actors in the court of justice from the observers. She faced the gallery, where she had so often sat on one of the pew-like benches, uttering silent prayers on behalf of her father.

The last time Liza was in this courtroom, Eli had been on her left, her mother on her right, and her father had sat with his lawyer just feet in front of her, with only the barrier of the rail between them. Langston had looked calm, but his bald head was sweating as they awaited the judge's entrance.

Today she sat in front of the rail with those who made their livelihoods in the justice system and those whose lives were at its mercy. On her left, sitting in the same seat in which her father had received his denial, sat Moses King—a man who'd known her father, a man whose life was in her hands.

"Take a breath, Ms. Liza." She felt his hand on her shoulder. "Deep breath. You've prepared for this. You're going to do just fine." She turned to face the judge's bench.

To her right, DA Taylor reclined, legs stretched forward, crossed at their ankles. He desired nothing more than to take Liza down a peg and to notch another win for his department and reelection campaign.

The loneliness of her battle was taking root. Her mother didn't know that she was trying to do for Moses what she, if she was honest with herself, felt she'd failed to do for Langston. Garrett would be furious if he caught wind of where she was. And Eli was gone. She had hoped they could work through their grief together and perhaps their hearts would find love on the other side. But that dream felt like a ship that had sailed to an unknown port without a map to guide it home.

"All rise."

Liza complied along with Moses, his hand still on her shoulder, and now they waited as usual for the judge's appearance. Today, like every day, he took his time. Liza believed he took joy in delaying his entrance as a show of power before he began his assent to the bench with a giraffe-like stride. She hadn't seen him since he'd dangled the carrot in front of her father's nose, only to snatch it away.

Lawyers knew his ego required more strokes than a needy lapdog, but Liza had little patience for men in power who needed those they ruled over to affirm their reign.

Finally, he appeared and surveyed his kingdom. Liza, at last, took a deep breath. Moses removed his hand from her shoulder and joined it to his other.

Liza set her jaw, squared her shoulders. The courtroom remained under the judge's gaze. Liza wondered what had gone wrong in his childhood that had him craving such affirmation and honor. Perhaps he was disappointed by the turnout. Besides those who had to be present for the proceedings, only a reporter and a high school student sat in the gallery, both taking notes. Moses's mother hadn't been able to make it. According to Moses, she couldn't put her shoes on because of the swelling in her feet.

Rumor was that the judge might step off the bench and onto the campaign trail to run for DA against Taylor. If so, this scene was the beginning of a phallic measuring contest between the judge and the DA. Liza had no intentions of holding the ruler.

The judge finally took his seat.

"Ms. Brown," said the judge.

Liza had never thought of herself as a *Ms.*; it had always felt like an odd, in-between way to reference a woman. But she was no longer young enough for *Miss* to be the obvious choice. In her heart she was a lady-in-waiting for a man who couldn't let go of his dead wife, which made her wonder if she'd ever be a *Mrs.* like she desired.

"Ms. Brown," the judge repeated.

Liza's eyes were on her legal pad instead of the judge. She was not there to give him whatever his parents had failed to provide. She counted to three before making eye contact.

"Yes, Your Honor. Liza Brown representing Mr. Moses King," Liza said, as she watched the judge's eyes register that she was, in fact, the daughter of Langston Brown. He was the first one to blink.

"And," the judge stumbled, "DA Taylor."

Taylor responded with mock deference.

"Ms. Brown, your motion. The floor is yours."

Liza looked back down at her notes, this time counting to five.

"Ms.—"

"Your Honor," Liza said as she walked to the center podium, leaving her notes behind. "Moses King is an innocent man. Almost three decades of his life have been lost because of the incompetence of the police department and the failure of the DA's office and judges preceding Your Honor." Liza paused and waited for an objection, but there was none.

"There are two victims in this case. First, a woman who was beaten, blinded, and assaulted. She deserves justice. We do not lay any blame at her feet. She was a wounded and traumatized woman who made her best attempt to bring resolution to a horrific situation. However, Mr. King is also a victim, and we do place blame on those who had a duty to investigate her claims. Simple fact is, we are here today because Moses King was convicted on a dream. How does one disprove an absurdity?"

Still no objection.

"Your Honor, counsel is well aware that this is a habeas case and that we are not here to relitigate old evidence. As you will hear, we have the real perpetrator, who will testify that he, in fact, was in the apartment, had sex with the victim, and claims responsibility for her injuries."

Liza sat. Moses offered an assuring smile.

"DA Taylor," said the judge.

Taylor stood and, with a side-eye to Liza, said, "Nothing, Your Honor. The state is ready to proceed."

No objections? No opening statement?

"Ms. Brown."

"Your Honor, the defense calls Levar Calhoun to the stand."

It was time to turn up the heat.

LEARNING PAINS

"Good morning, Mr. Calhoun."

Liza was standing at the podium, and Calhoun sat on the witness stand in his prison-issued scrubs. The jangle of chains echoed each movement of his legs or arms.

"Yes, pretty lady, good to see you again."

His demeanor and southern drawl felt even more repulsive in the courthouse than when she'd first met him in prison.

Liza looked to the judge for him to intervene, but he showed no intention of coming to her aid.

"Mr. Calhoun, we had an agreement about how we were going to address each other, and I—"

"Yes, Liza."

She gave him a stern glare.

"Ms. Liza Brown. I understand our agreement."

"Thank you, Mr. Calhoun. Let me begin by asking you to explain to the court why you are currently in prison."

Liza was expecting an objection with this question, but again, nothing.

"Let's just say I caught a charge that has me in for a while."

"Would it be accurate to say that the charge is in relationship to the assault and murder of a mother and daughter two miles from the case that has us here today?"

"Yes, Ms. Brown, that would be accurate."

"Your Honor, may I approach the witness?"

The judge nodded.

"Ms. Liza, you can approach me anytime you want."

This time Liza chose to ignore his antics and not to expect any intervention from the judge. She handed Calhoun the letter Moses had given her, now encased in a plastic sheath.

"Mr. Calhoun, does this document look familiar?"

"Sure does. I wrote it."

"Besides writing this letter, did you also send it to the defendant, Mr. King?"

"Ms. Liza, I did indeed do so."

"In this letter, you confess to the crime that Mr. King has served twenty-eight years. Why did you write that letter and send it to Mr. King?"

"Because he didn't do it."

Liza paused for another objection.

"Why did you wait so long to come forward?"

"Let's just say"—Calhoun looked at the judge—"I'm hoping when I meet the big judge in the sky that he'll offer me a plea deal or time served or something because I've done the right thing."

"Mr. Calhoun, did you know the victim in this case?"

"Yes, I did."

"Did you physically beat her on the night in question?"

"That was unfortunate, but yes, I did."

"And did you have sex with the victim on the same night?"

"Yes, I did, but that was consensual. I don't need to force no woman to lie down with me."

Liza turned to the DA.

"Your witness."

* * *

DA Taylor began speaking before he arrived at the podium.

"Mr. Calhoun, I have but two questions for you."

Liza sat with her legs crossed, pen in hand. Taylor shot her a smile, to which she did not respond.

"Did the police ever speak to you about this case?"

"Yes, there was a detective that stopped by my job and asked me a few questions."

What's his angle? Liza wrote and circled in red.

"Thank you, Mr. Calhoun. I don't want to keep you any longer—"

"Sir, I don't have anywhere to be. Keep me as long as you desire."

"I appreciate that, Mr. Calhoun, but I only have one more question. Was there ever a time that Mr. King's original lawyer had a conversation with you or made any inquiry as to any relevant and/or pertinent information you might have regarding this case?"

"No, not a one of his lawyers ever came to talk to me; that's why I wrote him that letter."

Liza shot to her feet.

"Objection, relevance."

"Overruled."

She was no longer breathing. Taylor's strategy was coming into focus, and she felt paralyzed. How had she not seen this until now?

"Thank you, Mr. Calhoun. Your Honor, we request that you dismiss this case so as not to waste any more of all of our time."

Liza stood.

"Your Honor, Mr. Calhoun has confessed to being there on the night in question, to physically assaulting and having sex with the victim. He has taken responsibility for every—"

"With all due respect, Your Honor, this is a habeas case in which the defense is to present, and I quote, 'new evidence that is not cumulative and was not available at the time of trial and could not have been discovered at the time by due diligence.'"

"Your Honor," Liza tried to interrupt.

"I repeat, Your Honor, 'discovered at the time by due diligence.'" Taylor continued. "And, as Miller makes clear, 'due diligence requires an attorney to be diligent in efforts to fully prepare the case for trial. The attorney must do everything reasonable but is not required to do everything possible.'"

Moses's hand was on her forearm.

"Your Honor, this is Habeas 101, and I implore you, for the integrity of the system, to dismiss this case. Ms. Brown has not filed her petition claiming ineffective counsel, but that she has evidence that was not available. We would argue that it would have been reasonable for original counsel to have at least had a conversation with Mr. Calhoun, and thus, Ms. Brown has misfiled her writ and now nullified all presented by her today."

Liza was horrified. Taylor was correct. She had squandered Moses's best and only opportunity for freedom.

"Your Honor, if you would please . . ." She attempted a rebuttal, but words failed her.

"Ms. Brown," the judge addressed her. The condescension dripped like honey from his voice. "Today is a learning opportunity for you. There is no doubt you will one day become an excellent attorney, but today is not that day, and this is not your finest hour."

Liza felt Moses's arm around her shoulders. He was now standing.

"Motion granted. Case dismissed." The judge struck his gavel, and the bailiffs escorted Calhoun from the witness stand and approached Moses to remove him from her side.

DA Taylor approached Liza as she determined not to let one tear well up in front of this man. She braced for a victory speech, but he spoke only one word as he departed.

"Rookie."

DON'T GIVE UP THE FIGHT

The *Rocky Mountain News* sat on the desk between Liza and Garrett.

The lead story, headlined "Lug Nut Task Force," was about more missing lug nuts on cars in Cherry Creek. The Denver Police Department was forming a special unit to address the problem.

On the bottom left of the front page was a picture of Luke Davies, the leader of the newly founded Denver division of the KKK. He was a tall, clean-shaven, all-American-looking thirty-year-old. His hair was cut short, but not so short that he could be called a skinhead. Davies's fresh face had recently become a Denver fixture. Over the last few months, he'd been organizing in Parker and Castle Rock. His rallies had garnered hundreds of those willing to own the KKK moniker without donning the white hoods. This new group didn't care if people saw their faces.

"We are ready, willing, and able to help," Davies said. "Starting this weekend, we will be on foot patrol in the neighborhoods that these hoodlums from Five Points have terrorized. If the police won't do anything, we will."

It was the third headline in the bottom right corner of the page that had Garrett's attention: "Liza Brown Strikes Out."

Liza's eyes were on her accompanying picture.

After the judge's decision and before they led Moses away, "Sorry" had been all she could say to her client. She must have repeated the word half a dozen times. This had been her first time filing a habeas petition and arguing an actual case. She agreed with DA Taylor's assessment: she had made a rookie mistake, and it cost her client dearly.

Liza knew Garrett wanted to make a speech about limited resources and focusing on the one while praying for the many. She had known this moment would come, but she'd hoped it would be from the vantage point of victory. Now she braced herself for a tirade about how their new project needed good publicity and how they needed some quick wins so they could raise money and someday be able to take cases like Moses's. Someday they would have an army of volunteers willing to read, sort, organize, and plead all cases, if only she would be willing to stay focused.

Garrett finally looked up from the paper. Liza straightened her back, fully expecting him to announce that he was relieving her of her duties as assistant director of Project Joseph. Instead, Garrett posed a question. "Are we now ready to move on to Dexter Diaz?"

Move on?

She didn't want to be here to begin with; she hadn't signed up for this fight.

Move on?

Her father was dead, her mother was barely surviving, and her daughter barely saw her. Liza had never thought she'd be a single mother, let alone a fatherless child trying to make up for her failure to save his life. And Eli was not being a good friend at the moment.

Move on?

Liza nodded.

Yes, she was ready to move on.

However, all she could think of were the last words Moses had spoken before they led him away: "Ms. Liza, I know you're not done. You'll figure something out."

PART III

To be a Negro in this country and to be relatively conscious is to be in a state of rage almost all of the time.

—James Baldwin

NOT YOUR MAMA'S MARADE

Eli forgot what day it was, or that the calendar had even changed to a new year.

When he'd closed The Roz, he didn't have a plan. All he'd known was that the five-year anniversary of Antoinette's death was about to arrive and that the holidays were coming. He couldn't keep up with managing the day-to-day of watching others celebrate while missing Antoinette.

She'd loved Thanksgiving, especially the giving part, so instead of cooking a big feast, they'd always volunteered to help Daddy Bruce feed the homeless from his restaurant on Thirty-Fourth Street.

This Thanksgiving Eli was again present at the restaurant, not as a servant but as a recipient. As he reached the end of the food line with a plate full of turkey, ham, greens, and stuffing, it surprised him that they didn't notice who he was. Even here, he went unseen by the children of Africa, who lived life unseen by the children of Europe. Eli, a Black man in the guise of a home-less man—an invisible man times two.

The only holiday that Antoinette had loved more than Thanksgiving was Christmas. She'd always dragged Eli down-town to stand out in the cold during the Parade of Lights at the

City and County Building. He'd loved watching her wonder at the floats and the high school marching bands as they passed by.

This year, Eli had skipped Christmas altogether, but he'd partaken in New Year's Eve as he sat alone at The Roz and rung in 1993 by emptying another bottle, this time from the top shelf.

He'd found it difficult to keep up with Liza, but due to a press conference held by DA Taylor where he touted the trustworthiness of the system, Eli had read in the paper about the outcome of her petition on behalf of Moses. He wanted to reach out, but shame and embarrassment kept him from dialing her number.

Eli had used the last couple of months to zero in on the scam the police were running. As a homeless man, it had been easy to track individual officers. He now knew that they were running a racket—investigating the very crimes they were committing. All he needed now was proof that he could share with the public, and had he been sober enough to make a New Year's resolution, it would have had something to do with this.

Today was the third Monday of the new year, January 17, Martin Luther King Jr. Day, and Eli lay in a doorway on Colfax after a frigid night of surveillance.

It was the marade that woke him.

For Antoinette, Martin Luther King Jr. Day had been the official end to the holiday season. Denver's celebration, second in size only to the one in King's hometown of Atlanta, was a time for the city's children of Africa to be together in one place. To be seen together, to remind themselves that in this city led by and dominated by the children of Europe, they were present and real and, contrary to popular belief, existed in significant numbers.

Jostling at the front of the pack were the usual suspects—preachers from the Ministerial Alliance, arms locked with the governor and mayor. They sang "We Shall Overcome" as they passed by, and Eli noted that DA Taylor marched in the second row; his voice was loud and off-key. Denver's pecking order of power was on full display for a front-page photo.

Eli stood, stretched his back, and wrapped his bed mat with a rope and slung it over his shoulder. The song of the politicians and preachers faded to his right as it moved toward the state capitol and Civic Center Park amphitheater for the endless parade of speeches.

To his left, another song echoed through the Colfax corridor. "No justice. No peace."

A group of at least a hundred children of Africa approached in tight formation with fists held high. They followed a tall, thin man with a bullhorn.

Tyrone.

Eli fell into formation.

* * *

To avoid being recognized, Eli walked at the back of the group following Tyrone. Behind him was a river of people, at least twenty thousand Denverites marching to show solidarity, but unity in the Mile High City was tenuous at best. The crowd was a mix of various coalitions with their own causes and matching banners and exclamation points.

"Republicans Love King Too!"

"King Baptist Welcomes You!"

"Kappas—Breaking Barriers, Building Bridges!"

"Gays for Non-Violence!"

Eli dodged a young white couple pushing a stroller while trying to keep up with their energetic five-year-old, who kept saying, "March plus parade equals marade."

Eli always wondered at the presence of the children of Europe at Denver's MLK celebration. Antoinette used to say, "I'm glad they're here. Just wish they were with us the other three hundred sixty-four days of the year."

"Today, they will hear our voice. We will not be silenced." Tyrone was walking backward as he spoke to the group through the megaphone. "We will not let them sanitize this man. King was more than a man with a dream; he was a man of action, and action is what we demand.

"As King said, 'Freedom is never voluntarily given by the oppressor; it must be demanded by the oppressed.' Today we demand change.

"No justice."

"No peace," the group thundered in unison.

As the children of Europe scurried after their child and toward the politicians and preachers and their melody of "We Shall Overcome," Eli noticed that at least half of those who marched in formation were from The Roz. They'd stood with Tyrone the night he returned, and they were standing with him now.

Out of fear of being noticed, Eli moved toward the curb and adjusted his hoodie and scarf. That was when he spotted her— Liza. She was walking briskly with Journey and her mother, Elizabeth, on the opposite side of the street. They slowed their pace as they joined Tyrone. Eli's heart wanted him to run to her and apologize, but he kept his distance.

They were approaching Broadway, a point where Colfax descended in elevation, creating a walled canyon. On the left was the state capitol building, and on the right was the Civic Center bus station. Normally it was a beautiful sight at the end of the two-mile walk, but today it felt like a trap akin to that of an old western movie.

Eli felt the danger before he could spot its source.

High on both sides of Colfax were hundreds of men and women wearing dark sunglasses and white satin jackets with red lettering. They too had signs with matching exclamation points as they shouted in unison.

"KKK is here to stay!"

RIOTSTARTED

His first thought was of Liza.

Slurs rained down on the marchers.

"Nigger" from the right.

"Happy King Coon Day" from the left.

There was no escape. The crowd from behind pushed forward, unaware of the danger that awaited. Forward, into the canyon of hate, was the only option.

Not all of the hate-filled agitators held signs; some brandished tire irons.

Eli jumped up on a trash can so he could scan the crowd.

"Liza," he yelled, pulling the hoodie from his head and the scarf from his face. "Liza!"

He spotted Tyrone, blood smudged red on his forehead. Tyrone was looking at something in his hand.

"What was that?" someone shouted.

"Take cover!" yelled another.

Only then did Eli see that between the marchers and the KKK was a wall of police. They too stood in formation and in full riot gear. For a moment, Eli felt hope, a fleeting sense that they were there to help. But they were not. The police stood, facing the marchers. Their backs were to the KKK.

Eli felt a searing blow to his left ear. He tumbled off the trash can and smashed to the ground. He jumped up and swung around, fists raised to confront whoever had struck him. However, there was no one to face off against. Eli felt his ear, and blood on his fingers confirmed he too was wounded.

"Liza!"

Eli was now frantic as he swung around and prepared to move forward into the fray.

"Lug nuts!" Eli heard Tyrone shout through the bullhorn. "Protect yourself. Cover your heads. They're throwing lug nuts!"

Eli stepped forward and felt something beneath his foot. He looked down, and lying at his feet was a silver, octagon-shaped lug nut.

He picked it up and stopped in front of an officer.

"Why aren't you doing anything?" Eli held up the piece of metal. "Stop them."

"Move along." The officer glared.

"What?"

"They have just as much right to be here as you. They have a permit for there and there"—he pointed—"and you people have the street. The right to protest for rights—isn't that how you say it?"

"Do they have a permit for this?" Eli dropped the lug nut at the officer's feet and turned. Journey's backpack caught his eye. Liza was crouched over her daughter, covering her head with her own body. Elizabeth shielded her granddaughter by offering her back to the white-jacketed mob. Liza and Elizabeth were bleeding too.

Eli ran to them.

"We need to get out of here."

"What . . . Eli? How did you . . . ?"

Eli took off his thick coat and held it up over his shoulders, a makeshift canopy over their heads. "Get under. I'll get Journey."

Eli scooped the child up as Liza and Elizabeth ducked underneath, each holding a side of Eli's jacket. He held her, tight and close. "Journey, baby girl, it's going to be okay."

With Journey cocooned by their bodies, they made their way to Broadway and turned north past Civic Station, out of the urban canyon and away from immediate danger.

In a nearby ally, out of harm's way, they stopped. Eli attempted to put Journey down while Liza checked her body for blood.

"You're good, baby girl. You're good."

Journey wouldn't let go, her arms held fast to his neck. Her tears mixed with the blood from his ear.

Eli looked at Liza, her face a mixture of gratitude and confusion.

Later they would check their own bodies; most likely they all had growing welts on their backs and legs beneath their clothing.

"Journey, you're safe now. I need you to go with your mom."

Liza took the handoff.

Eli hugged them all.

"You should be safe from here," Eli said. "Liza, I know you have questions and you deserve answers, but I need to go."

Eli then turned and started back.

"Eli, please, stay," Liza said.

"I need to get Tyrone. He's still in that mess."

* * *

Eli's rage swelled as he arrived back at the intersection of Colfax and Broadway. Much of the crowd had dispersed into the neighborhood streets of Capitol Hill, but a few hundred people remained.

Across from Eli, a child of Africa huddled over a trash can, yelling, "Burn. It all has to burn."

The smell of smoke arrived in Eli's nostrils.

The police, still on both sides of the street, now formed a protective bubble around the KKK as they escorted them into the bus station and capitol building.

"Let's go. This is for your safety," one officer said as he forced a man with a tire iron through a door.

Smoke billowed as flames now engulfed multiple trash cans. The fire starter flung a ball of flames into one of the portable toilets that lined the street.

Children of Africa, both men and women, surrounded two police cars about a block away.

Eli jogged in their direction.

One man was on top of one of the police cruisers, stomping the red and blue lights. Others had tire irons they must have confiscated from the KKK and were smashing the windows, headlights, and brake lights.

Another climbed inside. "Give me that iron." His focus was on the lock that secured the shotgun.

The second police car was rocking, swaying left and right, as a half dozen men tried to lift and flip it on its side.

Eli didn't need a moment of reflection, nor did he need to think things through. He was beyond sober and his mind was clear.

Eli took his place near the right front bumper of the patrol car.

"Together," he commanded.

"Count of three, lift."

Eli squatted.

"One, two three . . . lift!"

The men grunted as their muscles strained.

"One, two, three . . . lift!"

Eli looked to his left. Tyrone squatted and counted with him.

"Missed you, Unc."

"Missed you too."

The side of the car lifted above their heads.

"Push. Everyone together."

The car crunched on top of itself to the cheers of all who were present.

Gasoline poured out of the tank and pooled on the ground.

"Back away," said the fire starter as he held up a lighter.

Eli felt the same way.

Burn.

It all needed to burn.

BREAKING POINTS

When sunset arrived, two more police cars lay toppled on their lights, their metal charred and their tires melted by fire. The lyrics of Public Enemy shouted from an enormous boom box that sat in the middle of the street.

A few minutes earlier, two RTD buses had sped from the station packed with an escaping contingent of the newly rebranded KKK. The passengers took shelter beneath their white jackets as windows on the bus shattered due to some well-aimed lug nuts.

One of the lug nets rested in Eli's fingers, waiting for a worthy target.

"Up here," Tyrone announced through the bullhorn from the capitol side of the street. "They're still in there."

Eli responded along with the crowd, which had grown well past five hundred. He climbed the majestic gray front stairs to the capitol, pausing on the top step with its gold-medallion mile marker announcing 5280 FEET ABOVE SEA LEVEL. He made his way with caution to the front doors and looked through the windows. Gathered inside was another cadre of white jackets, outnumbered by police in riot gear protecting them.

Tyrone peeked over El's shoulder and announced through the bullhorn, "I say 'Protect,' you say 'Us.'"

"Protect!"

"Us!"

"Protect!"

"Us!"

The refrain echoed through the urban canyon where insults and metal objects rained down, wounding body and soul.

The crowd was now fully gathered on the front lawn beneath the gold-domed building. Behind them, a tree sprouted flames and the fire starter ran through the shadows.

"Don't let them leave," Tyrone charged the crowd. "Spread out. Surround the building."

Eli took another look inside at the assembled army, civilians and civil servants, white jackets and blue uniforms, all children of Europe. His thumb felt the angles of the piece of metal in his hand. It incensed him. Here it was Martin Luther King Jr. Day, and the same group that had burned a cross on the lawn of the King family home was still terrorizing the children of Africa all these years later. Denver and the Klan had a long, unbroken history of friendship that included governors, mayors, and police chiefs among its devotees. Eli had seen black-and-white pictures of the streets of downtown Denver packed with thousands of hooded Klan members marching as a show of power. But today felt different. These terrorists had attacked a peaceful march without a shred of cloth covering their faces. Even though they wielded tire irons and committed assault with metal projectiles, the police were giving cover and protecting them.

After one last look inside, Eli back away from the front door, the lug nut warm in his hand. He zeroed in on the Colorado state seal on the window. Eli had found his worthy target. He took aim and released the lug nut like a pitcher aiming a fastball down the center of home plate. The window shattered upon impact.

Overhead, two helicopters hovered with spotlights—police or news crews, he couldn't tell. Tyrone now stood on the mile-high step, bullhorn in hand. Eli stepped to his side.

"Didn't I tell you?" he whispered. "Lead, and we will follow."

Eli descended the steps and took his place in the circle of children of Africa standing three deep, surrounding the state capitol building.

Because of the efficient work of the fire starter, every tree burned bright, giant torches beneath the night sky.

Tyrone started another round of "No justice," "No peace."

Eli stood in solidarity with his people. He could retreat no longer. Today was an awakening, and his long hibernation needed to end. The only thing that burned hotter than the trees was his anger, and tonight it demanded satisfaction.

"We ain't here for peace."

The fire starter interrupted Tyrone. First, he shouted, then he wrestled the bullhorn from Tyrone.

"It all needs to burn."

The crowd cheered.

"Let it burn!"

They all joined in.

"Let it burn!"

Eli joined in too.

"But this is just the beginning. When I say it all needs to burn, I mean all. This whole city, let it burn."

"Let it burn!"

And then the fire starter spoke words that Eli's heart could not support.

"To Five Points. Let's start with the Points."

Eli's heart stopped cold.

The Roz. He couldn't let them burn The Roz.

Eli ran home.

* * *

At The Roz, Eli locked the door behind him. Even with heavy boots, he'd beat the crowd back to Five Points, but he knew they were on their way. He would not let them take The Roz without a fight.

The irony wasn't lost on him. The place that he despised was now the place he would die to protect. Removing his jacket, he surveyed the room that he'd once thought would be his salvation. The banister that he'd sanded and polished, the floors he'd scrubbed, and the bar top that had taken him a week to rebuild so it was solid and able to take the weight of ten drunks leaning on it hoping to stop the room from spinning. The back bar display with only a few, top-shelf bottles remaining, evidence of his three-month binge.

He looked out on the empty five-pointed intersection, where he and Antoinette used to sit and dream of a day when they could restore The Roz for the sanity of their people. Little had he known then that it would be the insurance money from her death that would make that dream a reality, and now their people were on their way to pillage their own neighborhood.

"Let's do this!"

Shouts rang through the night air, and a few shadowy figures ran past the windows. Eli pushed the sleeves of his hoodie to his elbows. The very crowd he'd joined just a few hours ago in the daylight, he was now willing to fight through the night. Willing to die for the place he'd walked away from just a few months ago.

Strengthening his resolve was the fact that losing The Roz was nothing compared to losing the files for Moses's case. Liza had made The Roz her second office, and tonight Eli was surrounded by files, pictures, and legal pads organized on the bar, stage, and various tables—the fruit of her labor. He needed to protect these artifacts, for they might possess the clues to Moses King's freedom.

The bulk of the crowd now filled the intersection. The hundreds were now thousands, ready to continue the destruction that had begun at the capitol building.

* * *

Eli paced from window to window. He needed a plan. He thought about the unfinished floors above. Perhaps he could position himself in a room and launch a defense from an upstairs window. Or maybe the roof might give him the high ground on the mob. But what could he do from there?

He looked down the block at the firehouse with its dark windows. Most likely Bear and his crew were tending to the torched trees and making sure the capitol building didn't suffer the same fate as the firemen's neighborhood.

Eli's former mob now shouted in unison outside his place. He moved to the front door, only to see the fire starter with the bullhorn working them into a frenzy.

"Burn it, now! Burn it, now!"

At once, the crowd scattered. Eli wasn't sure what the cue was, but their intentions were clear. He ran to the utility room and grabbed the mop. After ripping off the cloth head, he snapped the long wooden handle in two with his knee.

Eli met the throng as he exited the front door to defend his place person by person on the sidewalk.

Trash cans were ablaze, and a bonfire now glowed in the center of the intersection. In the distance, he could hear windows shattering.

"Don't even think about it. Get away."

Eli swung his mop sticks at anyone who came near.

"Mr. Stone?"

Eli spun around, arm raised, ready to swing.

"Mr. Stone, what are you doing?" The fire starter cowered in front of him. He was just a teenage boy, not even close to drinking age.

"Son, don't you come near my place. I'll take you—"

"Mr. Stone, we ain't here for you or Mr. Freeman's place, none of our people's. We are here to take our neighborhood back. All these interlopers come in here buying up our grandmas' houses and pushing us out. We here to tell them we didn't ask them to come here and it's time for them to leave."

The fire starter ran east down Welton Street.

Eli lowered his arms and, with barely a thought, dropped the mop sticks and ran inside The Roz. His target was a bottle of tequila. After unscrewing the cap, he stuffed a rag down the opening. In a drawer full of tea light candles, he found a box of matches and made his way back to the sidewalk.

The interlopers.

The uninvited.

The invaders.

They all needed to leave.

Eli eyed the bright sign with its shining neon-blue hat. Public enemy number one, the supreme invader of Five Points—Chance.

Eli lifted his hoodie over his head and struck a match.

The flame began its slow crawl from the tip of the cloth toward the tequila in the bottle. He walked with steady purpose to the opposing sidewalk.

The white-and-blue lettering—*Chance's Place*—obscured his reflection in the front door.

Eli raised the flaming cocktail, took aim, and with all his might, he released his rage.

As the fire exploded on the facade, Eli reveled in the light of his destruction.

NEVER TOO LATE

City Park, east of downtown Denver and Five Points, was a sprawling oasis, home to the Denver Zoo, the Museum of Natural History, and hundreds of geese that had stopped migrating and decided that the two lakes and three hundred days of sunshine were what they were looking for. Year round, runners, walkers, and moms with strollers put in their miles. A family comprising children, parents, and grandparents—children of Asia—huddled, catching crawdads from the small lake to sell as the special of the day in their family restaurant.

City Park was also home to Denver's Martin Luther King Jr. statue. After setting fire to Chance's place and with the night nearly exhausted, it was here that Eli ran, partly out of fear of getting caught, but mostly out of fear of what other destruction he might perpetrate.

Eli sat on one of the many meditation benches, each flanked with slabs of granite etched with the words of Dr. King. The benches and slabs encircled a majestic tribute to Black history, itself complete with statues of Mahatma Gandhi, Frederick Douglass, Sojourner Truth, and Harriet Tubman. Above them, as if standing on their shoulders, rose a bronze statue of King in an oratory pose.

It was here, the morning prior, that the marade had started. Little had the participants known that flying projectiles and vile words awaited them at the hands of the newly formed KKK.

Eli needed a solitary place to sort through what he'd done. The list was long and included helping Liza, Journey, and Elizabeth find safety; toppling a police car; breaking the front window at the capitol building; and launching a Molotov cocktail at Chance's Place. With his adrenaline subsiding, his ear throbbed from the lug nut that had struck it, and his fingers found sore spots on his legs, arms, and back, no doubt bruises from other flying lug nuts the KKK must have been throwing by the handful. What worried him was not what he had done but his lack of remorse. Eli's rage was far from finished, and he would have wreaked more havoc had he not run here to this place of solace.

As the sun peeked over the horizon, Eli rose and made his way around the edge of the circle, reading the words of King etched in the stone.

The choice is not between violence and nonviolence but between nonviolence and nonexistence.

Eli looked up at the statue of King.

"How did you do it? They threatened your wife and kids, burned a cross in your front yard. Didn't you want to fight back?"

Eli thought about King's secret infidelities.

"Coretta, how did you not lash out at and leave your husband when the FBI sent you the tapes of his indiscretions?"

Eli's own secrets were piling up. Was it just a matter of time before his past infidelities were exposed? Would Fredricka expose him? What would Liza do? And then there were the crimes committed over the last day and night—destruction of government property, vandalism . . . would they come to light?

Eli also knew that the police had their own secrets. Secrets that he was hell-bent on bringing into the light.

As the sunlight awakened the city, the morning news was about to inform everyone about a peaceful protest that had turned to destruction. Would they tell the complete story about how the police had protected the agitators, or would they focus on the response to the agitation? Agitation that those in Five Points had endured in Denver for more than a century?

Come what may, Eli could no longer hide. It was time to emerge and move forward. He had to face reality. Antoinette was dead. His pain was real. The Roz, while it was a reminder of his past life and a burden on the present—he still cared and was willing to fight for it.

Another quote by King affirmed the path that he was now choosing: "It's always the right time to do the right thing."

To move forward, he knew what he needed.

Eli needed Liza.

TOGETHER AGAIN

"I see you made yourself at home," Eli said to Liza.

She had turned The Roz into a full-fledged second office. One table was clearly her workspace, with pens, highlighters, and a half dozen legal pads scattered across it. Besides the boxes stored at Eli's living space, she had another five or six here in The Roz, their contents unpacked and organized along the length of the bar. Crime scene photos lay strewn across the front of the stage.

"Turns out you had enough space for me to move in after all," Liza said with a smile.

Eli topped off Liza's coffee and poured himself another cup. They sat across from each other at one of the free tables.

"No whiskey?" Liza tested the waters between them.

"No, I think I've had more than my fair share of whiskey, and . . ." Eli scanned the near-empty back bar, then continued. "And vodka, rum and tequila as well."

He was having a hard time making eye contact, so he stared at Liza's reflection in his coffee.

"Eli, all of us . . . I've been worried about you. Thought you were . . ."

She deserved answers, but he wasn't sure where to start.

"Were you really living on the streets?"

"Yes—well, kind of." He hesitated. "It was by choice, but I showered, if that matters."

"Was that a whiff of Irish Spring I noticed when you swooped in and rescued us?" Again she smiled. "And your five o'clock shadow hasn't grown past seven or eight."

"Liza. I'm sorry. But I don't know how to move on, to get out of this—"

He wanted to say *depression* but couldn't bring himself to admit it out loud.

"I feel like I'm in a deep cave surrounded by dark clouds, heavy clouds pressing in from all sides, making it impossible to breathe sometimes. You must feel the same way. You've lost your father, and then I . . . I disappeared, leaving you . . ."

Eli's tears flowed as he looked up and met her eyes. Tears were also streaming down her cheeks.

"Alone. I'm sorry for leaving you alone."

He reached out to wipe her tears.

They both leaned forward and bowed, resting their foreheads on each other. Eli slid his right hand behind her neck and felt hers on his as they pulled closer, burying themselves in an embrace of grief.

There they rested in each other's warmth and sorrow.

Two broken pieces fitting together, not like a jigsaw puzzle but more like a mosaic held together by the grout of grief, despair, and the desperate need to find hope.

When they released their embrace, Liza cupped Eli's face with both of her hands. Her touch soothed and her eyes forgave. Eli clasped his hands around hers. He was grateful for her kindness.

To compose himself, he leaned back and looked out the window. Yellow tape and orange cones marked Chance's Place as a crime scene. Scorch marks striped the front of the building, leading up to the melted neon sign. A new yet unnamed feeling seemed to be dissolving the rage that had driven him that night.

"Liza, I've needed you. Whatever this is, I've needed more than I can admit."

As he now looked into Liza's face, he noticed she wasn't wearing makeup. Her tears left no mascara in need of a touch-up or lines in her foundation. She'd been beautiful before, but the face he was beholding now was unvarnished, pure and natural.

"Liza, where do we stand?"

Silence filled the space between them. He'd been gone long enough for weeks to turn into months, leaving her alone. They were not a thing, and yet they were something. He wasn't ready for her answer, nor did he sense she was ready to deliver it. What he knew was that somehow Liza was connected to his moving forward. Antoinette was the love of his life, and she'd been right when she told Eli he had loved her so well because he, in his soul, needed to love.

Eli rescued them both from the weight of the moment.

"With all of this . . ." Eli nodded at Liza's work that filled The Roz. "Where do we stand with all of this?"

"Eli, I've failed, and I'm failing."

While Liza struggled with inadequacy, Eli marveled at her competence. She was a good woman and loving mom, but she was also an excellent lawyer. If the police ever caught up with him for his mounting misdeeds, he was convinced that it was Liza he wanted at his side, arguing his case. What he didn't know was whether she would want to stand by him. She worked for the innocent, but after what he'd done to Chance's Place, Eli was guilty.

"What's next? How do you move forward?"

"Well, The Roz isn't the only thing that's been shut down over the last couple of months. During the holidays the court system pretty much comes to a halt too. But I've been making headway on both cases. I tracked down Dexter's so-called accomplice."

"The guy who picked him up for the joyride in the stolen car?" Eli asked.

"Yeah, Carlos Ruiz," Liza said. "And get this. He was never charged with murder. Once Dexter confessed, they decided to pin the more serious charges on him, and in exchange for cooperation, they only charged Carlos with stealing the car. Only did a few months in juvie and then probation for a couple of years."

"What did he say about Dexter?"

"Confirmed the story. Says he stole the car and picked Dexter up the next day so they could cruise Federal Boulevard."

"Did you ask him about the murder?"

"Yeah, asked him point-blank if he did it, and he denied it. Said he didn't see anything unusual when he took the car and that he would have seen a dead body in the front yard if it was there. Which makes sense; he could have just been there before the murder went down. I don't think he did it, and if the police did, they would have charged him too."

Eli nodded in understanding.

"Plus, I saw the look in Taylor's eyes when I mentioned the boyfriend. If we can find that rock and submit it for DNA testing, we might be able show Dexter didn't do it. I need to give my attention to Dexter. He deserves it."

"And what about Moses?"

"It took a while, but I found the retired detective who worked on King's case," Liza said. "Old-school kind of guy who knows what he knows. Even though he recognized me immediately, he was more than willing to talk. It was like he wanted to convince me that they got the right guy. Said that Moses lived next door to the victim and she said that he did it. I pressed him on why he didn't corroborate her story; didn't he think he should have additional objective evidence? He didn't budge—case closed as far as he was concerned. But you should have seen what happened when I told him Calhoun had confessed. Clammed up immediately and asked me to leave.

"My heart wants to keep fighting. But after losing on habeas, the only hope he has is if we can find the victim and see if she's still holding to her story. I don't want to, but I think she's the key that will unlock his cell."

Eli reached in his pocket and placed the note Liza had left him on the table.

"CC—Claudette Cooper."

"Yes, I need to find her."

"Divide and conquer," Eli said. "You stay focused on Dexter, and let me take a shot at finding Claudette."

He could sense her hesitation.

"Liza, I'm here to stay. Not going to leave again." Eli reached his hands across the table. "Together."

Liza placed her hands in his.

"Forward together," she said.

BEAR NEXT TO NOTHING

"How have you been, man?" Eli asked Bear.

"Feels like I should ask you the same question."

It had been three days since the eruption on Martin Luther King Jr. Day, and while there was relative quiet during daylight hours, the evenings were eventful.

"You holding up?" Eli asked.

"Can't keep up, man. We haven't had a full night's sleep since this all started."

Bear looked exhausted, and most likely there was no rest in sight. City officials were not responding, the KKK was regrouping, and the protesters were now divided into two groups: one led by Tyrone, applying pressure through protest, and another led by the fire starter, bent on destruction.

"Man, I get it," Bear said. "Things here in the Points aren't right, haven't been for a while. We show up after the police, and we see things aren't kosher. But we can't report anything because we didn't actually see anything. We arrive and care for the victims and only hear the well-rehearsed story of the cops. For one of us to say something would be to risk our jobs. Usually all we can do is treat the injured and render them aid. So we get it, but we're tired."

Eli had appreciated that, of late, every firefighter at the Five Points station was a child of Africa.

"To tell the truth, we'd all want to be out there in the streets, not setting fires but protesting alongside everyone else. While we're here at work, they ticket our cars too. So much for being brothers in blue."

Eli made a mental note to page Tyrone and check in on how he was holding up. He hadn't seen him since things started at the capitol.

"Man, I know you're busy and could use some shut-eye," Eli told Bear, "but I'm following up on that note you left on my door."

"That was over two months ago. You still on that?"

"I'm back on it," Eli responded. "You said you had a lead on the victim. Her name's Claudette Cooper. I've been through all the Coopers in the phone book, even called every one that lives here in Five Points, Park Hill, and Whittier. So far nothing—can't find any kin."

"Well, I did some asking around," Bear said. "Don't have much, but there is this white guy, used to be here at the station back before all of us. Looks like he would have been part of the responding crew that night."

It wasn't much, but it was worth chasing down.

"Got a name? Is he still with the department?"

"Raymond Murphy, and yeah, he's still on the job. Scored one of those cush early-morning gigs out at Stapleton babysitting those afraid of flying and putting Band-Aids on boo-boos."

"Stapleton," Eli said. "Looks like I'm off to the airport, then." Eli clasped hands and bumped shoulders with his childhood friend. "You take care, man, and stay safe. I appreciate you."

Eli walked away but turned back at the sound of the chief's voice.

"Eli, we're all glad your back. Hasn't been the same without you."

STAPLETON

The cab driver glanced in his rearview mirror in order to see his passenger.

"To the airport, please."

Stapleton Airport was on the edge of Denver's Black community, and while the constant noise of low-flying jets left these neighborhoods less than ideal, it was the reason they remained affordable.

Eli enjoyed the airport, especially since Stapleton had started accepting international flights. Seeing travelers from all around the globe in one place was a pleasant change from the segregated neighborhoods of Denver, where the children of Africa, Europe, Asia, and South America crossed paths only when necessary. The irony of seeing such a variety of people in this airport named after a KKK member was lost on most who traveled through it. Benjamin Stapleton was a former mayor of Denver who had also been a proud and prominent member of the KKK back when the Mile High City boasted the second-largest membership in the country, only Indiana claimed more white hoods. With the current renaissance of the new, unhooded members of the KKK, Eli wondered what future Denver municipal projects would be named after the lug nut terrorist.

The cab driver, a child of this land, asked what airline.

"Doesn't matter, whatever's convenient when we arrive."

The man nodded in the mirror.

"And my brother, if you don't mind me asking, what tribe do you belong to?"

"Lakota."

"Rosebud or Pine Ridge?"

"The Bud," the man answered. "You know about my people?"

"I know a little—spent a week at Pine Ridge when I was a child. My mentor, a Catholic priest, took some of us from the Points to play ball and throw gloves against some of your finest."

"And how did our finest do?"

"They held their own. We handled business on the court, but things were more even in the ring."

Another nod.

Ten minutes later the driver found a spot outside the American Airlines ticketing desks, and—as Eli offered the fare plus a tip—he clasped the man's forearm and pulled him near.

"I know enough to recognize that we're fighting the same battle against the same forces. Please, my brother, be safe."

The man gripped Eli's forearm in return.

* * *

Not knowing what Captain Murphy looked like or where he might be, Eli thought he'd ask around and hope to find a lead. It was midmorning on Monday, and Eli blended in with the business travelers, as he had put on his funeral suit to fit in and upgrade people's assessment of him.

He planned on passing himself off as an investigator of sorts who was trying to get ahead of the impending legal challenge in Moses's case. He figured Captain Murphy would be on the side of the prosecution, so Eli decided not to volunteer anything that would cause suspicion or get him arrested for impersonating a police officer.

After asking a couple of customer service representatives and a janitor, to no avail, Eli joined the line that snaked through the security checkpoint. He dropped his wallet and keys in a bowl and placed it on the conveyor belt along with his suit coat.

"Okay, honey, raise your arms, please."

She was a thirty-something-year-old redhead with a bright smile and an even happier heart.

As she checked his legs, waist, and arms with the wand, he spotted her name tag and her occupied ring finger.

"Mrs. Barbara, I'm looking for Captain Murphy. Any idea where I might find him?"

"Murph?" She glanced directly into Eli's eyes. "Yeah, this time of day he usually hangs out down on Concourse A. Check the coffee shop."

"Thank you, Mrs. Barbara. Appreciate your help."

"No worries and no guns or knives. You're good, dear."

Eli put on his suit coat and grabbed his keys and wallet.

"If you find Murph, tell him he owes me a coffee."

"Will do." Eli raised his right hand. "Promise."

Two men in Denver Fire Department uniforms sat in the coffee shop, both with bellies over their belts, one balding with red hair—Murphy, Eli assumed. He approached with confidence.

"Captain Murphy, my name is Eli Stone, and I'm an investigator on the Moses King case. I was wondering if I could have a word with you."

The two men paused their conversation. Murphy looked up, confusion in his eyes.

"Do I—"

"Claudette Cooper. Years ago, you attended to her at an apartment building in Park Hill. He assaulted and beat her—"

"Blind. He beat her blind." Murphy shook his head. "That was one of the worst. Jim, remember when I told you about that call?"

The other man lifted his head in acknowledgment.

"Captain, I don't want to take up too much of your time, but I'm sure you've heard that the case is back in court."

"Yeah, I saw that. DA Taylor sure did slam the door again on that SOB. Hope he rots in prison for what he did."

Eli sat down.

"Captain, this is not over. Additional motions are coming, and we're trying to stay ahead of things. I was wondering if you could help."

Eli plowed forward.

"I got your contact from Chief Barrinton. He said you might help us with a problem we're having."

Seeing no objections in Murphy's demeanor, Eli continued.

"Claudette Cooper. With everything going on, we're trying to reach out to her, but we don't know where she is. We want to check in on her to see how she's doing but also to prepare her for what might be next."

"Not sure I can help you. We were just first responders; we don't stay on after the initial call."

"Kind of figured, but we're getting desperate. She seems to have dropped off the radar. We want to get to her before the other side does—can't imagine how this is resurrecting old wounds for her."

Murphy seemed like a nice guy and—to Eli's surprise—wasn't putting up any resistance. Eli didn't sense Murphy had any information and didn't want to overstay his welcome, so he stood.

"Captain, I won't take up any more of your time, but allow me to express my gratitude for your decades of faithful service."

Eli turned to leave.

"Down south."

Eli turned back.

"I remember hearing something about her moving south, like Colorado Springs or Pueblo. I'm not sure."

"That's more than we had. Glad you remembered something," Eli said, but Murphy wasn't finished.

"Who did you say sent you?"

Eli smiled.

"Mrs. Barbara sent me. Says you owe her a cup of coffee."

FOUR WOMEN

After meeting Captain Murphy, Eli needed to further narrow his search for Claudette Cooper. Murphy had said that she'd moved south of Denver, perhaps Colorado Springs or Pueblo. He left the airport in another cab and headed straight for Shemekia Turner.

* * *

Shemekia was the branch president of the Unity Bank location that sat catty-corner from The Roz. She'd also been Antoinette's maid of honor in their wedding. His hope was that she could look up financial records that might help him find Claudette, but Shemekia was in no such mood. She was the reason Eli had been able to purchase The Roz. After Antoinette's death, the life insurance money had provided the down payment, but he was still a high-risk loan. Shemekia had advocated for Eli, put her reputation on the hook with her colleagues.

"Eli, since that night when you abruptly exited The Roz, you haven't sent a smoke signal—let alone called—to let me know what's going on, and now you want me to do what?"

Shemekia was angry, and rightfully so. When Eli closed The Roz, he should have warned her about what was coming instead of letting her hear the news along with everyone else. Over the last two months, he'd failed to call, write, or stop by with any sort of explanation.

"Mrs. Turner," Eli said, "I'm sorry, I should have called or something, but as I'm sure you've noticed, I haven't missed a payment. My loan is still current."

Eli wasn't behind on payments, but what Shemekia needed was a plan. Was he going to sell, reopen, or something else?

"I had noticed. Yes, you are correct that you have yet to miss a payment, but I also know that you only have three months of money in your account, and then what will you do?"

He didn't have a good answer for her, and that effectively ended their meeting. Until Eli gave Shemekia a solid plan, she would remain a dead end in his search for Claudette.

* * *

Eli moved on, and against his better judgment, he called Fredricka. The conversation was short and contentious.

"You want *me* to help *you*?" Fredricka's laugh pierced his ear through the phone's receiver.

Calling Fredricka was a bad idea, especially after their last conversation at The Roz.

"Eli, you made it clear that you want nothing to do with me. I accept that, but you remember that if you are not my friend, you are my foe. Don't call me again unless it's to give me what I want. If you don't give me the journals, and soon, I will have to resort to other means. And if it comes to that, I cannot promise that your face will not be on the front page of my paper."

Eli didn't like the sound of that, but—for now—he didn't have the capacity to worry about such a possibility.

* * *

Roberta Messay was Eli's next attempt to find an additional clue to Claudette's whereabouts. He waited for her in the parking lot of the *Weekly Word*, hoping to recruit Fredricka's secret weapon from underneath her nose.

"Ms. Messay. We've never met, but I'm—'"

"Eli Stone. Yes, I know who you are. I've seen you when you drop by on occasion."

Eli needed to approach her with honesty and without guile, for Roberta Messay's beauty was exceeded only by her intellect.

"I was hoping you would be willing—"

"To help you with the Moses King case? Mr. Stone, Fredricka could walk out here at any moment. You know as well as I that if you cross her, you will get burned."

"Then I'll make this quick. Moses King is an innocent man. Though we lost our appeal, we know beyond any doubt that he didn't commit the crime, because we have a confession from the actual perpetrator."

Roberta unlocked her car with her key fob.

"Her name is Claudette," Eli continued. "Claudette Cooper. She is the key; without her, Moses will die in prison. We need to find her."

Her car door was now open.

"Please, Ms. Messay, you wrote the story that exposed what was happening with the accelerated executions and the expired death drugs. You know that the corruption of this city runs deep. We—that is, me and Liza Brown and Project Joseph—are just getting started with plumbing the depths of depravity in this city, and it starts by making things right for people like Moses. We need to talk with Claudette—"

"Mr. Stone, I'm sorry, but I can't."

"When we solve the case, we'll give you the scoop. You can write the story."

"You know she wouldn't allow that."

Eli sensed an opening.

"Ms. Messay . . . Roberta, I know your motivations are different than hers."

Roberta stood still, one leg inside the car. She was a queen of Sheba. Her dark skin revealed zero nervousness; not a drop of sweat glistened. Eli often thought about the plight of the new arrivals from Africa to America. They weren't descendants of the oppression of America. While they knew the horrors of colonization, they, by and large, hadn't experienced Blackness as the means of their subjugation until they arrived on these shores. How difficult to wrestle with life as a direct child of Africa in a land designed to erase their very existence.

"I know you are different. Fredricka does this out of a base sense of fear and power, but we can hear it in your stories—this is about something deeper and more substantive for you. Fredricka enjoys exposing the wrongs of the powerful out of vengeance. You, however, are in this to make things right, for all of us."

Roberta sat, started her car, and drove away.

Eli turned and ran . . . to Liza.

* * *

"Do you really think she was there to take a bath?"

Eli and Liza had scheduled a meetup that evening to share progress reports. They were back at The Roz, at the same table where they'd shared their embrace. A bottle of wine sat between them. Eli had vowed privately to no longer drink alcohol alone and to drink only as much as the person he was with. The only exception was when he shared a bottle with Antoinette; then he allowed himself one glass.

Tonight, as the golden hour arrived, Liza was still feeling overwhelmed by the prospect of finding freedom for both Dexter and Moses.

"Pharaoh's daughter . . . what are you talking about?" Liza asked.

"Father Myriel used to tell the story all the time. He'd ask the church, 'Do you think she really went down to the Nile River to bathe? Don't you find that odd? It was her father that ordered all the Hebrew boys be thrown into the Nile River, and then she says, "I think I'll go down there to take a bath." Really?'

"Why would she take a bath in the river next to all the bodies of the dead babies floating by? She wasn't there for a bath; she was there to see if she could make a difference. To see if she could save just one."

Eli paused before he continued. "Liza, you are her."

"If so, then I've failed. Couldn't save the one I came for; the river got to Daddy before I could. And now I'm neck deep and drowning trying to save two more. I can't do this by myself."

"Pharaoh's daughter wasn't in the water by herself, and neither are you." Eli reached for her hand; Liza reached back. "Liza, Pharoah's daughter had help in the water, and you've got the folks at the project helping you with Dexter. And me, I'm here to help with Moses."

Eli gently squeezed her hand. "Liza, I'm here, in the water with you."

Their hands slid from each other to their glasses as they took sips. The first time Eli had been alone like this with Liza, he'd felt an immense amount of guilt for being with a woman who was not Antoinette. But tonight, he didn't feel like he was betraying his wife. At some level he felt like she approved, that Antoinette wanted him to move on and find purpose.

"I have something," Eli said. "It's not much, but I talked to one of the first responders in the case, and he thinks Claudette is in Colorado Springs or maybe Pueblo. Not sure how to narrow the search within those cities, but I'll figure something out."

"Eli, I hope you can find her. I'm not sure if we can convince her to help Moses, but we need to try."

"What about you?" Eli asked. "How are things with Dexter's case?"

"We've requested the evidence for DNA testing, specifically the rock which was used as the murder weapon. You should've seen the look on DA Taylor's face when I mentioned the boyfriend. We're onto something."

Eli offered another pour, and Liza accepted, so he poured another glass for himself as well. They both leaned back and looked out the window.

"Do you think he's going to reopen?" Liza asked.

Eli's abdomen tensed. Liza was looking across the street at Chance's Place.

He shrugged.

"And what about you?" Liza leaned toward him, her forearms on the table. "Has The Roz seen its last day? Have I sung my last song here?"

Eli wanted to say no. His heart wanted to reopen just so he could hear Liza sing again, but one thing he hadn't missed over the last few months was the headache of managing the place.

"Well, whatever you decide," Liza said. "Take your time; this has been an incredible second office for me."

SICKENING

Liza paused the VCR.

The image on the screen was a timid, scared teenage boy—Dexter Diaz. Wearing white pants and a black T-shirt, he slouched in a chair. His eyes were closed, his head turned so far to the right that his chin sat atop his shoulder. What struck Liza most were his arms. They were crossed in an embrace, a self-soothing hug for a terrified young man separated from his mother and trapped with two predators.

Earlier that morning, Liza had gone to see Dexter, and while he'd greeted her with his usual "How you doin', chica?" this time felt different. Almost like an act. She'd pressed on, determined to look passed the facade of this young man raised—as Eli had put it—by wolves.

Liza was his advocate, not by assignment but by choice. She was the one who'd read his application and presented his case to the team. Dexter deserved her best, though after what had happened with Moses, she doubted her best was even close to good enough. At least with Dexter, she had her team by her side, providing support.

"Tell me about what happened." Liza had wanted to hear the full story from his perspective.

His guard softened. "Lady, I wish I could tell you, but to be straight with you, I'm still trying to figure that out myself."

"Haven't you read your files?" Liza asked.

"You think I know how to read?" Dexter's laugh was almost a giggle. "Chica, you funny."

Liza spent the good part of an hour quizzing Dexter about his case and the crime he'd been convicted of. While he was clear on the details of his arrest and conviction, it shocked her that he seemed clueless as to what had actually happened to the victim.

Their time together bolstered her belief in Dexter's innocence, but as she drove back to her office at the project, she worried about how well he would fare if she gained his release. She had to trust his life post-exoneration to his family; her job was just to give him a chance to succeed or fail outside prison.

Which was why she now sat alone in the conference room watching the video of the taped confession. The offices were dark, and she needed to get home to Journey, but she wanted to watch every minute of the multi-hour interrogation from start to finish.

On a legal pad, she kept a tally of how many times Dexter had denied involvement. Garrett was right—sixty-five times Dexter had claimed he wasn't involved, but the police had worn him down both physically and psychologically.

The video began with Dexter and his mother sitting together in the small cramped room with two detectives speaking in calm, almost friendly tones.

However, after an hour, one of the detectives asked the mother if she could go back with him to the office because there was some paperwork that needed her attention.

In her absence, the remaining officer's tone changed from friend to foe. On more than one occasion he leaned down close to Dexter's face, his words too soft for the microphone to pick up but clearly disturbing to the boy. In each of these situations, Dexter dug his heels into the tile floor and pushed, but his chair, wedged into the corner, prevented any retreat from the detective's words.

Dexter had filled in the whispered words when Liza met with him early that day. "The cop said, 'We ain't leaving this room without a detailed, signed confession. You are going to make a pretty girlfriend for someone when we send you to Stratling.'"

Over the course of three hours without his mother in the room, the detectives tag-teamed Dexter. The second of the men returned to the room and added physical intimidation to threats about his future.

When Dexter was unable to outline the details of the crime, they fed him facts and lied to him about the evidence they had against him. Not only did they tell him they had his fingerprints on the rock and shoe prints in the snow, but they also made the absurd claim that hair prints on the body matched Dexter's.

They also told him that if he confessed, he'd go to juvenile jail and be out by the time he was old enough to drink, but if he made them go to court, they were sending him to adult prison.

That was when he leaned back, turned his face away from the two detectives, and hugged himself. With his mother out of the room, they broke him.

Liza pressed play on the remote.

"Okay, I did it," Dexter mumbled.

"Say it again."

"I did it."

"Louder."

Dexter sobbed as he attempted to pacify himself with his self-embrace in the absence of his mother.

Liza was out of her seat, pacing, remote in hand.

"Write it down," the detective said, pushing a pad and pen in front of Dexter.

"I can't."

"You will do what I say." The detective stood.

"I can't write!" Dexter blurted.

The detectives seemed stunned for a few moments until one of them reached for the pen and paper and wrote. Ten long minutes passed without a word from any of them until the detective slid the pad of paper back in front of Dexter.

"You know how to sign your name, don't you?"

Dexter nodded.

"Then sign here and here and here." He pointed to the bottom of each page.

It was then, as the detective looked at the camera and pressed its off button, that Liza took aim at the wall with the remote and threw it, adding to the previous dents inflicted by Dr. Garrett.

MOTHER TO MOTHER

Dexter's mom brought Liza a cup of tea.

The night before, after she viewed the video of his so-called confession, his mother had been all Liza could think about.

She'd stopped by Dorothy's house on the way to the office and been glad to find her alone.

They sat at the kitchen table, their tea between them.

"I wanted to let you know we continue to work on Dexter's case. He is the team's top priority, but these things move slowly, so while there's nothing to report, I just wanted you to know we . . . I am focused on fighting for your son. We have some promising leads."

Dexter's mom dabbed the corner of her eye with the sleeve of her housecoat.

"I also came by because I wanted to tell you that I believe Dexter. I'm convinced that he is not responsible for the death of the teacher."

Liza gave Dorothy time to cross herself, but this time her hands remained still.

"I've seen the tape of his confession," Liza said. "He didn't have a chance. They manipulated him, lied to him, and took advantage of him. It was psychological warfare, and there's no way he could have prevailed."

"Mi hijo."

"And you, Dorothy. I saw what they did to you."

This was the real reason Liza had stopped by. After Dexter signed the confession, the detective brought his mother back into the room. When she sat down, Dexter whispered in her ear not to believe them. The detectives announced that they were arresting him for murder. All she'd done was leave the room to sign some papers, and four hours later she returned to find her son in handcuffs.

"They tricked you. You are not to blame. You did not abandon your son."

Dexter's mother leaned forward so far that Liza thought her head would hit the teakettle. She buried her face in her hands. The weight she carried—already feeling like a failure for not being around for Dexter when he was young, and then when he'd needed her most in that interview room, she'd failed him again.

Liza reached across the table to comfort her.

"It was not your fault, and I'm doing everything I can to bring him home."

"Mother's Day," Dorothy said, looking up from her hands.

Liza loved spending Mother's Day with Journey. Her daughter was her joy, but the day was wrought with pain. Mother's Day was the marker for the loss of her father. The Mother's Day Massacre was what had brought the police to their door and ultimately left her and her mother alone in their fight.

"Liza, I want to spend Mother's Day with my Dex. Not at the prison. Here." She motioned around, and then her hands settled on her chest. "I want him right here with me."

Liza thought of the rock that needed to be tested for DNA. If the police had preserved it along with the other evidence in the case, there was hope. Liza was certain it would show the boyfriend's blood.

"This one, this year," Dorothy said. "Please bring him home by this Mother's Day."

As Liza drove away, she hoped she wouldn't regret nodding yes.

BLIND LUCK

Eli was on a bus from Denver to Colorado Springs. The Air Force Academy passed by the bus window to his right. Gliders carved the crystal-blue sky, future fighter pilots at the helm, and far below them the academy's signature glass chapel glistened in the morning sun—all framed by the mountains of the front range. *Purple mountain majesties* was more than a line in an anthem for people in this part of the country.

Eli's long shot, Roberta Messay, had come through. She had knocked on his door the evening before with her car parked behind her, door open and still running. She handed him a note that read *Colorado School for the Deaf and Blind in Colorado Springs*.

"There are records that after the trial, Claudette spent some time there, learning how to navigate her new reality," Roberta said.

Eli thanked her and promised to keep her in the loop for an exclusive, but she declined. "Mr. Stone, you know there's no way Fredricka would allow for that. You are anathema, untouchable,—and we all know it."

"Then why are you helping me?"

"Let's just say that I too believe that the corruption in this city runs deeper than Detective Slager, but this is it. Please don't call me for anything else." She'd glanced down the street. "And, a little advice, Mr. Stone: watch your back. When you're on the double-barrel side of Fredricka, it's only a matter of time before you feel the burn of lead in your back."

The bus arrived in Colorado Springs. Eli exited and checked the chart for a connecting bus going east of downtown and then, with transfer in hand, he sat down on the bus that would take him to his final destination.

He didn't know what he was going to do when he arrived at the school. He couldn't just walk in and ask for Claudette's records or address, but it was the only lead he had, and he hoped to catch a break.

As they neared Prospect Park a few blocks away from the school, they passed a lone man walking confidently on the sidewalk, a white cane bouncing back and forth in front of him, serving as his eyes.

Eli pulled the string to alert the driver. He exited at the next stop and waited for the man to catch up, the nib of his cane tapping and scraping the sidewalk as he approached. Eli shifted to be outside the man's radius and, when the man was about twenty feet away, verbally greeted him so that the blind man would know he was there.

As the man passed, Eli's eyes followed him from north to south. It was then, as Eli looked past the man, that he realized he was the last in a long line of confident, striding walkers. About every hundred yards there was another person making their way, their cane serving as radar.

Eli crossed the street and followed the dispersed group of walkers, assuming they shared his destination, the Colorado School for the Deaf and Blind. A half mile later, he found the walkers gathered on the lawn in front of an almost-castle-like four-story stone building. It was a co-ed group of students of all ages, and he could hear them comparing notes about their adventure. While Eli was in the right place, he felt no closer to knowing where Claudette might be.

After the attack, she must have moved to Colorado Springs not only for the resources the school provided but also to get away from Denver and all that it represented. If Moses King was innocent and Claudette had any doubts that he was, in fact, her perpetrator, then she most likely was trying to put some distance between herself and the actual attacker. Eli also figured that she stayed in close proximity to the school and the help it provided.

It was midmorning, and the last bus back to Denver didn't leave until eight PM, so Eli continued on foot. For the next three hours he searched the neighborhood around the school, walking in ever-widening circles, not sure what he was hoping to find as he meandered through the mostly residential community. About a mile from the school, he stopped at a grocery store for something to drink and sat outside to gather his thoughts.

If he helped Liza, then Liza could help Moses. Not only was Moses innocent, but Liza needed a victory. Eli knew what it was like to feel trapped by one's dream, unable to wake up from the tyranny of what you once hoped for. The reality was that Eli needed some sort of victory as well. After putting all his hope in The Roz and coming up empty, he was now all in on Liza.

He took another mouthful of juice, and as he did, a figure, black and white in motion, snatched his attention. Off in the distance, on the other side of the parking lot, a daughter of Africa moved with swiftness, a white cane guiding her steps.

Eli hesitated. Could this actually be her? He'd hoped to find something that led to the elusive Claudette Cooper, but he hadn't expected to actually find her.

The woman was stocky but moved with the swiftness of a gazelle.

Eli got up and began walking in her direction, but as the distance grew between them, he broke into a jog. He lost sight of her as he exited the parking lot and she turned the corner into the neighborhood. Eli sprinted for a stretch and then slowed to a walk again as he approached the corner. The rubber soles of his boots were virtually silent, and he was confident that whatever sounds they might have made were drowned out by passing cars. Eli turned left where he had last seen the woman, but he was not prepared for what awaited him.

She had turned and was facing him directly. Less than a half block of sidewalk lay between her and Eli; it was as if she were waiting for him. There was an empty field to his right, her left, and behind her was an apartment complex. She stood still, her cane resting on the ground in front of her. A dark-blue cotton sweatsuit covered her solid but not overweight build. Her dark skin glistened.

Eli froze.

She inhaled deeply through her nose. Eli checked the leaves on a nearby tree, thankful he was downwind.

Another deep breath, this time through her mouth. She shifted her grocery bags and retrieved something from her pocket, then pivoted with the agility of a point guard and resumed her pace.

Eli kept the woman in sight and followed her to the multi-building complex. Upon reaching an open-air stairwell, she stopped, turned, and took another deep breath through her nose.

Again, Eli froze. In her right hand, he caught the glint of what looked like an open pocketknife with at least a three-inch blade. She turned and made her way up the stairs with surprising agility. By the time he reached the bottom stair, he'd heard a door shut, but he couldn't tell where or what floor the sound had come from. His instinct was to keep following, but better judgment kept him on the first step.

To his left he spied a bank of mailboxes, three rows of four, apartment numbers listed but no names. However, Eli's eye settled on one mailbox that was unlike all the others—3B. Across the top of it was a black label, and as Eli moved closer, he could see that its message was written in braille.

NOW WHAT?

Back in Five Points, Eli exited the bus near Freeman's Furniture about a block from The Roz and his place. As he was getting off, two young men dressed in hoodies and holding signs entered, flashing their bus passes to the driver.

"Mr. Stone, you coming out tonight?" asked the taller of the two.

With temperatures back above freezing, the protests had resumed, still strong in numbers but with less destruction. Aside from an occasional burning dumpster, the removal of lug nuts, now from police officers' personal cars, was the new tactic.

"Can't," Eli responded. "Relying on you. Hold down the fort for me, but be safe, okay?"

They bumped fists and parted ways.

Eli needed to resume his tracking of the police. He knew that besides writing frivolous tickets and harassing people in Five Points, they were also running a racket of their own. He needed to get proof, and he had a plan for doing so.

However, Liza was his priority. Reuniting with her had awakened him from his malaise and reignited his resolve. Liza was now his purpose.

As he approached the front door of The Roz, he thought about using the phone behind the bar to call Tyrone and Liza. However, Tyrone was most likely on his way to lead the protest, and Liza was at home with Journey. He would call Liza in the morning to let her know that he might have found Claudette Cooper. He turned right toward his place.

His mind raced as he thought about what might happen next. If he had found Claudette, then Liza could reach out to her, and if Claudette had doubts about Moses being the one who had attacked her, then Liza could realize her dream of walking an innocent man out of prison and back to freedom.

Eli's mind snapped back to the present.

The door to his place was ajar.

Liza must be inside. He could tell her the good news tonight and in person.

However, as he entered, it was dark. It was then that it occurred to him that Liza's car was not outside.

"Liza?"

Eli closed the door and flipped the switch for the lights. His fists clenched as the hatch in the center of the room caught his eye. The portal that led to his underground quarters was open.

Eli no longer suspected Liza.

He locked the door, set down his backpack, and removed his coat.

"All right," Eli said with a firm voice that filled the room. "I can either come down there or, for your own good, I'd suggest you meet me up here."

His heart rate responded to the increase in adrenaline.

"Have it your way."

After a deep breath, Eli dropped down the ladder into the darkness.

He braced for a blow of some sort—fist, pipe, knife, something—but nothing came his way.

The light from upstairs spotlighted him. He jumped to his left into a dark shadow and waited for his eyes to adjust.

A few moments of silence passed, and he could now see the outline of his sleeping cot, space heater, and heavy bag.

He sensed no movement.

Eli pulled the cord on the single lightbulb. The worst thing about making a mess was having to clean it up. It had taken him a few weeks to put things back in order after the chaos he'd created the night he'd closed The Roz. Tonight, everything was as it should be, his books especially. Nothing seemed out of place.

He checked the bathroom. Finding it clear, Eli reached up, pulled the hatch shut, and turned toward the three rows of bookshelves.

"All right, it's just you and me. Let's do this."

Eli checked the first. Empty.

The second row—nothing.

He steadied himself with a deep breath and stepped into the third and final row, the last place for someone to hide.

No one.

Maybe Liza had come down and then left in a hurry, forgetting to close and lock things up. He would ask her in the morning.

His heart rate, however, increased even more. The hair on his arms stood at attention. For a moment, it felt like his lungs were on strike, no longer accepting oxygen. Dizziness swirled in his head. Eli's subconscious had registered a truth that his conscious mind had yet to become aware of.

He buckled at the waist as if punched in the solar plexus. His knees followed suit.

Finally, his eyes saw what his mind already knew.

The bottom shelf of the last bookcase on the right was empty.

Slager's journals were gone.

The journals that contained the confessions of a good cop gone bad. The pages that contained the secret that cleared the name of Liza's father, but only after they'd executed him. The brown leather covers smudged with Eli's fingerprints. If his fingerprints were on the stolen property of the dead detective, then he could be linked to the mysterious Black priest who was on Slager's balcony when he fell to his death. It wouldn't be long before someone connected the dots from the priest to the gardener, caught on video, who'd found the missing evidence in Langston Brown's case.

If Liza had the journals, they would devastate her. If the police possessed them, then Eli was headed for death row.

A solitary note card lay on the empty shelf.

Eli retrieved it and read: *Don't say I didn't warn you.*

He recognized the handwriting.

Fredricka.

ROAD TRIP

"There." Liza pointed at a sign on the side of I-25 headed south toward Colorado Springs. "I don't know how many times I made this drive."

The sign read *Stratling Correctional Facility*.

Eli nodded.

"This old car is wondering why we're not turning. Daddy's no longer there, but Moses still is, and Dexter is about another hour past it."

When Eli called that morning to let Liza know he might have found Claudette, he hadn't expected her to rearrange her day and pick him up for a trip back down to Colorado Springs.

"Eli, are you okay?"

He wasn't.

The missing journals had him rattled to the point that he'd almost barged into Fredricka's office instead of calling Liza. However, when a snake is coiled, the last thing you want to do is reach for it. Eli hoped that if he didn't agitate her anymore, perhaps Fredricka might slither away.

"I'm good," Eli said. "Just a little preoccupied."

Besides Fredricka, Eli was concerned about Tyrone. The morning news had reported that the police had arrested at least a dozen people at the protests. He'd tried paging his nephew but had heard nothing in reply.

"Do you want to talk about it?"

Eli shook his head and focused on the subject at hand.

"Liza, I don't want you to get your hopes up; the chances that we've actually found Claudette are slim to none. That said, what's the game plan?"

"Kind of winging it. But thinking that I'll knock on her door and, assuming it's her, see if I can convince her to talk."

Eli didn't know if he'd actually found Claudette. He'd followed Roberta Messay's lead to the school and then followed the only blind middle-aged daughter of Africa that he'd seen. Yes, there was braille on her mailbox, but there was nothing that explicitly identified the woman he'd followed as Claudette. However, she'd displayed the alertness of a rabbit aware and on the lookout for a fox and had a knife at the ready in case she encountered one.

"There, West Bijou Street." Eli pointed to the off-ramp. "This is our turn."

"If she will talk, my goal is to be gentle. She's been through a lot. I'm hoping to gauge how confident she is that Moses is the right man. She has to have doubts."

This morning the grounds of the Colorado School for the Deaf and Blind were quiet, no groups gathered on the front lawn. Eli guided Liza to the grocery store and explained where the woman had been when he spotted her. They retraced the route and parked with a view of her apartment building.

Liza turned off the car and looked toward Eli.

Eli pointed to the third-floor window.

"It's right there, 3B."

"Eli, this is it! I can't believe you found her." Liza grabbed his hand. "If this works, then we've done it. Moses will be a free man."

She hugged him in excitement.

"Liza, we don't know this is her yet. We're searching for a needle in a haystack, but we don't know if we're even in the right haystack."

"Yes we do. This is most definitely her place."

Eli raised a question with his eyebrow.

"Don't you see?" Liza pointed to the window.

Eli didn't.

"Eli, look closely. There are security bars on the window. Who puts bars on the windows of their third-floor apartment?"

Only someone who was still living in fear.

LIKE A SCREEN DOOR ON A SUBMARINE

Liza left Eli behind in the car.

She assumed that the presence of a man would cause undue consternation for the traumatized woman, so she climbed the three flights alone.

Apartment 3B looked like the others she had passed except for two details. First, there was no welcome mat to greet any visitors. More importantly, there was a screen door in front of the regular apartment door. Not the run-of-the-mill variety, but a thick wrought-iron framed door, the heft of it matched only by that of the locks that fortified it.

Liza knocked directly on the painted black metal. The metal dulled the sound more than the wood door on the other side, but Liza didn't attempt to open the iron door. Something told her that it was locked; there was no way Claudette was taking any chances.

She knocked again.

What would she do if Claudette wasn't home? Sit in the car and wait? Approach her on the sidewalk outside? Leaving a note with contact information wasn't an option.

"I don't want anything. Please leave now."

Liza wasn't sure what she'd expected Claudette to sound like, but a woman speaking in a forced deeper voice was not it.

"Ma'am, my name is Liza Brown, and I hoped that I—"

"I said please leave." Claudette's voice was louder, deeper still.

"Ms. Cooper, I mean you no harm. I'm a lawyer with Project Joseph. We . . . I am looking into a case you were involved in."

Silence.

"Please, Ms. Cooper, I just have a few questions, and then I'll be—"

"How did you find me?" Her voice boomed but then cracked.

"Please, Ms. Cooper, this is . . . you could help save someone's life." Liza struggled for words. She didn't want to mention Moses King for fear of pushing Claudette away, but how could she avoid the obvious?

"I'm sorry. You've got the wrong place. I won't help you."

"Ms. Cooper." Liza rested her forehead on the cold iron. She softened her voice. "Claudette, there's been a horrible mistake. It's not your fault, but Moses King is an innocent man. We have proof that he's not the one who hurt you."

Liza could only imagine what was happening on the other side of the door. The confusion. Claudette must feel trapped. Her second-worst nightmare.

"Claudette, please open the door. You don't have to let me in. Just five minutes, that's all I'm asking for."

Nothing.

"I'm here alone. There's no one in the hallway with me. It's just us."

Liza could hear her breathing.

"I can't help you. If you don't leave now, I'm calling the police."

Liza took one last shot.

"Claudette, if you were sure that Moses King was the man who hurt you, then why are you still afraid? Why do you have bars on the windows of a third-floor apartment? Why do you have a fortified screen door?"

Liza allowed for the silence to do its work.

She would wait a minute or two more, but then she needed to leave in case Claudette followed through with her threat to call 911.

Liza was about to walk away when she heard the slide of a chain and the click of a dead bolt lock.

SEEING IS BELIEVING

Liza stood face-to-face with Claudette Cooper, separated by the distance of the secured, reinforced screen door.

Claudette doubled-checked the locks.

She was a woman of medium build, five eight to Liza's five ten, with short, tightly coiled hair. She wore a dark-blue sweatsuit, Adidas bottoms with a Nike top. She wasn't wearing sunglasses as Liza had envisioned. Instead, her eyelids were open, revealing lifeless brown eyes staring back—prosthetics.

Claudette took a deep breath through her nose.

"It's just me out here. I'm alone," Liza repeated.

Claudette smelled the air again.

It was only now that Liza noticed the knife in her right hand, gripped with the force of a pit bull's jaw.

"How did you find me?"

"Like I said, my name is Liza Brown, and I'm an attorney with Project Joseph, and we're working on the case of Moses King because we—"

"I moved down here to get away. How did you . . ." Claudette trailed off.

Liza didn't want to lose her.

"Thank you for opening the door. I won't take much of your time, but—"

"Langston Brown your daddy?"

Liza nodded but then realized the futility of the motion. "Yes, ma'am."

"He was a good man . . . sorry about what they did to him." Claudette loosened her grip on the knife.

"Thank you, that means a lot. After fighting for my father, I came to realize that there were many more innocent people in prison in need of help, and that's why—"

"Moses King is guilty; he did this to me. Jury said so. Judge said so."

"Claudette, are you sure? Moses has been in jail for twenty-eight years, and the only real evidence against him is your testimony about the dream you had."

Liza had read every page of Moses's case multiple times. It still left her dumbfounded that the evidence the prosecutors had put forth and that had resulted in a man losing his freedom was so scarce. Juries wanted to believe victims, and rightfully so. Compassion compelled them to do so even if the story was as thin as a desperate woman holding on to a dream.

"Are you absolutely sure it was him?"

Claudette lifted both hands and put them on the crossbar of the door to brace herself as she leaned forward, face toward the ground.

"All I wanted was to get away. How did you . . . ?" She shook her head. "Why did you do this?"

"Are you absolutely sure? Do you have any doubt at all? DA Taylor will understand. Perhaps I could come in and write something down for you to sign, or we could even make a recording."

Claudette stood up straight and began to close the door.

Liza had one last shot.

"Another man confessed!" she blurted. "Levar. Claudette, Levar Calhoun wrote a letter and testified in a court of law that he was the one who did this to you."

Claudette turned back. Stunned.

"He's in prison for kidnapping and assaulting a mother and daughter just a few blocks away from where you lived in Park Hill. Levar Calhoun did this to you, not Moses. Moses King is innocent."

Liza felt guilty for her next question, but she needed to ask it, needed to see the look on Claudette's face.

"Calhoun says he was in your apartment that night and even took responsibility for what he did to your eyes, but"—Liza's mouth went dry—"he says everything else was consensual."

Liza couldn't bring herself to actually form the words *Did you have a voluntary intimate relationship with Levar Calhoun?* The revulsion on Claudette's face rescued her from asking the question out loud.

The two women stood stock-still, both desperate for different reasons.

"Ms. Brown, I can't help you. I know what I saw."

NOTEWORTHY

Liza sat at her desk with the door closed. Awaiting her judgment, a new stack of letters from hopeful inmates sat alongside the two boxes marked NOW and LATER. She pushed everything aside and turned her attention to the two pieces of paper her assistant had handed her when she arrived.

The first was another letter from Moses.

Ms. Liza,

I am worried about you. You were as low as I've ever seen you. Just wanted to write to say that I'm going to be all right.

After her failed meeting with Claudette, Liza had stopped by Stratling to see Moses. Eli sat in the car for an hour while she visited her client. She shared everything she'd seen with Moses, from the bars on the windows to the reinforced screen door. She described how it appeared that Claudette had doubts, and how it wasn't that Claudette wouldn't help but that she couldn't. To do so would unravel any sense of security she had.

Prison is my home, has been for almost three decades, and while I hoped to get out, please know that I'm at peace. I will make the most of the life I have. My value as a man and my meaning as a human is not determined by the neighborhood in which I live nor the softness of the bed in which I sleep. Not sure how long I will survive, but I will thrive. If there's any way you could try to keep me in Colorado, that would be helpful so I can stay close to my mom.

Liza dabbed the corner of her eye with a tissue. First her father and now the man her father had promised she would help.

Ms. Liza, I couldn't have asked for more. You fought with valiance and grit. Langston would have been proud. There are still more who need you in their corner, so I leave you with these words—fight the good fight, finish the race, don't lose faith.

Forever grateful,
Moses

Claudette had been Moses's last hope, and now Liza was out of ideas.

Eli, however, still had his gloves on. When she dropped him at his place, he said, "You. Me. We got this. You focus on Dexter, and I'll keep grinding for Moses."

She wasn't sure he would find a way for Moses, but she believed Eli was back. Over time, they would figure things out together.

Liza put down Moses's letter and picked up the second piece of paper.

CONFIRMATION OF RECEIPT OF OFFICIAL PROPERTY—
CHAIN OF EVIDENCE.

It was from the DNA lab in Chicago. Liza's team had located all the evidence in the Diaz case, and the bloody rock was about to share its secrets. There was still hope for Dexter.

PART IV

. . . history . . . it may be that nightmare from which no one can awaken. People are trapped in history and history is trapped in them.

—James Baldwin

MOUNTAIN MADNESS

"You look like you're feeling better," Eli said to Sister Francis.

That morning he had taken the 15 Limited bus west on Colfax from Five Points to the Mother Cabrini Shrine in the foothills of Denver, just outside the city of Golden. The Mother Cabrini Shrine was a home away for home for Eli. It was here, after the murder of Father Myriel, that he had spent his teenage years under the tutelage of the nuns and in the tender care of Sister Francis.

"Thank you, Eli. Told you I'd be okay. That little stint in the hospital was just a speed bump, slowed me up but didn't keep me down."

Two cups of tea steeped as they sat down in their usual chairs next to the fireplace.

"So, I see there's been quite a ruckus going on down there."

Eli nodded.

"Been on the news ever since King's Day. The 'Fires and the Fury' is what they've called it. But I've been around long enough to know that where there's fire, there was first dry kindling."

Sister Francis was a child of Europe who lived with her eyes wide open. She had a knack for understanding the world from the perspective of others, often to the detriment of herself.

Today was no different, and Eli was not surprised by what she asked next.

"Eli, have you noticed how when Black people destroy something, the media puts up some talking head to condemn your actions, but when we do the same thing, they talk about us like we're patriots standing up for freedom, like righteous revolutionaries?"

Eli had noticed. Following what happened, the media had made the destruction sound like a spontaneous event, unrelated to current reality. Radio talk show hosts fed their listeners a daily narrative of Black people destroying the city and even their own neighborhoods like Five Points without thought or cause. Eli knew from personal experience that the selection of targets was far from random. What he had done to Chance's Place that night was a well-aimed surgical strike.

"Reminds me of Killdozer," Sister Francis said as she took a sip of the Earl Grey. "Yup, up in Granby, Colorado. That old boy got his panties in a wad because the city council wouldn't give him what he wanted. Felt slighted. Let his anger get the best of him, and do you know what he did?"

Eli loved history lessons with Sister Francis.

"Made himself a tank out of a bulldozer, that's what. Then one morning locked himself inside and went on a rampage through the small mountain town. Destroyed Main Street, the police station, newspaper building . . . leveled everything. Destroyed his own community."

Eli had been young at the time but had a vague recollection of the event.

"I can still remember the headlines," continued Sister Francis. "They treated him like an unheard, misunderstood victim. Even the politicians said, 'This is what happens when government isn't responsive to the people.' If he hadn't taken his life when the tank ran out of gas, they would have made him mayor or senator or something."

Eli took a sip of his drink but mostly held the mug for the warmth and aroma. Tea wasn't his thing, but tea with Sister Francis was.

"Eli, let's talk about you. Liza called up here looking for you when you disappeared. We were all worried, prayed for you."

He didn't respond.

The smoldering logs in the fireplace still warmed the room.

"Anger has to come out. It will come out. If you don't give it an escape door, then it will eat its way out and destroy you. You hear me?"

Eli nodded. Smoke ascended up the flue.

"Son, what are you doing with your anger? From the looks of things, it's getting the best of you."

Eli didn't hide things from Sister Francis. She knew about his panic attacks after Father Myriel's murder. When he fell in love with Antoinette and decided to propose, he'd taken the same 15 Limited bus to show her the ring he'd bought. He'd always shared the unvarnished truth with her, and it didn't make sense for him to start hiding things from her now.

"I haven't been dealing with it well at all."

Eli told her about The Roz and how things had fallen apart when Liza left.

"I've been drinking way too much. After I closed The Roz, I emptied all but one of the liquor bottles."

He explained what the police were doing in Five Points and about Tyrone. He even admitted to helping with the overturning and burning of the police cars, but he stopped short of confessing what he'd done to Chance's Place.

When he finished, they sat in silence, his tea now cold. The old woman leaned forward. Her eyes lacked judgment or condemnation. But when she asked her question, Eli's soul unraveled.

"My son, you are angry at a lot of things and a lot of people, but I noticed you left someone out. Eli, why didn't you mention Antoinette?"

Eli sank into his chair as if to escape into the cushion.

"Could it be that you're angry at everyone else, including yourself, so you don't have to admit that you're angry at her? Eli, Liza didn't leave you; it was Antoinette who did."

* * *

That had been this morning.

Tonight, Eli sat at his kitchen table with candlelight and his last bottle of whiskey to comfort him as he stared at the empty chair draped with Antoinette's burnt-orange scarf. His wedding ring sat on the table between them.

WHO THEY?

Eli didn't know what to say to her.

Sister Francis was right. Eli's exasperation with life would remain even if The Roz, Liza, the police, and Chance disappeared. His three months on the streets showed him that as he turned his aggravation inward while trying to avoid the inevitable truth: Antoinette had left him.

Her departure was not out of volition or malice, but she'd left him feeling empty and alone to navigate a world in which he'd become dependent on the stability of her love.

Eli had liked himself when he was with Antoinette. Her presence had improved him, and he increasingly despised who he'd become in her absence. Without her, he was an underground rodent blindly searching for a way out of the darkness.

The bottle of whiskey invited him to soothe his sorrow as the candle flame flickered through the brown liquid. He wanted to drink every ounce, fast. Perhaps this would be the way to end everything. How much more could his body take? How much longer could he share dinner with an empty chair, a ghost for a wife?

Sister Francis's words rang a true and certain note in his mind: "Anger has to come out. It *will* come out. If you don't give it an escape door, then it will eat its way out and destroy you."

Eli stood and walked to Antoinette's chair. He picked up her scarf and buried his face in it. Her smell still lingered. He draped it around his neck like one of the stoles Father Myriel used to wear with his robe on Sunday mornings.

The liquor summoned him.

Eli reached for the bottle. His fingers gripped the neck. He clutched it to his chest, held it like a precious artifact that belonged in a museum. He knew he couldn't let himself drink it, but he also couldn't bring himself to pour it out.

Deep inside, something gave way, like a shift of the earth plates but more violent. His grip tightened on the bottle.

"Why?" It was a faint whisper, but he said it—to her.

The question felt like a betrayal of the one he lived for.

"Why?"

A tear fell on to the table in front of him, next to his wedding band.

Rage rose inside like trapped steam.

Eli opened the door, offering it a way to escape.

He raised the bottle high above his shoulders and with both hands brought the thick bottom down on his teardrop. A dent appeared in the table, and his wedding band jumped. The noise must have echoed, but he couldn't hear it. Eli threw the gold band down the open hatch into the darkness of his underground catacomb.

"Why?"

He returned to the table and sledgehammered the same spot. Again and again.

The candle bounced high off the table and onto the rug. Eli stomped the flame with his boot.

The bottle was still intact, and Eli continued to slam it down on the makeshift altar, the centerpiece in the temple dedicated to his dead wife.

"Antoinette." He finally said her name.

Three more blows to the table, and then five more, one following each word.

"Why—"

Thud.

"—did—"

Thud.

"—you—"

A crack.

"—leave—"

The wood splintered.

"—me?"

The bottle shattered, slicing Eli's hand as it gave way.

Eli threw the remnants aside as the alcohol saturated and burned in his wound. He continued his destruction with his bare hands with blows from his palms angled down, pounding the table, smearing his blood on the altar to his god.

He paused long enough to remove the orange silk scarf now hanging from one of his shoulders and wrapped it around the cut on his swollen hand. His blood soaked through the thin silk in an instant.

Eli returned to the weakened table, flipped it on its side, and kicked it. The heft of his boots caused chunks to break away. For a moment, an image flashed of Father Myriel's bloodied face after the murderer stomped him to death, but Eli kept going. Only after he snapped the legs and tossed them aside did his body give way.

The desecration was complete.

Eli spent the next hour caring for the cut on his hand and throwing the remnants of the table in the dumpster, but then he was at a lost as to what to do next. He was too amped to sleep and too tired to process the meaning behind what he'd done.

He settled on the boxes of files from Moses's case and set out to read every word of every page. If there was an unturned stone in the trial transcripts, police reports, or evidence notes, Eli was determined to find it.

The break came when he opened an envelope labeled *Detective notes* and reread the familiar pages containing references to Moses and Calhoun. As Eli turned the page, one sentence glowed like a neon sign in the night.

How had he missed it?

Five words: *They moved out of town.*

Was this a reference to Claudette when she'd escaped Denver for Colorado Springs?

As far as Eli knew, Claudette had lived alone then as she did now.

If so, then who was *they*?

THE ROCK

Liza wasted no time.

First, she called the media, both television and print.

The DA was next. After informing Taylor of the news, she let him know that he should expect calls from reporters.

"The city is watching. Everyone will be wondering what you're going to do," she said.

The DNA results were back on the weapon used to murder the teacher. The blood on the rock was a mixture of two people's, one male and one female. As expected, the victim's DNA was present. However, highly relevant to the fate of Dexter Diaz, the male DNA was not a match to the man convicted for the crime.

This was enough to get a new trial and hopefully enough to provide a jury with reasonable doubt. There was still the issue of why Dexter had been in the passenger seat of the victim's car a day after the murder, but Liza believed her team could explain that away, given the opportunity. Namely, Liza envisioned highlighting for the jurors that there had been two crimes: the murder and the car theft. Dexter riding in a stolen car that—unbeknownst to him—belonged to the murder victim did not mean he'd been involved in her murder. It would require a legal argument with the precision of a scalpel, and while Liza knew she lacked the experience needed, she felt confident that Project Joseph's lead trial counsel, Lee Goldstein, would be up for the task.

However, there was a reason Liza had called the media first. It wasn't just to inform them that her client was innocent but also to make them aware that her team had discovered who the real perpetrator was and that she would leave it to DA Taylor to announce the findings to the media.

The male DNA on the rock was a match for the victim's boyfriend. While detectives had failed to explore him as a suspect during the original investigation, they'd had the foresight to get a swab from him before they shifted their attention to Dexter.

* * *

Liza sat at the defense table next to Dexter Diaz. He was nervous and kept turning to see his family, who lined the rail behind him. She put her hand on his shoulder and whispered reassurance.

DA Taylor had responded as she had hoped—held a press conference extolling the work of Liza and Project Joseph and promised "to continue our track record of transparency for the good of all." He'd also announced that his office was in support of Dexter's exoneration and that he was "calling on the courts to expedite the process." Liza assumed that Taylor had also made a few personal calls, because ten days after she'd called the media and made him aware of the DNA results, they had a court date.

The bailiff called the court to order, and as they stood, Liza looked toward Dexter's mother. Dorothy's tears flowed freely as she smiled and clasped her hands.

"Ms. Brown, you may address the court."

Lee Goldstein remained seated beside her. Earlier he'd reminded her that he would not be around forever and that she needed to learn how to do these things.

"Your Honor, you have received the documentation, but for the record, Dexter Diaz was arrested at the age of fourteen and forced to endure what we can only describe as psychological torture. He asserted his innocence and denied his guilt sixty-five times. It was only after they isolated him from his mother and lied to him about the evidence they had against him that he succumbed to the pressure.

"We are here today for *you*, Your Honor, to right a wrong. We tested the murder weapon in this case—something, I might add, the police should have done in the beginning. Not only do the test results clear Dexter Diaz, but they point to the real perpetrator—a man that lived in the house at the time and is now on the run from the US Marshals due to this recent discovery.

"Your Honor, we ask that you set Mr. Diaz free today to go home with his family and begin life as a free man."

The judge turned his attention to DA Taylor.

"Your Honor, the people have no desire to pursue this case regarding Mr. Diaz, and therefore no objection."

The judge waited a beat.

"Mr. Diaz, please stand to your feet. I have reviewed the evidence in this case, and because the state desires not to pursue this matter, you are free to go. Bailiff, remove Mr. Diaz's handcuffs. Court is adjourned."

The judge stood.

Dexter's family erupted.

Liza was perplexed. That was it. No apology. No *We hope you can move on and make the most of your life*. Colorado didn't have a compensation policy, so Dexter was in for a long battle to get any apology, let alone remuneration for the loss of his childhood.

Liza felt Dexter's hand on her shoulder.

"Ms. Brown, I was wrong about you. I'm sorry for what I said when we met. You ain't no B-team."

"You've been through the unimaginable. I want to say on behalf of everyone that we are sorry. You did not deserve what happened to you. We are beyond happy for you."

The Diaz family hopped the rail in celebration.

Liza stepped aside and packed her briefcase.

DA Taylor attempted to slip through the swinging barrier doors, but Liza pivoted, forcing him to acknowledge her. He did with a nod.

Liza held her tongue and decided not to gloat, though all she could think was *Not bad for a rookie.*

WALK OF FREEDOM

Liza hadn't known it would feel this good.

Garrett nodded for her to take the lead, so she walked shoulder to shoulder with Dexter down the long corridor toward the front door, flanked by Dexter's family and the small but mighty team from Project Joseph.

Reporters with cameras and microphones greeted them as they exited the City and County Building.

Liza stepped forward.

"Today is a good day for Denver and an even better day for this man, Dexter Diaz."

Cameras clicked, and Dexter's family gave a collective hoot.

"Today is a day of justice for all of us. For Dexter and his family but also for the victim in this case, Kathy McCarver. Let us remember that when we convict the wrong person, the real perpetrator walks free."

Liza took a moment and looked up. The gold dome on the state capitol building glistened, surrounded by scorched trees, the final remnants of what had happened on Martin Luther King Jr. Day. To the left was the tallest building in the skyline, Unity Bank, the place where her father had worked nights to supplement his day jobs as a maintenance man and barber.

The location of the Mother's Day Massacre, where four people had lost their lives and the nightmare of false imprisonment had begun, eventually resulting in the execution of her father. She stood on these steps with a juris doctorate because of the unchecked injustice in this city.

"My father, Langston Brown, was not the first, and I'm sorry to say Dexter Diaz will not be the last. There are more. It's been well documented that the corruption in this city reached the highest levels of government, and it's going to take years to unravel."

Liza looked to her right and exchanged nods with Fredricka, who stood next to Roberta Messay. At the back of the crowd, Liza could see that Eli had come to celebrate her big day.

Liza acknowledged her team and highlighted the patience and vigilance of Dexter's family.

"No family should have to endure what they have." Her voice almost cracked under the weight of those words, for they betrayed what she and Journey and her mother were still bearing.

"So I've got all your pager numbers—stay tuned. There are far more wrongs to right than you can imagine, and we will be back.

"Denver, it is my privilege to introduce you to your newly freed son, Dexter Diaz."

Dexter stepped forward as the applause erupted and began to field the reporter's questions.

Liza turned to Dexter's mother.

Dorothy hugged Liza. "Thank you. Thank you for bringing my hijo home."

"Happy Mother's Day," Liza said as they hugged again.

She then stepped back next to Garrett as Dexter told his story.

"Our first exoneration." Garrett smiled. "So," he whispered as he leaned down, "who's next in your box of prospects?"

There were more, many more that she wanted to present for consideration. Many that fit their criteria.

But all she could think about was the one who didn't, Moses King.

BLIND LEADING THE BLIND

The next day, after seeing Liza stand next to a free Dexter Diaz, Eli pressed on with the King case.

He had a hunch.

The note had said *they* had moved out of town.

Which was why he was back at Claudette Cooper's apartment building.

He was standing at her mailbox, eyeing the braille letters on the label. It was made with some sort of sticker-labeling machine. He had assumed that the label read 3B, but now he wasn't so sure.

Eli removed a piece of paper from his pocket, the kind that the waitstaff used to take food and drink orders at The Roz. He didn't want to remove the braille sticker, so he placed the paper on top and pressed firmly with his thumb until small raised bumps appeared.

After a glance up at Claudette's window with its security bars, he left on foot. The Colorado School for the Deaf and Blind was his next destination.

* * *

The smiling face of the middle-aged receptionist met Eli as he walked in the school's front door. She wore dark glasses and a headset for answering the phone. Her fingers poised to type on an odd sort of typewriter, most likely for braille.

"Hello, sir, how may I help you?"

Eli wondered how she'd guessed he was a *sir*.

"Yes, ma'am, I was wondering if you could do me a favor."

"I'll help if I can."

"I have this bit of braille that I'm unable to read." Eli slid the paper on the desk in front of her, and the receptionist reached out with both hands. Her fingertips found the paper and the raised lettering.

"I'm not sure what it—" he began.

"*Theo*. It's somebody's name. Theo."

Eli had expected an apartment number or perhaps Claudette's last name, but his hunch was paying off.

"Ma'am, you are a lifesaver. Might you have a phone book I could borrow?"

"We do—would you like braille or no braille?" She laughed as she turned in her chair and rolled herself to the bottom drawer of a nearby filing cabinet. Wheeling herself back, she lifted two volumes onto the desk.

Eli set the yellow pages aside and flipped through the white pages, searching for Claudette's last name, Cooper. There weren't many, and one entry caught his eye: Theo Cooper at 20265 E. Sage Brush Ave.

He flipped to the back of the book and scanned the maps. Theo Cooper lived just a couple of miles from Claudette Cooper.

"You have been most helpful, and when I said that you've been a lifesaver, I meant it."

* * *

Theo Cooper's house was in a working-class neighborhood on a street that butted up to a busy thoroughfare. Eli sat in a McDonald's, sipping coffee in a booth that gave him a view of a convenience store on the corner and Theo Cooper's front porch just three doors down.

He'd been there for a couple of hours, shifting his gaze between the unlit porch and a book, *If Beale Street Could Talk*, by James Baldwin.

A blue car arrived, and a tall son of Africa in his late twenties along with an average-height daughter of Africa and a bouncing elementary-age girl stepped out of the vehicle and bounded her way up the steps. They disappeared into the house.

Things were quiet for another hour as dusk settled into darkness. Eli was on his second order of fries when the porch light turned on and the same man stepped out and lit a cigarette.

The little girl bounded out of the house, and Eli watched as they played tag, the glow of the cigarette intact until they headed back into the house.

After one last drag, the man extinguished the cigarette in what Eli assumed to be an ashtray of some sort.

Eli ordered an apple pie and refilled his coffee. Then, after finishing the final chapter of Baldwin's book about a man falsely accused of a terrible crime, he walked across the street to the convenience store and purchased a box of ziplock bags.

BUTT WHY?

Eli popped the cork, and champagne fizzed and overflowed onto the floor of The Roz.

He poured and raised his glass.

"To justice and freedom and the ever-talented Liza Brown."

It was just the two of them. The night before when Eli returned from Colorado Springs, he'd called Liza and asked if they could meet in the morning. While it was too early for a drink, Eli couldn't help but celebrate.

"Eli, I cannot tell you how amazing it felt to walk Dexter out with his mother and family. It was beyond belief. Thank you for coming."

"You know I wouldn't have missed being there for that moment."

But Eli also didn't want to see Fredricka—or rather, for Fredricka to see him. That was why he had kept his distance at the back of the crowd.

"Liza, I am beyond happy for you. I know this is not the life you would have picked for yourself, but it is the life that providence chosen for you.

"To *the* Liza Brown." Eli raised his glass. "One sensational, hardworking, and brilliant woman."

In his heart he wanted to say more. He wanted to tell her about his conversation with Sister Francis and how it felt like his anger—toward her, Antoinette, everyone—was dissipating.

"I just wish I could have done the same for Daddy."

"Your daddy, Langston Brown, was and is proud of you. Liza, I'm proud of you. Dexter is home eating home-cooked meals provided by his family and basking in the love of his mother."

"But . . ." Liza looked around at her stacks of notes and the papers spread out across the bar and tables. "But Moses has a mother too. She deserves to have her son with her, especially now."

Eli smiled as he walked behind the bar and retrieved a plastic ziplock bag.

"I have something for you," he said as he placed the bag on the table.

Liza picked up the bag of ashes and a dozen or so cigarette butts in various state of completion.

"Well, Eli, I don't know what to say . . . you shouldn't have." Liza laughed as she began to open the bag.

"Wait, don't do that. I have something else for you too."

Eli handed her the detective note he'd discovered and directed her attention to the page that read *They moved out of town*.

"They?" she asked.

Eli explained about the mailbox, the braille, the kind receptionist, Theo, and the ashtray on Theo's porch.

"Wait, are you telling me that Theo and Claudette are connected?"

"More than connected. Related."

"And this"—she pointed to the plastic bag—"what am I supposed to do with it?"

"Test it for DNA."

Liza turned her head to the side in thought.

"Liza, this is why Claudette is not cooperating. It's not that she's unwilling to help Moses but that she's protecting Theo."

"From what?"

"From the truth."

"How do we know he's not an old boyfriend or something? Wait . . . Eli, how old is Theo?"

"Late twenties."

"Are you saying that Theo is Claudette's *son*?"

Eli nodded as Liza assembled the puzzle.

"But then that means that Theo is the child—"

"—of a violent and vile man," Eli finished. "My guess is that she hasn't told him, and for her to help Moses would mean that Theo would learn the secret that she's kept from him all these years—Levar Calhoun is his father."

DO THE RIGHT THING

"Ms. Brown, what now?"

Liza was back in DA Taylor's office.

"Just a rookie here for another lesson," Liza replied. "How am I doing, Coach?"

"Ms. Brown, let's not play games."

"Moses King. I'm here to talk about the release of Moses King."

"Give me a break. Don't let Dexter go to your head; we aren't running some two-for-one special."

"You know Moses is innocent. Calhoun confessed."

"You've already lost that battle."

"In court, maybe, but currently you are losing in the court of public opinion. What's going to happen to your reelection bid when the city finds out that not only did you oppose the release of an innocent kid but now there's another wrongfully convicted man that you're stubbornly opposing? You sure you don't want to get out in front of this one before I call the media again? I'm giving you the chance to be the hero."

Liza retrieved the plastic bag of cigarette butts from her purse and placed them on the desk between them.

"Ms. Brown, what's this?"

"*That* is proof."

"Okay, I'll play along. What do you think you have now?"

"Claudette's son."

DA Taylor stopped breathing.

"Wait a minute. You knew?" Liza charged. "Now who's playing games?"

"I don't know what you're talking about."

"His name is Theo, his birthday is almost nine months to the day after the assault on Claudette, and he takes a smoke on his porch every night. And what is this? This is DNA evidence that will show Moses King is not his father. How much do you want to bet it matches Calhoun's sample that is already in the state database?"

Silence.

"Would you bet your next term on it?"

"Calhoun testified that what happened was consensual. This proves nothing."

"But what will Claudette Cooper say when I put her on the stand?" Liza let the weight of what she'd said settle for a moment. "Do you think she'll confirm Calhoun's story, that she had a relationship and child with a man who is in prison for the kidnapping and violent assault on a mother and daughter? Do you think Claudette will agree that it was consensual?"

Taylor finally spoke. "We can't do this to her. She has endured too much."

"On that we agree."

"Ms. Brown, it devastated her. I've never seen a woman so broken. No, I didn't know about the kid at first, but I know she barely got through the trial."

"She's still living in fear. Has security bars on her third-floor apartment windows. Saw them with my own eyes."

"You found her?"

"Moses needs justice."

"And Claudette needs peace. Ms. Brown, are you really prepared to disrupt her life and now the life of her son on a whim?"

Liza didn't want to cause more pain to Claudette or to introduce pain into Theo's life. But Taylor needed to believe she was prepared to do exactly that.

"Not only am I willing to get this tested, but I'll subpoena the son to get a proper swab of his cheek so there are no doubts."

"Ms. Brown, please." Taylor was pleading.

"Why are you willing to let an innocent man . . ." Her voice cracked. "Moses and his mother have been separated for almost thirty years. She doesn't have long to live."

The ashes drew both of their attention like an urn full of missed opportunity and regrets.

"Alford."

Liza looked up.

"I'll offer him an Alford plea."

"That's not good enough," Liza shot back.

"Ms. Brown, it's an elegant solution, and you know it."

Now Liza wasn't breathing.

"Do I need to remind you that you are obligated to take all good-faith offers to your client?"

Liza put the plastic bag back in her purse.

"I will take your offer to Mr. King, and I will advise him against taking your deal. But if he does, there's one thing I want in return."

ALFORD WHO?

"But again," Liza said to Moses, "the choice is all yours. As your counsel, I advise against taking this deal."

"They would let me go though, correct?"

"Yes, you would be free to go. But I've seen a picture of Theo Cooper. He's most definitely Calhoun's son, and I have no doubt that DNA will show exactly that."

"So there would be another trial?"

"Yes."

"At our last trial, I had no doubt the truth would prevail, and look where that got me." Moses gestured around the meeting room. "Ms. Liza, what's stopping them from saying that while Calhoun may be the father, that doesn't prove he was the perpetrator, especially when the victim says I did it?"

"We would call Claudette to the stand—not to ask her about the dream but whether she ever had a relationship with Calhoun."

"Claudette would have to testify again?"

Liza nodded.

Moses bowed his head.

*   *   *

"The state wouldn't have to admit to any wrongdoing or make a statement clearing Moses' name?"

Liza was back with Eli at The Roz.

"I know, that's the thing about an Alford plea. Moses will get credit for time served and released, but he'll still be a convicted felon, on probation, and can't vote. But he's free and we can still fight, if he wants to, for a complete exoneration."

"Freed but still fighting for exoneration. What about compensation? Will they have to pay him back for what they did to him?"

"Nothing. With an Alford plea he's still treated as guilty, can't even apply for food stamps or Medicare."

"Liza, this is not right."

"What would you do?" Liza asked. "Wait for months while the DA stalls and then, at trial, roll the dice with a jury of your so-called peers?" Liza made air quotes around that last word. "Or, if you had a chance to get out of prison, would you take it?"

The question felt personal for Eli. Did he want out of his hole of a house? If he could move on from the prison of his grief, would he want to?

"What did he decide?" asked Eli.

"Moses took the deal. He'll be out in a few weeks. All that's needed is some paperwork and an appearance in court for the judge to sign off."

"I'm happy for him, but it just feels wrong."

"I feel the same way, but you want to know what he said?" Liza took a sip of wine and wiped a tear from her eye. "Moses said it felt more wrong to put Claudette on the stand again."

SAFEKEEPING

Eli lay still and did his best not to react when the officer kicked him.

He wasn't drunk, but he'd made sure he smelled like it.

The officer removed his baton from the loop and struck the shopping cart that Eli had filled with junk to complete his ensemble.

"Get up. Move on."

Eli did not move. He could see the man's shadow through the slight crack in his eyelids.

It was Officer Winston. The same officer who had confronted him in front of Freeman's Furniture Store and failed to give chase.

Winston leaned down and jabbed Eli in the ribs with the silver ball on the butt of his nightstick. It took everything in Eli to not react to the bruising pain. He gave no response, not even a groan. Officer Winston walked back to his car, satisfied that Eli was too inebriated to be a problem. As the patrol car drove away, Eli pulled a disposable camera from his pocket and snapped a picture before it turned the corner a block away.

Tonight was the night. For months, Eli had monitored the movements of the DPD's late-night crew. He knew what they were up to, and he was determined to get the evidence needed to expose the whole squad.

Besides harassing people in Five Points, they were committing crimes, specifically robbing businesses and then investigating the very crimes they had committed only hours before. Their MO remained unchanged. Officer Winston would clear the streets of loiterers and potential witnesses. Then two officers in plain clothes would break into a business and blowtorch the bolts that anchored the store's safe to the floor. Together, they'd carry it to a vehicle they'd borrowed from the impound lot earlier that night.

Across the street was their current target, a Rent-A-Center on Broadway. While the city slept, the light of a flashlight made its way through the showroom toward the back office. Eli waited until the light disappeared into the back room. With no sign of Winston, Eli ran across the street and snapped a couple of pictures into the darkness of the store. He then made his way to the side of the building, where a Ford sedan waited outside. The side door was open, the lock busted. Eli snapped multiple pictures of the door and the car, both inside and out.

"Can you believe it? It wasn't even bolted down," a voice said from inside the store.

Eli ducked around the front corner of the store and watched as Officer Winston's accomplices struggled and shoved the square package into the back seat and then slammed the door.

"Check the cash register, and I'll get my tools."

They disappeared back inside the building.

Eli decided it was worth the risk and snuck back into the alley. He knelt beside the car and opened the back door for a clear shot. The shutter snapped, but before he could close the car door completely—

"Freeze."

It was Officer Winston.

"Stand. Slowly."

Eli complied. He could see Winston's face and the outline of his gun.

"Let me see your hands."

Eli raised them, the camera in his right hand.

"Bravo. Abort. Now." Winston radioed the others.

Eli took the opportunity to press the middle button on top of the disposable camera and could hear the high-pitched sound as the flash charged.

When the sound stopped, Eli pressed the shutter button.

The flash went off.

He hoped it captured Winston's face, but he still needed to get away.

Unlike the first time they'd met, Eli ran straight at Winston, hoping the flash had temporarily blinded the man. Winston moved into Eli's path, and as they collided, the gun fell from Winston's hand.

Eli attacked with a shove that put Winston on his back. Eli no longer wanted to get away; he wanted to teach this man a lesson. To exact retribution for Tyrone and those in Five Points who'd lived in fear because of this man.

Eli jumped on him, but Winston was strong and bucked.

Eli still had the upper hand. Winston gave up his back as he turned to get his feet under himself and attempted to stand. That was the mistake Eli was waiting for; he grabbed the nightstick from the officer's belt loop and, with both hands, secured it around Winston's neck.

Eli pulled tight and squeezed. Winston flailed. Eli could feel the cop's strength fading. He squeezed even tighter.

The roar of the car engine and the screech of the sedan's tires startled Eli as it skidded around the corner. The rear door flew open and the square metal safe tumbled out to Broadway, crashing on the asphalt.

Eli loosened his stranglehold and pushed Winston away as he snapped a picture of the two police officers in plain clothes, who had exited the car to wrestle the evidence of their crime back into the car.

"You've got to be kidding me," Winston gasped.

Eli gave him another push and ran.

* * *

That had been last night, about three AM.

Eli now waited in the parking lot of the *Weekly Word*.

Shortly after dawn, a white Mercedes pulled into the parking space by the door. Fredricka. Eli still felt his best option was to lie low and out of her sight. She had yet to make a move to expose him, and while he knew she could, he wasn't convinced that she would.

Fredricka unlocked the front door, always the first to arrive and the last to leave.

About twenty minutes later, Roberta Messay arrived.

"Ms. Messay."

She jerked around.

"It's me. Eli Stone."

She took in his attire.

"Mr. Stone, you shouldn't have come."

"I know, but I need to give you this. I don't know who else to turn to."

Eli handed her the disposable camera.

"You know she won't let me run a story from you."

"She doesn't need to know."

Eli explained in broad strokes what was happening and offered to fill in the blanks for her at a later date.

"Please, develop the film. You'll see that what I'm saying is true."

"If it is, Mr. Stone, then what do you want in return?"

"Ms. Messay, I need to know that I can count on you to have my back." Eli nodded toward the white Mercedes. "Best as you can, help me with her."

TAKING A CHANCE

Eli needed sleep, but the adrenaline coursing through his body dictated otherwise.

After giving the evidence to Roberta Messay, he made his way to The Roz. He wasn't sure if he had found Slager's partner in Winston, but he was confident that the Denver police were about to clean house. Hopefully, that would be good news for Five Points.

He made a pot of coffee and drank a glass of water. As the pot brewed, he removed his heavy coat, hoodie, and hat. The warm sun radiated through The Roz's windows; his T-shirt and cargo pants were now enough both indoors and out.

He poured a cup and leaned with his forearms on the bar. In front of him were an empty stage and a sea of empty seats. Through the window and across the street, Chance was on his sidewalk. Today he lacked his typical attire—no white designer sneakers or blue hat. Instead, he was dressed for manual labor as he unpacked items from his trunk.

Not much had changed with Chance's Place since Eli had set the facade on fire. Boards covered the windows, and shattered glass still littered the sidewalk. Black burn marks lined the red brick. While the lobby had sustained smoke and water damage, the inner parts of the club were still intact.

Eli paged Tyrone and left a message for Liza. He wanted to meet up with them the next morning so he could fill them in on what he'd decided to do with The Roz. He wanted both of them to hear his plans directly from him. While the future felt uncertain, one thing that was clear was that he wasn't willing to go back to the way things were before.

Chance removed his shirt, in part because of the rising sun but mostly because he'd done too many push-ups not to. Shirt off and his blue hat back in place, he began removing the boards that covered the windows.

Eli didn't feel anger against his unwelcome neighbor nor regret for what he had done to him. Today, he mostly pitied him and wished his neighbor didn't see the children of Africa as products to be imitated but rather a people to be respected. As far as Eli was concerned, if Chance humbled up, he was welcome to stay.

After he finished his coffee, he placed the mug in the sink and headed to the back room. Eli retrieved his work gloves, tool bag, and push broom.

Eli made his way to the sidewalk and stepped out into the morning sun.

At the sound of The Roz's door, Chance turned toward Eli.

Their eyes locked.

Chance squared his shoulders.

It was time for Eli to heed his own advice. He was the one who needed to clean up the mess he'd made. So Eli crossed the street to pick up his own trash.

ONWARD AND UPWARD

"You got DA Taylor to do what?" Tyrone grilled Liza about the news she'd just shared.

Eli was speechless.

"So let me get this straight," Tyrone continued. "The city of Denver, with the support of DA Taylor, has canceled all parking tickets and fines handed out to residents of Five Points over the last three years. Am I hearing you correctly?" Tyrone was standing on the stage at The Roz. Liza and Eli sipped coffee at the bar.

"Sis, when I said we needed you to help, I had no idea you could pull off something like this."

"You didn't think your girl was going to leave you all hanging? Us single moms know how to multitask."

"Props," said Tyrone.

"But before I can take all the credit," Liza continued, "word is that there's a big story dropping about the crimes and misdemeanors of Denver's finest."

More like felonies, Eli thought.

The day before, after Eli finished helping Chance clean his place, Roberta Messay had dropped by. She'd had a few questions of clarification before she published her exposé based on the evidence Eli had provided—complete with a perfectly framed shot of Officer Winston pointing his gun at the camera.

"So, Tyrone, what's next?" Eli asked, "We followed you once, and while things got a little out of hand, we'll follow again."

"I don't know, Uncle. I'm not sure what we should tackle next."

"Well," Eli said as he walked to a table in the middle of the room. "Perhaps I can help with that."

Liza and Tyrone joined him.

"I want you to hear it from me. I've decided not to return The Roz to the way it was."

Liza's shoulders slumped.

"It was too much, and something had to give. That being said, I've run the numbers. We make most of our money and have all of our fun on Friday and Saturday nights. So . . ."

Smiles crept onto their faces.

"When we reopen . . ."

"Yes." Tyrone pumped his fist.

"The Roz will reopen, but only on those two days of the week. Only opening on Friday and Saturday nights feels sustainable for me. Tyrone, I'm hoping this means that you don't have to choose between your bullhorn and your saxophone. You can have both."

"Sis, the band is getting back together," Tyrone said as he shoulder-bumped Liza.

"And Ty, I'd like to give you the opportunity to make some extra money around here. Would you consider becoming The Roz's new assistant manager? It's a part-time gig, but you could keep organizing in the streets and help me stay organized in here."

"Uncle, yes." Tyrone stretched across the table for a hug. "I'll do it. Promise I won't let you down."

Eli turned his attention to Liza.

"I know you love singing, and we love and enjoy hearing you do so, but I also want to recognize that you are doing needed and necessary work at the project. Dexter, Moses, and the cancellation of the parking tickets—you are on a roll."

Eli reached for her hand.

"Liza, I need to apologize to you."

"For what?"

"For how I've blamed you for my problems. You've been nothing but a true friend from the day you walked in here."

Liza squeezed his hand, her eyes heavy with tears.

Eli raised his mug.

"To the future."

Their mugs clanked.

"When do we reopen?" Liza asked.

"If it works for the two of you, I was thinking Friday after next."

"Works for me," Tyrone said as he jumped up and gave Eli another hug and headed for the door.

"Where are you going?"

"Down the street to KDKO radio, the voice of the community." Tyrone pointed. "Dr. Daddy-O is on the raddy-o, and your assistant manager needs to talk to him about getting the word out."

Tyrone set out jogging down the sidewalk.

Liza turned her head and then her full body toward Eli.

"And what about you, Mr. Stone? With this place only open two days a week, what are you going to do with all your extra time?"

"Ms. Brown, follow me," Eli said. "I have something to show you."

The Roz was a jazz club on the first level, but back in the day when it was in full operation, it had also served as the Baxter Hotel on the upper two floors.

Eli led Liza up the stairs.

"Keep your eyes closed. I got you."

He was holding her hand and beholding her beauty at the same time. Liza's nail polish matched the blue water in the tattoo on her chest. And today, long braids flowed down her back, stopping at the top of her jeans. Her signature boots announced her arrival on each step.

"Almost there. Keep 'em closed."

They reached the top of the landing, and he guided her to the center of a large, empty room. Her boots echoed in the space.

"All right, you can open your eyes."

Originally, there had been eight rooms on the second floor. Eli had knocked down the walls between the larger rooms to create an open space that joined with the smaller rooms.

Liza scanned the room, whose windows looked out over the five-point intersection. Across the street, Brother X offered a bean pie to a passerby.

"Eli, this is beautiful. When did you do all of this?"

"Well, you don't think I was just drinking and laying on the streets that whole time, do you?"

"What are you going to use this for?"

"Liza, all of this is *yours*."

"I'm sorry, what?"

"And these are yours too."

Eli held up a set of keys.

"You already have a key to the front door downstairs. These give you access up here."

"Eli, I don't—" Liza covered her mouth.

This was the moment Eli had imagined as he scraped, cut, and hammered. Seeing the look on her face gave him a feeling that had eluded him for too long. Antoinette was right: love was his only path to happiness.

"I don't understand."

"This is for your side hustle—your extra projects at the project. Seems to me you're always going to have cases that don't fit neatly into your boxes."

Liza's tears flowed.

"You are the lawyer with the expertise and training, but I realized that I was able to help you because I had time to go through the boxes of files and search for what you told me you needed."

Eli looked out the window. Brother X was gone.

"Liza, I can read. Your mother can read. There's an entire community here of people who can read their Bibles in the morning and case files here throughout the day. Not only that, there's a wealth of street smarts and common sense in these neighborhoods. We may not understand habeas, Brady, or Alford, but we do know when the math isn't adding up. Teach us what to look for, and we will find it."

Eli walked her around and described where he thought she could put cabinets for her case files, then showed her the side room that would make a perfect law library. There was enough space for tables, desks, and chairs for an army of volunteers.

"There's still a lot of work to do before it's ready. Framing is mostly finished, but I could use some help with electrical, plumbing, drywall, and painting. I was hoping we could call on some of your dad's friends from the shop to help with the finishing touches, and I'm sure Mr. Freeman would cut us a break on the furnishings as well.

"And I've run the numbers. Liza, with the money I'm saving on staffing at The Roz, we could afford to hire someone to manage this place. The choice is up to you, but I was thinking Moses King might be perfect for the job. As for me, I'm discovering I'm a pretty good at snooping around and digging up details. Think of me as your own personal PI."

"Eli, I don't know what to say. No one has ever put this much thought into something just for me."

"Liza, you deserve it. All we need is the perfect name. I was thinking we could call it the New Underground Railroad, because you are our Harriet Tubman."

"Underground." Liza laughed. "Eli, I think you've got that whole underground thing wrapped up."

Propped in the corner was a large piece of wood that Eli had painted and fashioned into a sign. He picked it up and turned it so Liza could see the other side.

"Actually, I was thinking this could be the name."

THE LANGSTON BROWN READING ROOM

Liza dropped to her knees, For a moment he thought she had fainted. Eli leaned the sign against the wall.

He knelt and wrapped his arms around her.

"This is too much, way too much." Liza said, looking up at him as she returned his embrace.

As he held Liza, this strong, smart, beautiful daughter of Africa, Eli knew he could not allow himself to go back to the darkness and despair that flowed like lava from the volcano of his rage. Liza was his ticket out of bondage.

Eli joined her on the floor as she looked at the sign.

"The Langston Brown Reading Room," Liza said. "Eli, all of this . . . it's perfect. But I do have one question: Does this mean I have to move out of your place?" Her laughter filled the room.

"Yeah," Eli said. "All those boxes are cramping my style. Consider this your eviction notice."

One of her hands still held the keys; the other held Eli's.

"Liza, you . . ."

Eli was now the one with tears in his eyes.

"You have saved my life. You don't know the half of it, but if it weren't for you, I wouldn't be here."

Eli wiped the tears from his cheeks.

"Liza, I don't know what we are, but I know what we are not."

It was time for Eli to make his intentions known.

He placed his hand on the side of her face and leaned in for a kiss. Liza's warm lips delivered her RSVP to his invitation to a new, uncertain future together.

THE NIGHTMARE OF FREEDOM

Liza was almost to Colorado Springs, but her mind was still at The Roz.

That morning had been unexpected in so many ways. The reopening of The Roz meant she would sing again, and the Langston Brown Reading Room meant she didn't have to choose between the "nows" and the "laters." Garrett would have to understand that with an army of readers carrying the load, Project Joseph could handle a broadening of its scope.

Then there was the kiss.

She and Eli were no longer friends, but what were they now? What could they become? She felt ready for love, but Eli was still living underground and barely back on his feet.

Two things were clear. First, as she had concluded long ago, Eli had loved before, and once he healed, he could love again. Not only was Eli healing; today he'd proved that he knew how to meet her needs. Second, there was still the unfinished third floor at The Roz, which, if things worked out, would be a wonderful place to raise a family.

Liza parked in front of Claudette's apartment building, climbed the stairs, and knocked on the wrought-iron screen door.

"Ms. Cooper, it's me, Liza Brown."

The solid wood door opened, leaving only the screen door between them, which Liza assumed was locked as usual.

"Why are you here again?"

"Ms. Cooper, I'm sorry to bother you, but I was hoping we could talk."

"About what?"

"About your safety."

"My safety." Claudette laughed. "What are you talking about safety to me for?"

"Ms. Cooper, I know you've heard the news about Moses. I wanted to . . ."

Claudette took a deep breath through her nose; her hand was in her pocket.

"You don't need to live in fear anymore, and I want to help. I'd like to offer you more than this screen door and that knife in your pocket."

"How you gonna help me?"

"Well, for starters, I know people. Daddy had a lot of friends. What if we installed a security system? The kind that beeps and automatically calls the police if you ever need help.

"And with Moses out, I hoped I could explain to you how we know without a doubt that Levar Calhoun was the man who hurt you and how he will never get out of prison to harm you again. And . . ." Liza paused for a breath.

"And what?"

"Your son . . ."

Claudette stiffened.

"We know about Theo. He's a good man with a beautiful family. Claudette, I imagine that one of your greatest fears is that he would find out the truth about his real father."

Claudette's prosthetic eyes shifted up and down slightly.

"Ms. Cooper, here in my bag I have the only pieces of paper that link the case to you and Theo: the detective notes we used to find you. I'd like to give them to you for you to destroy as you see fit."

Claudette took a deep breath, this time through her mouth.

"Ms. Brown, like I told you, I knew your daddy; we all did. Langston would be so proud of you. We all are so very, very proud of who you are."

Claudette removed her hand from her pocket and unlocked the door.

* * *

Smith Road was a forgotten wasteland on the outskirts of Denver's oasis.

People came here to visit loved ones serving short time at Denver's men's and women's jails. The other reason people arrived here was to start a new life. Smith Road was where Colorado's prisons brought loaded buses of people who had finished their time and were now being released back into society.

Men and women were dropped off wearing the same clothes they'd had on when they were arrested, carrying plastic bags with their belongings. In their pockets was a check for whatever money they'd earned while on the inside.

Smith Road was twelve miles from the closest shelter and even farther from a former prisoners' probation officer, whom they were mandated to contact in person within twenty-four hours of release. If people knew you were coming, they could pick you up. If you were released in haste, like Moses King, the buses left you on the side of the desolate road to fend for yourself.

Moses stepped out of the bus and onto the dirt shoulder. Twelve miles to the west were the homeless shelters. If he was going to make it to them before they shut their doors for the day, he needed to walk now without delay, but he also needed money. Rumor was there was a liquor store to the east that would cash the checks of the newly freed if they first agreed to make a purchase.

Moses headed east to the liquor store. Perhaps, in exchange for buying a bottle of juice, they would cash his check of $987.13—all he had to show for twenty-eight years of work. Tomorrow he'd figure out a way to the halfway house where he was to start his new life, but for now he'd catch a cab from the liquor store to one of the shelters.

That was when Liza found him.

She jumped out of her car with balloons and a big hug.

"Sorry I'm late, but when I called to see when you were getting out, they said they had already released you."

She gave him a hug.

"Look at you. Hungry?"

McDonald's was what he wanted; he'd been craving the fries. Liza told him she'd scheduled an appointment with his probation officer and they could take care of things at his office if they hurried. Moses's Alford plea meant his reentry back into society was still as a convicted felon and he'd endure all that went along with that label. He would have regular check-ins with a probation officer and would have to start off at a halfway house before he could get a place of his own.

After a Big Mac and two large fries, she drove him to a large windowless building by Mile High Stadium.

"Mr. King, I need you to read this," the probation officer said. "Initial here and sign here and here. It's an acknowledgment that you understand that you may not leave the jurisdiction of the State of Colorado without first getting permission from me and that you are not, under any circumstances, to remove your ankle monitor."

Moses initialed and signed. Once the monitor was attached, it beeped.

"This is the new kind. This unit will vibrate and beep once every six hours. If it does not beep or vibrate, then that means we do not have a location on you and you must call us to check in."

"Are you serious?" Liza exclaimed. "He's supposed to know if it doesn't beep, even when he's sleeping, and then call you?"

Moses reached out to calm her. Her days of fighting for him were over. Liza had done all she could. For Moses, the monitor wasn't a significant concern. The worst part of his Alford plea was that he was still considered guilty even though he was free.

His probation officer slid another paper across the desk with the heading *Sex Offender Registry*.

"Mr. King, you'll need to renew this annually or each time you change residence. Failure to do so could result in reincarceration."

"How long does he need to do this?" Liza asked.

"Ma'am, this is a permanent feature of his agreement. He needs to register for life."

* * *

Moses wanted to see his mom, but there was a small check-in window at the halfway house. He'd rather go there than the homeless shelter, but if he and Liza were going to make it, they needed to move fast.

Upon their arrival, Liza was informed that she could not enter.

Moses hugged her and thanked her.

"Please, let Mom know where I am."

At the front desk he read, signed, and initialed more forms acknowledging the house rules, the no-drugs-or-alcohol policy, and the list of expected community chores.

They directed him to his room. Thumbtacked to the wall was his daily schedule.

5:30am—Wake up
6:00am—Breakfast
7:00am—Community chores
8:00am—In-room time & enrichment
11:00am—Enrichment groups
Noon—Lunch
1:00pm—Groups and classes
6:00pm—Dinner
7:00pm—Community chores
8:00pm—Free time
10pm—Lights out

Moses unpacked the contents of his plastic bag and placed what few clothing items he had in the top drawer of his dresser and his toiletries in the bathroom.

He sat on the edge of his new bed. The room was slightly larger than the cells that had defined the last twenty-eight years of his life.

But at least now, he was free.

Free to follow their schedules.

Free to apply for jobs, only to be rejected because he was and always would be considered a convicted felon.

Free to register as a sex offender for the rest of his life.

His eyes darted.
    His jaw clenched.
        His fists tightened.

For the first time since his ordeal had begun, Moses felt something he should have felt from the beginning—pure and complete rage.

AUTHOR'S NOTE

Separating Fact From Fiction

From Langston's Dream to King's Nightmare

In my debut novel, *They Can't Take Your Name*, I sought to explore what happens to our deferred dreams. Langston Brown was a wrongfully convicted man who not only shared a first name with Langston Hughes but quoted his poetry as well.

Many have argued, and I agree, that there is a direct link between the poetry of Langston Hughes and the rhetoric of Martin Luther King Jr. Hughes's question "What happens to a dream deferred?" had an influence on King's dream of what America might become. It was W. Jason Miller who said, "Langston Hughes's poetry hovers behind Martin Luther King's speeches and sermons, the way watermarks show through bonded paper when it's held up to the light."

A Dream in the Dark is my attempt to hold the American dream up to the light so that we might wrestle with what happens when we realize our deferred dreams, only to see them become our nightmares.

Most people know of the dream of Martin Luther King Jr., but few know of his nightmare. In 1963, King stood in the shadow of the statue of the man who authored the Emancipation

Proclamation and called the nation "to live out the true meaning of its creed." With wondrous words and compelling cadence, he delivered one of the greatest speeches of all time. He called Americans to be American, and few remained uninspired by a vision of what life could and should be. Yet only four years later, Martin Luther King Jr. spoke of the same dream in very different and disturbing terms. On Christmas Eve 1967, before his home congregation, he said, "Not long after talking about that dream, I started seeing it turn into a nightmare." Malcolm X and James Baldwin offered similar refrains, and collectively they point us to a singular conclusion—our deferred dreams can also become our lived nightmares.

To explore this theme, I wanted to move from the fictional victim of my debut, Langston Brown, to two real-life victims in Denver who endured the nightmare of the greatest injustice in our justice system.

Moses Is Real

Moses King was inspired by the real-life wrongful conviction of Clarence Moses-El, who, in 1987, was arrested and subsequently convicted on the basis of a dream. The victim was attacked when she returned home after an evening out at a bar with some friends. She suffered broken facial bones and lost sight in one eye. Initially, she told police it was too dark to identify her attacker, then named three men from the bar as possibilities that the police never investigated. A full day and a half later, she told the police that the identity of her attacker came to her in a dream and that it was her neighbor, Clarence Moses-El.

At trial, Clarence was convicted because of the dream-influenced testimony of the victim, and the jury sentenced him to forty-eight years, even though his blood did not match a blood sample from the scene.

An assault kit was collected but never tested, and in the 1990s, an innocence project took the case and gained a court order to test the evidence. Yes, like Moses, Clarence did indeed raise $1,000 from fellow inmates for the DNA testing. However, even though the kit was labeled *Do not destroy*, the police had thrown it away. Clarence remained in jail.

In 2013, Clarence received a letter from LC Jackson, one of the three men originally named by the victim. The letter began, *Let's start by bringing what was done in the dark to light . . . I have a lot on my heart.* Jackson was in prison for assaulting a mother and daughter less than two miles away and said that while he had in fact beaten the victim, the sex was consensual.

Even with a confession from the real perpetrator, the DA declined to retry the case. The innocence project moved for retrial, and the judge vacated all prior convictions and granted a new trial. After twenty-eight years, they released Moses on $50,000 bail. The same day, the DA set a date for a new trial.

In 2016 Mr. Moses-El was acquitted of all charges and the Colorado legislature passed the first compensation bill to address the financial losses of the wrongfully convicted, including Clarence Moses-El, who was sixty-two when ultimately freed.

While maintaining the essence of Mr. Moses-El's account, I did fictionalize significant portions of the narrative for the sake of the story. For example, they did not move Clarence to Huntsville, the death penalty capital of the United States, nor was he released on an Alford plea.

The nameless victim in this saga, represented by Claudette Cooper, is also real. My hope and prayer is that she has found peace and security, wherever she may be.

Dexter Is Real

The ordeal experienced by my fictional character, Dexter Diaz, is based on the real-life nightmare endured by Lorenzo Montoya. He was sentenced to life without parole at fourteen.

What ultimately led to his conviction was a false confession obtained by the detectives who used the Reid technique. As described in *A Dream in the Dark*, this technique encourages officers to tell a person they have evidence that in reality they do not possess; to ask loaded questions such as *Did you plan on killing her, or did it just happen?*; and to downplay the crime using *It could happen to anybody* scenarios. It's psychological warfare that, over time, wears down a subject while making a confession preferable, practical, and inevitable. The technique works on guilty suspects, and it is also extremely effective with innocent people. Fourteen-year-old Lorenzo Montoya didn't have a chance.

In Mr. Montoya's actual videotaped confession, the detectives fed him facts he didn't know, lying to him about fingerprints, shoe prints, and, yes, hair prints that they claimed to have found. Also, after Mr. Montoya's mother left the room, they threatened him with adult prison. Young Lorenzo Montoya stood strong for hours and denied his guilt sixty-five times before he succumbed to the adults in the room.

Thankfully, attorney Lisa Polansky took Lorenzo's case. After meeting with Lorenzo, she realized he had little grasp of the basic facts about the murder. She watched the confession video, in which the detectives swung from loving, fatherly tones to intimidation and menace, and recognized that this was a case of a coerced false confession. When Polansky's investigators uncovered DNA evidence that contradicted Mr. Montoya's conviction, the DA offered a plea deal for time served. After thirteen years behind bars, Lorenzo Montoya walked free in 2014.

Emily Johnson, the murder victim in this case, was a twenty-nine-year-old special-education teacher who loved her students at Skinner Middle School in northwest Denver. May all who loved her find peace.

The Marade Mayhem of 1992 Was Real

I was there.

Skinheads along with the KKK got a permit to gather on the grounds of the Colorado state capitol building to stage a counterprotest to the Dr. Martin Luther King Jr. Day celebration. As those of us in the marade approached on Colfax Avenue, I, along with the peaceful crowd of fifteen thousand, was met with Nazi salutes, Confederate flags, and vile and hate-filled words, including shouts of "White power."

A police helicopter hovered overhead, while on the ground over two hundred officers stood in formation, clad in riot gear. Seeing what was brewing, I immediately made my way back to my car, almost two miles away, and returned home.

Lug nuts didn't fly that day, but rocks, bottles, and snowballs did when, after the marade, some of the young people, frustrated with the presence of the KKK, confronted them. Older marchers attempted to stop the confrontation with talk of nonviolence, but tensions escalated when state troopers escorted the KKK and skinheads into the capitol for protection and eventually rushed the white supremacists across the street, where buses sat ready for their escape.

That's when the powder keg of frustration exploded and resulted in overturned and burned police cars and the smell of tear gas in the air throughout the night.

It was another chapter in Denver's long history with the KKK.

Killdozer Was Real

On June 4, 2004, Marvin Heemeyer locked himself inside a homemade tank and set out on a mission of destruction in the small town of Granby, Colorado. Secure in the yellow bulldozer covered in gray plates of steel reinforced with concrete, he crashed through the walls of his own business, crushed cars, and terrorized his neighbors for over two hours.

Heemeyer rammed and smashed into and through thirteen buildings, including the town hall and local newspaper, and in the end he took his life, after causing more than $7 million in damage. He left behind a two-hour audiotape detailing his grievances behind his rage-fueled revenge tour.

To this day, Heemeyer remains a hero to some.

Denver's Burglars in Blue Were Real

In the early 1960s, over fifty Denver police officers were arrested and sentenced to prison for participating in a large-scale burglary ring. They scouted their victims while on duty and broke into the businesses at night while other officers provided lookout, communicating with each other via their police radios. The same officers investigated the crimes. The racket was finally exposed when a stolen safe tumbled out of a getaway car and onto the street in front of a police officer who was not involved in the racket.

The year 1961 was labeled "the year of shame" for the Denver police, as it was heralded as the most corrupt department in America. Besides burglarizing businesses, the officers regularly rolled drunks and people living on the streets for their Social Security and veterans benefits. Even worse, these officers appeared to delight in delivering "street justice." It was not unusual for these public servants, sworn to serve and protect, to

A Dream in the Dark

administer physical punishment as they saw fit; being stopped for petty theft could result in every cop on duty having the opportunity to take a swing at you.

Smith Road Is Real

Denver is a beautiful place to live. As a Denver native and one who has only ever lived in the Mile High City, I love the city I call home. However, part of my aim in setting my novels in Denver is to shine a light on the fact that in this beautiful place to live, not everyone is living beautifully.

Case in point: Smith Road. As I described in the final chapter of *A Dream in the Dark*, Smith Road was the place that authorities literally left people to fend for themselves. For years, they simply dropped formerly incarcerated individuals on the side of the road with zero services in sight. The closest place for shelter was over ten miles away; the only belongings of those dropped off were contained in the plastic bags in their hands.

I had the privilege of being a part of a group that organized a crisis response team on behalf of those who had served their time and were now attempting to start anew. We met newly released people on Smith Road with survival backpacks complete with food, water, maps, blankets, hats, gloves, and toiletries. Additionally, we offered coats and rides. Thankfully, after a few years of these tactics, the system responded to the shame it had created and changed the drop-off location.

Read a Book, Right a Wrong Is Real

If you've purchased a book in this series, you've already made a difference through my Read a Book, Right a Wrong initiative. Simply put, I donate a significant portion of my advance and royalties to innocence projects, and I'd like to encourage you to give to them as well. These organizations are on the front lines of the fight to free the wrongfully incarcerated.

In my first novel, *They Can't Take Your Name*, I spotlighted the Korey Wise Innocence Project at the University of Colorado. They work tirelessly to free those whom the legal system has failed and push for reforms to prevent wrongful convictions at the front end.

With *A Dream in the Dark*, I'd like to turn your attention to the Pennsylvania Innocence Project. They are doing valiant work in a hotbed of wrongful convictions.

Some have wondered if the injustice described in my books—systemic corruption that leads to mass wrongful convictions—is realistic. Unfortunately, this kind of corruption is all too real and recent, and there are places in our country that seem to convict innocent people at a rate disproportionate to the rest of the country. Philadelphia is one of those places. Thankfully, the Pennsylvania Innocence Project seeks to exonerate those convicted of crimes they did not commit, prevent innocent people from being prosecuted and convicted, and help those wrongfully convicted transition to freedom. Proceeds from *A Dream in the Dark* will go to support this worthy work.

Please visit my website (RobertJusticeBooks.com) for more information about my Read a Book, Right a Wrong initiative.

Thirty Thousand years is Real

Wrongful convictions can happen anywhere. I've set my novels about systemic injustice leading to wrongful convictions in my hometown of Denver because I must not assume that what happens in other places is not also happening in my own backyard.

According to the National Registry of Exonerations, we have passed a grim milestone in America—time lost to false convictions has now exceeded thirty thousand years. With over three thousand exonerees who served on average eight years and eleven months each, there is still work to be done. Black people served the overwhelming majority of these thirty thousand years.

There are more, and they are why I write!

ACKNOWLEDGMENTS AND THANK-YOUS

Each step of the way, even during moments when I wondered how this story would make its way into the world, I was accompanied by supportive companions. For each of you, I am deeply grateful.

To my Father who art in heaven, hallowed be thy names.

To my children—you are hidden within these pages. Even more so, you live in my heart.

To my mom, my own CC—I miss you.

To my beta readers, David, Chris, and Judith—in addition to your insights and honesty, you gave me the gift of time, and for that I'm grateful. You made this book better.

To those who provided Spanish language assistance, Amy, Cleofé, and Cleide—muchísimas gracias!

To Andrew—you were a trusted guide through every twist, turn, and dark tunnel, a true friend in the trenches.

To Crime Writers of Color and the listeners of the Crime Writers of Color podcast—when I found you, I found my tribe.

To the team at Crooked Lane Books, Matt, Terri, Rebecca, Dulce, Thaisheemarie, Elizabeth, Rachel, and Mikaela—working with you is a dream.

Acknowledgments and Thank-Yous

To my beloved bride, Barbara—thirty years going on forever, I'm beyond grateful for each moment, second, day, and decade. A lifetime with you is not enough!

To all who read—you believe the power of words and lean into their siren call. Thank you for taking time with my words. May you never lose the joy that comes with the cracking of a spine and the wonder of *Once upon a time*.

Robert Justice
Micah 6:8

INDUSTRIAL SNOW

It was too cold to snow in Denver, but today in the Five Points neighborhood, flakes fell softly. One landed on Eli's face as he lounged on the sidewalk across the street from The Roz and his home—watching Liza.

The Suncor refinery in Commerce City, just north of Denver proper, was a maze of steel pipes. The massive flames that topped the chimneys burned night and day to provide electricity for the two and a half million people of the region. On most days, Suncor's smokestacks billowed towering white clouds into the atmosphere of the Mile High City, marring the picturesque skyline. In the winter, on days when the temperature hovered around freezing, the warm humidity-saturated air and the water particles from the smokestacks mixed to produce fake snow that fell on the surrounding neighborhoods, which comprised mostly children of Mexico. On days like today, the slight southerly wind carried the Suncor snow as far as Five Points, where Eli sat, propped against the wall of the fire station.

Eli ignored the flake on his cheek as Liza locked the door to his home and walked passed her car toward The Roz. She didn't recognize him when she arrived, and even now, as she glanced the official witness list from the trial with the complete name of the victim, which she had also confirmed with Moses. She scribbled a note and put it on the seat of Eli's chair.

It read:

CC—Her name is Claudette Cooper. We must find her.